CLOUD
NINETEEN

Also by William Stanley

Mr. Holroyd Takes a Holiday
One Spring in Picardy

CLOUD NINETEEN

WILLIAM STANLEY

Walker and Company
New York

Oz Edition

First published in the United States of America
in 1984 by the Walker Publishing Company, Inc.

Library of Congress Cataloging in Publication Data

Stanley, William.
  Cloud nineteen.

  1. World War, 1914–1918—Fiction. I. Title.
PR6069.T293C55 1984   823′.914 84-13221
ISBN 0-8027-0816-1

Printed in the United States of America

10 9 8 7 6 5 4 3 2 1

Dedicated to the airshipmen of the Royal Naval Air Service who between 1914 and 1918 flew and maintained the largest fleet of airships the world has ever known. Perhaps it was because their function was to prevent losses rather than cause them that their achievements have been overshadowed by the more spectacular branches of the services. The men and women in this book are all fictional but the statement 'that no merchantman escorted by an airship was lost during the war' is true.

CHAPTER ONE

The frightening thing about the attack, apart from the surprise, was the normality of the surroundings. The world inverted, the laws of logic shattered. One minute Shepherd was walking down the steps of the Admiralty, muttering at the February rain beating in his face, secretly relishing the freshness after a night in that smoke-filled attic. He was tired, almost enough to sleep. Perhaps all day. It had been another one of those nights. Jerry had changed the cipher again, for the second time in ten days: perhaps they were beginning to smell a rat. But it had come out all right. A twelve pots of coffee problem, Tregarron had called it. From midnight, when the first of the U-boat traffic came in from the triangulation stations, until 5.30 in the morning.

A night about which he could be contrary. Hard work was an anodyne for his personal grief. In it he could hide from himself this new awareness that his work, the job he had slogged at for three years since late '14, the job that had killed Jennifer, was a pointless paperchasing accumulation of data for the sake of having it. Not for fighting, not for cutting the appalling, and still rising, merchant ship losses – 800,000 tons last month. For filing. A piece of bureaucratic tidiness.

Sometime in the future when there was nothing but routine stuff coming through, messages cleared by reference to the code-book like a cipher clerk, sometime in the long night hours this new awareness would fester and grow.

But last night had been good, difficult without being impossible, the three of them racing each other. And it had come out all right before the end of his stint on duty. No time to brood. He had a satisfied feeling, a job needing a peculiar talent had been well done. He should sleep like a log. After bacon and eggs and salty farm butter newly sent from home in York.

Henry, Dr Henrietta Talbot MA, had slipped on the steps and clutched his arm. A little woman rounded into a ball by her fur coat and that ridiculous dumpling of fur on her head. She had eyed the overflowing gutter and had said, 'If I submerged in there, Richard, you would decode my screams and whistle up a destroyer before thinking of lending me a hand.'

He had laughed at the silly joke as she hung on to his arm. Richard Peter Shepherd, Lieutenant (Interpreter) RNVR, and he was going to have the most enormous breakfast. Bacon and eggs and toast swimming in butter, the parcel that his mother had sent down with Jennifer. Jennifer ...

The riding crop hit him across the right forehead, curled across the left side of his face and drove him down on to one knee. He looked up. An ordinary scene. The dirty greystone pillars; an open-mouthed doorman; half a dozen startled pigeons exploding upwards; early morning office workers on the pavement below, heads down against the rain; Henry rolling down the steps like a furry ball; a policeman ... The crop lashed down again and again, beating aside his raised arms to rake his face and hammer across his shoulders.

'Murderer. Pampered swine. Hiding in Whitehall with your whore – my poor gel not settled in her grave. I'll teach you to laugh – spit in her face.'

Jennifer's father, Alderman Jervis, senior partner, JP, seventy, grey haired, his clipped moustache flecked with spittle, lashed down with the crop again. Desperately Shepherd threw himself upwards to butt him in the stomach.

The crop thumped across his shoulders but the old man was now off balance. The butt-end jarred into Shepherd's nose, blinding him with tears. Shepherd, two steps lower, butted him again, and clawed at Jervis's thighs as the blows hammered down on to his shoulders. They fell over, rolling down the steps as Shepherd struggled to lock his arm over that of the old man. A punch on the jaw rocked the old man's head against the pavement. The riding crop dropped as Shepherd rolled on to his chest with his fist upraised.

'That's enough of that,' the policeman said in his ear, taking a firm grasp on his fist. 'You young hooligan, hitting a man old enough to be your grandad. What's going on?'

Someone in the little crowd that had gathered helped old Jervis to his feet. He pointed a bony finger at Shepherd. 'Ask him why he is polishing a desk in Whitehall instead of being at the Front, Officer. Shirker. He murdered my daughter.'

An umbrella prodded Shepherd in the ribs. He tried to rise but the constable's grip on his arm held him down. A walking stick rapped his knuckles.

'That's enough of that,' growled the policeman. 'Stand aside,' he snapped at the onlookers. 'Well, have you got anything to say for yourself?'

Shepherd nodded at the doors into the Admiralty. 'I work there. Ask the chap on the door. I've been there since '14.'

'So does my missus. She cleans the floors. I suppose you dirties them ... ' A row of medal ribbons coloured the policeman's left breast. 'Not much fighting in there. Not for a fit young 'un like yourself. You'd best come along; we'll sort this out at the station.'

Effortlessly he forced Shepherd up. 'And you, sir,' he said to Jervis. 'Nah then, move along. Show's over.'

With a firm grip on Shepherd's arm the policeman took the two of them away. Still dazed by the sudden attack Shepherd stared at the angry faces around him. It was a ghastly mistake, a dream. Where was Henry? She would explain. He stumbled and the constable's grip tightened.

Jervis led the way, head erect, his military bearing impressing the onlookers. Someone picked up his homburg, brushed the rim on their sleeve and handed it to him. A trickle of rain dribbled from the lock of hair displaced over his forehead. It was so damned unfair, thought Shepherd. The old man had never been more than a volunteer in the Yeomanry. A picnic soldier.

At the police station they had to wait while a drunken soldier was helped into the cells. Someone with a bucket and mop swabbed the vomit off the floor. It was cold, and the institutional dirty cream and brown paint was dreary. Jervis and the constable tried to tell their stories at the same time until the desk sergeant told them to shut up. Shepherd was still in a daze, expecting to wake up at any minute. His face was smarting, one eye was beginning to close and his shoulders had begun to stiffen.

'Now, sir, you say that this chap Shepherd murdered your daughter. It's a serious charge, sir, o'course you'd be the first to realize that.' The desk sergeant straightened the charge sheet and held his pen poised for the third time.

'The man is a shirker. Look at him. Why isn't he at the Front?'

'Yessir, that's as maybe. It's not a crime to work in Whitehall. Else we'd have all the politicians in jail. What I want to know is what's all this about a murder?'

'The last time I heard my little gel she was crying. Crying over the telephone. Her last day before she left for France. She was going to France, not him ... ' The bony finger waggled with fury. 'Her fiancé, that shirker, was too busy at the office to see her. She cried to me over the telephone.' He turned back to address the sergeant. 'The general she was to drive in France, a true English gentleman, gave her permission to catch a later boat. From Folkestone.'

Suddenly the sergeant caught on. 'The packet boat, the one Jerry sank leaving 'arbour. It were a crime all right, sir, but not agin this gentleman. It's the captain of that U-boat you wants to see in the dock. An' so you shall ...'

But Jervis had not done. He shouted, 'I want him in the dock. I want everyone to look at a man who can hide behind a desk while his future wife sails for France.'

'What the devil is all the noise about?' An angry inspector strode out of his office. Hastily the sergeant explained. The inspector turned to Shepherd, 'Well, young man, you must have something to say. What is it, flat feet or cold feet? Say something ... '

Shepherd stared at him, tongue-tied by the suddenness of everything. The attack ... no, not just the attack, everything that had happened in the past week. Not that there was anything that he could say. Three years of working in OB 14 had stilled his tongue as effectively as though it had been cut out.

'You serve in the Royal Navy. You serve your country as effectively as any lieutenant on any one of His Majesty's ships.' In his mind the stocky little admiral, Director of Naval Intelligence, eyelids blinking in a nervous twitch, snapped, 'You will not under any circumstances tell anyone your function in this building. Tell 'em you are a lieutenant in the Royal Navy and you go where their Lordships tell you. And refer them to me.'

Now he could not remember his own telephone number. The policemen were staring at him. He must look a sight. Tie askew, coat torn, rain-soaked. Jervis glared at him with his lip curled. Not very long ago he had been the apple of the old man's eye.

'One moment, Mr Pollock, if you please. I think I am in a position to clear up this little misunderstanding.'

The sonorous voice, the gold-rimmed pince-nez, had been worth over £10,000 a year at the bar before the war. Shepherd relaxed. It was Bart Tregarron, his section leader, arm in arm with Henry, who was still wearing her rain-bedraggled fur coat.

The inspector shook hands, 'Nice to see you again, sir. With respect, sir, I am sure that you have more important things in hand now, but your presence has been sorely missed.'

'Much to your delight and profit, eh, old chap,' Tregarron said. He twitched the charge sheet towards him and raised his pince-nez. There was nothing on the sheet.

'Excellent, Mr Pollock. This whole unfortunate affair, Mr Pollock, did not occur. It never happened.'

The inspector bridled, 'Really, Mr Tregarron, I can't 'ave that. There was an assault. Charges of murder, exaggerated perhaps, heat of the moment, but there was an assault.'

'Had there been an assault, Mr Pollock, it would have been witnessed by the two naval pensioners on duty at the door. And by this good lady, Dr Henrietta Victoria Talbot, ex-headmistress at Roedean, Girton and a graduate not only of Oxford and Cambridge but Heidelberg and the Sorbonne as well. Had there been an assault she would have made an excellent witness. But, Mr Pollock, had there been an assault, Lieutenant Shepherd, who was a gentleman before he became an officer, would never have embarrassed his late fiancée's father by charging him. So it is as well that what we

11

are talking about never happened.' He scribbled a name on his card. 'Ring Scotland Yard. Special Branch. Ask for that man. He will agree with me that nothing happened. Or you can ring Mr Villers at that number. He is private secretary to Admiral Hall. I'd rather you didn't. He's a stinker.' He took Shepherd's arm. 'We have all suffered grievous losses in recent days, Mr Pollock. Each of us in our own way has been hurt. Mr Jervis's son will be here shortly to look after his father.'

As they moved to the door, with Shepherd moving like a man in a dream, Tregarron said over his shoulder, 'He also works in Whitehall, Mr Pollock. But Lieutenant-Commander Jervis needs a stick and his list to port is not due solely to the medals on his left breast. Good day to you.'

All the fire had drained out of Jervis. He slumped on to a chair, buried his head in his arms and began to cry.

Working irregular hours had given Shepherd a sailor-like ability to fall asleep anywhere at anytime. Not today. And his appetite for eggs and bacon had gone. So much of what old Jervis had said was true. It was his fault that Jennifer had died.

The work in the U-boat section usually started late at night as the boats surfaced to recharge their batteries, report their successes and get their orders. Sometimes it seemed as though they had a need to chatter. The triangulation stations around the coast intercepted the transmissions and plotted the bearing of the transmitter. Plotted on a chart the three bearings made a neat cocked hat about a couple of miles across. Inside was a U-boat, at the time it made the transmission.

The bearings and positions went to the Operations people. Shepherd's group was interested in the content of the message. They had had copies of the German Naval Code since late '14. It was one of the few things of real value which had been given by the Russians. By now they were expert at unravelling the changes in the ciphering of the code.

There was more to OB14 than decoding U-boat skippers' lists of sinkings. Germany had been dependent on wireless to communicate with the world outside Europe since the cable ship *Telconia* had slid through the morning mist off the German coast the day after war had been declared to lift and cut the German transatlantic cables. Out of that had sprung OB14. A peculiarly British collection of amateurs with minds tuned to the solving of acrostics and deciphering ancient languages. Even now the diplomatic room was finishing off a long cable from the German Foreign Secretary, Herr Zimmerman, to Mexico. If the rumours in the office were true it contained enough political dynamite to blast the Americans into the war.

It was some vacation work that had got Shepherd into OB14. Some assistance translating Sumerian scripts and two unsuccessful years' work on some Minoan tablets had been remembered by the right people. He had been press-ganged into the Department late in '14. Since then he had worked like a mole in a scruffy low-ceilinged office under the roof of the Admiralty Old Building.

His requests for a transfer to a job on active service had gone to every quarter. And were refused unread. So he had accepted his lot. The work was interesting, and a challenge to his wits.

It was only in the last six days that he had come to realize how much of it was wasted effort, a reflex action loading the files with information unread, too profuse and too secret to allow anyone to take action on it. This despite the grim reality that the U-boats might starve the country into submission while the armies remained locked in futile, murderous battles along the length of the Western Front.

Well, now he knew how valuable his work was. The message he had deciphered six days ago had been a precise operation order. A U-boat, code-name *Der Dichter,* the Poet, would proceed to Folkestone Roads and at high tide on Wednesday night she would torpedo a French destroyer carrying the Combined Anglo-French Anti U-boat Committee across to Dieppe. The day, the time, the place and the objective. What more could they want?

And the provenance. He, Richard Peter Shepherd, had given them the lot, a brief as neatly tied up as anything Tregarron had been handed during his days at the bar.

It had started with a man being knocked down outside a Harwich public house. And an alert policeman who wondered why a half-illiterate potman should have kept a copy of a letter to his aunt in Amsterdam. And checked his place of employment. A hotel. And the guests. Scientists, naval officers. The Anti U-boat Committee.

They had spent eight head-splitting hours working on a telephoned copy of the letter without any headway. Then Tregarron's pleading had got them the original. Shepherd had taken a few isolated figures, and the fact that the potman carried a celluloid rule in his pocket, and made a mask. The slots spelled the message. The day, time, place and objective.

Then they had to wait for the orders to be wirelessed to a U-boat. The day he should have been with Jennifer, Shepherd spent in a draughty Nissen hut on a Yorkshire sandspit. That message was too important to entrust to a dispatch rider,

It had come, code-word *Der Dichter*. It had been pre-planned. They had been waiting for the letter from the spy.

Place, time and objective. But no U-boat. Nothing plotted in the Channel within range. One off the Suffolk coast, but it was impossible for a U-boat to get through the Dover barrage. So the Navy said. The nets, mines, hydrophones and the patrolling trawlers were impregnable. It was not the first time that a coup had been planned without the means to execute it.

Grudgingly they had changed the departure point. So that the first ship out of Folkestone on the tide took two torpedoes and sank in ten minutes. The Folkestone-Dieppe packet, the ship Jennie had joined after her extra twenty-four hours' leave. 300 dead – men, women and children. Witnesses had seen the prow of the UC62 tip a lifeboat full of women, nurses and drivers into the freezing water. The files said that Kapitänleutnant Otto Schiller was in command of UC62. The Poet? Was it Schiller who murdered Jennifer? Or the Navy doing nothing? Or himself, too engrossed in deciphering that message, organizing her another day's leave? If they had married in the spring of '15 ... ? Instead she sailed on a boat destined to take two torpedoes at top speed at 10.30 pm in the darkness of a February night.

14

Shepherd pushed the congealing breakfast aside. There was no chance of him sleeping. He rummaged through his small store of wine. Tregarron educating the provincial youth. A bottle of Burgundy slipped and fell, the heavy bouquet turning his stomach. He was after stronger meat. The brandy was finished but he found a quarter-full bottle of Scotch. He sipped it from a tumbler as he bathed his face and gingerly shaved.

His face was criss-crossed with weals, the right eye half-closed. He was going to look a mess for the next couple of weeks. The real wound went deeper. Some of what old Jervis had said was true. It was humiliating to have your fiancée killed on her way to France while he ... what had he done? Accumulated a dozen bottles of wine?

His Harris tweed suit was a mess, soaked with rainwater and mud, a torn pocket exposing the lining. His uniform lay on the bed, newly pressed by the woman who 'did' for him. He put it on feeling like a fraud, as though he was going to a fancy dress ball.

Alec Jervis found him in the local public house an hour later. The landlord whispered in his ear as he went in. Half a bottle of Scotch on an empty stomach was beginning to have an effect on Shepherd.

'My God, you look a mess,' Alec said. 'The Old Man sends his apologies.'

'How is he?' Shepherd called for a pink gin.

'I put him on the train for York. There is a nurse with him. They are travelling with the coffin. He is really sorry for what happened. The strain of waiting for the bodies to be found. And that idiotic coroner whipping up a bit of hate. No sleep. He was going to see you about the funeral. Something came over him when he saw you and Henry laughing on the steps.'

'Don't be so mealy-mouthed, Alec. He has hated my guts since I got stuck with the Department. And a lot of what he said was true. If I hadn't been so bloody noble – doing – doing that job for the bloody Department. If we had got married as we planned. If ... She'd still be alive. I killed her.'

'Keep your voice down, you chump.' Alec waved a newspaper in his face. 'The coroner named the man who killed her. The captain of the UC62. I got his name from the Intelligence bloke.' He lowered his voice to a whisper. 'Kapitänleutnant sur Zee Otto Schiller.'

Shepherd reached for the paper, missed and grabbed Alec's shoulder to steady himself. The pain on his friend's face momentarily sobered him.

'Come to the club for lunch,' Alec said. 'I've got to meet a chap there. Got a chance of a job, a real job.'

'You really know how to twist the knife in the wound,' Shepherd said.

'You know what I mean. I'm not one of you slide-rule merchants up in the attic. I don't even know what you do. I'm a messenger boy. This new job is not much, but it is better than that. A flotilla of converted trawlers minesweeping off the east coast. Sort of poacher turned gamekeeper.'

Shepherd screwed his eyes up, trying to focus on his friend. 'I'd have thought the doctors would have kept you there. A sort of walking testimonial. All right, let's go to the club and get you a real job.'

Shepherd fell asleep in the taxi, but a wash, a meal and a pot of black coffee sobered him. Then he sat in the bar, willing himself to drink slowly while Alec started to pull strings with a couple of old friends from his class at Dartmouth. His eyelids began to droop. It seemed a lifetime since he last slept properly.

Someone joggled his elbow, spilling whisky over his sleeve. A voice squeaked apologies and hastily had the glass refilled. Shepherd stirred. A knot of midshipmen, six of them, had drifted into his corner. One of them smiled nervously and edged the refilled glass nearer Shepherd's hand.

He raised it in salute. 'You all look very excited and pleased with yourselves. I know, their Lordships in their wisdom have given each of you a battleship to command.'

'Exactly, sir. Well, not a battleship capital B but a command. A fighting command. Well, not even that, really. 'Cos we're really only halfway through training. But we will be passed out on the Station. Flying airships.'

'Zeppelins? Didn't know we had any that were any good.

And I did think that the commanding officer would be, er, a little more senior.'

'A Zeppelin, sir, is a rigid airship. The airships we fly, blimps we call them, are non-rigids. Quite small as airships go. Just a pilot and a wireless operator in a converted aeroplane fuselage. 70,000 cubic feet in the envelope, which is self-shaped with ballonets.'

'Put a sock in it, Gassy,' the eldest of them said. Their youth made Shepherd catch his breath. Eighteen? Four of them seemed barely old enough to shave. 'Sorry about that, sir. Gassy blinding you with science. We all tend to get carried away about them. Marvellous things ... '

'What do they do? Can they carry bombs?'

'Oh yes, sir. Two of the new 100lb depth-charges. On anti U-boat patrols. They are the last vessel in the Royal Navy where a chap can fight a personal battle. I mean, even a destroyer needs a hundred chaps to stoke the engines, cook the meals, fire the guns. The captain just stands there directing things. Some other chap pulls the trigger.'

One of the others butted in. 'And the chap that pulls the trigger may not see what happens to the shell. The gunnery officer up in the director tells him to wind it up a few degrees. But in a blimp you have to do everything yourself. Just you and a wireless johnny sniffing out U-boats.'

'With two dammed great depth-charges. Boom ... '

A loud voice cut across their chattering. 'That's right. Get that rubbish out of your system before you get to my station.'

Shepherd glared up at the newcomer, angry at him putting down their enthusiasm. He was a squadron commander in the Royal Naval Air Service, although the ribbons across his chest told of an earlier career in the Royal Navy. He was tall, six foot two and a bit, and about the ugliest man Shepherd had ever seen. He grinned at the midshipmen and Shepherd revised his opinion. He was the most attractively ugly man he had ever seen. His face was seamed with scars and one of them cut across his broken nose, leaving an absurd blob of flesh at the tip. But the steel-grey eyes, red-rimmed with fatigue, said that this was no clown's face. His uniform was stained, and across one arm he carried a fur-lined leather coat that swamped them with the stench of petrol and oil.

'You can leave those ideas in the bar or at Scapa Flow where they belong,' he boomed. 'When you fly blimps from my station you will clearly understand that sinking U-boats is the lesser part of your job. Your top priority is to see that every merchant ship in your area or convoy gets safely into port.'

'But, sir. How— '

'Don't "But, sir" me, boy. You heard the message. I don't give a damn if the U-boat crews die of boredom, as long as they don't sink any of my ships. Is that clear?'

The voice was loud enough to be heard across the length of the room. It was deliberately offensive. Shepherd fought back the temptation to stand up and cheer. Two of them against the mob. He and Bart had often wondered whether the dashing exponents of hunting down the U-boats ever saw the weekly sinking rate of merchant ships. Did they realize that unless something different was done it would be too late to get America into the war. At the rate the U-boats were sinking ships the country would grind to a halt in six months. And unrestricted sinkings had been authorized by the Kaiser only since the beginning of the month. And we were still building battleships when the need was for more and more escort ships.

'Three of you,' the squadron commander said, 'the two with the most flying time and the one with the least, he goes with me, will take a couple of Zeros up to Howden after lunch. Flying kit and overnight bag only. And belay the giggle juice. The other three can look after the rest of your gear. Porter's desk, half an hour. I'll be in the dining-room if I'm wanted.'

Shepherd was green with envy as he watched him stride away. The midshipmen looked as though they had been patted on the head by God.

The normal chatter round the bar restarted as though switched on by the man's exit.

' ... disgrace to the Service. That sort of rubbish destroys public confidence ... '

' ... damned air people are all the same. Irresponsible enthusiasts tossing panaceas to a gullible public ... '

' ... gullible politicians, that is worse. And damned dangerous. The C-in-C ought to have him muzzled ... '

' ... the man's an ass. No historical perspective. Command of the sea is the Navy's job. Not wet-nursing a mob of stinking Greek freighters ... '

' ... bloody fool. I'd like to see his gasbags nursing his precious ships through a force 9 gale ... '

Shepherd watched the cheeks of the midshipmen flush with anger. 'Well, I agree with him,' he said loudly. 'But who is he? And pray, what is a Zero?'

All six of them spoke at once. The tallest won. 'Squadron Commander Carberry, sir,' he drawled. 'He's about the oldest blimp pilot flying. Frightfully tough egg. Refused promotion. He says that there are too many old fools flying desks and killing young fools.'

'It's terribly hush-hush and all that,' the one called Gassy said. 'But he has just got back from France. Chased a U-boat halfway across the North Sea. Didn't have enough petrol to fly home, so he turned round and made it to Marquise. Wind from the north-west, y'know.'

Shepherd shrugged his shoulders. 'Sensible fellow. I don't get the point.'

'Our chaps put the kibosh on the Zeps after we invented incendiary bullets to light up the hydrogen. Ordinary bullets just make a hole. Jerry has got bullets like that now. The seaplanes operating out of Zeebrugge use them.'

'We can't climb the way the big Zeps climb, so if you get caught you are a dead duck. They got one of our big Coastals last month.'

'Even 70,000 cubic feet makes a jolly big fire.'

Shepherd nodded. 'And the Zero?'

'Super,' Gassy said, unable to contain himself. 'The latest. No more cast-off aeroplane parts. The nacelle is built like a boat and it's got a Rolls-Royce Hawk engine with a mechanic to look after the plumbing.'

'It's faster. Carries more petrol. Twelve-hour patrols.'

'And a wireless operator?' Shepherd asked.

'Of course. They are turning them out like sausages.'

'It's one thing to churn out airships but it must take ages to train the crews.'

'It's not a large crew. Three on the Zero, only two on the old SS blimps. People like us volunteer for pilot training. Anything to get away from Scapa Flow. And direct entry civilians. Takes them a bit longer. How to salute, and eating your peas the Navy way. Wireless operators are mostly direct entry. A lot are ex-amateur wireless fans. It's more fun than foot-slogging with the poor bloody infantry.'

A porter sidled up to Shepherd. 'Excuse me, sir. There is a call for you from the Admiralty.'

Shepherd followed him, feeling even more of a fraud than usual as he felt the midshipmen's eyes follow him to the door.

'You have been drinking again,' Henry said when he reached the office. 'You should wear your uniform more often, it suits you.'

'I'll keep that in mind for our next fancy dress ball. What is the flap? I thought the place was falling down.'

'It's Mr Tregarron. He is the duty officer and I cannot find him. Villers wants to see the pair of you. I wish someone would drown him. He was complaining again about the time I spend here. And there is a pile of signals waiting for attention.'

It was Henrietta's favourite bone. Despite her qualifications, her command of four languages, she was officially in charge of the filing room. Only Tregarron and Shepherd allowed her to help them on decoding.

'Pull the other leg. Poor old Villers is terrified of your piercing glare of disdain. You've covered up for Bart before. He's probably entertaining half the chorus from Dalys. And I'm not on watch until ten. Now, try again.'

Henrietta stared at him, looking like a doll with her pink and white complexion. The years had dealt kindly with her, leaving her face unlined. The baby blue eyes dissolved into tears.

'You damned fool, Richard Shepherd. Thank God he was not present to hear you say that. I've been to his rooms in Albany. He's gone I tell you. Packed a bag. And he's taken his guns.'

'What guns, what the devil are you hinting at?'

'He had a gun, a poacher's rifle. It breaks into three pieces. And a revolver. He has taken them. That horrible old man shouting filth at you this morning upset him terribly. I'm afraid ... I think I know what Mr Tregarron is going to do. And they are bound to catch him.'

Shepherd gave her a clean handkerchief and a glass of brandy from the bottle in Tregarron's desk.

'Why should Bart, of all people, want to shoot himself?'

Henrietta snapped at him. 'Don't be so damned selfish. 300 people were killed on that boat. Jennifer was not the only young woman who died. And one not so young. Molly McCready, the musical comedy actess. She had been Mr Tregarron's mistress for over fifteen years. You are so wrapped up in your own misery that you cannot see that every victim left someone bereft of the pleasure of their company.'

Shepherd had never heard Henry talk like this. Who had she lost, he wondered? And what the hell was a 64-year-old KC thinking about doing with a rifle and a revolver? And where did one start to look?

'Ah, Shepherd. I thought Mr Tregarron was on watch.' Villers, the Admiral's private secretary, stood in the doorway. 'Where is Mr Tregarron?'

Hubert Vereker Villers was a fleshy little man perpetually on the point of becoming fat. He was not quite the English gentleman that he liked to affect. South Africa, the diamond fields and the Boer War had brought him home to retire. The war and Admiral Hall had given him a chance to secure a niche in the Establishment. Shepherd did not like him. Few in the Department did, although he seemed to be at work twenty-four hours a day. Administrating.

'Are you all right? You look dreadfully pale and your face is in a mess,' Villers said. 'You have been drinking. The Admiral was most displeased to hear about the brawl in which you were involved this morning. It won't do, y'know. You have a position of great responsibility in a very sensitive area of the national effort. Well?'

'It was my fiancée's father. The shock of having to identify

21

the body made him ill. He's an old man. If I had been allowed to go he would have been spared that. He's all right now. Alec Jervis arranged for a nurse to accompany him back to York.'

'A most unfortunate affair all round. You and Mr Tregarron have the sympathy of the Admiral and the whole Department. It is unfortunate that at this time the Diplomatic Section should be handling material so delicate that the entire course of the war could rest on its successful outcome. We cannot, we must not, jeopardize that affair no matter how grievous the affliction.'

Shepherd sat down. The too clean, too smart, unctuous old man made him feel sick.

'I've been to see my doctor,' he lied. 'I can't sleep, I can't work and I don't think I've eaten properly since it happened. Because I blame myself and the Department for my fiancée's death. My doctor says I should take a complete break. Right now. And for several weeks.'

Villers pursed his lips. 'You are as much on active service as a naval officer on the bridge of his ship. I dare say they feel the need for a complete break, eh? Well, you are overdue for leave. See Mr Tregarron. If he agrees, then you must do as the doctor orders. I dare say Miss Talbot will be only too pleased to help out during your absence.'

'Of course,' Henrietta said. 'And I have no doubt that for a short while I could cope with the ladies in typing and filing as well.'

'What are you up to?' she asked when Villers had gone.

'I don't know. Just a hunch, something I heard. How do we find Bart. He might have pushed off to Truro to have a quiet brood and sink a barrel of cider.'

He was lying in his teeth and Henry knew it. The missing guns did not make sense. How could Bart, sprightly old gentleman though he was, get within range of a U-boat captain. There was only one way and the thought of it made Shepherd feel sick. They would catch him and then ... ?

'We'll shift this paper,' he said. 'If there is no news by dinner I'll go round and have a word with his man.'

The cipher had not been changed, so the work was

straightforward, a matter of rooting out of their home-made code-books the plain text equivalent to the code groups. Then making a rough translation of the German text into English.

Shepherd held on to a sheaf of messages. They were all the same, the Flanders Flotilla calling 'the Poet' to reply immediately. Once an hour, every hour through the night. And last night the most powerful transmitter in Europe, at Nauen, on the outskirts of Berlin, had repeated the request half a dozen times during the night. There had been no reply from 'the Poet'.

Carefully Shepherd spread the array of messages across his desk, arranging them in time order. Why were they so keen to get Schiller to support the official story that the ship torpedoed in Folkestone Roads was a minesweeper. Five days. Where was UC62? Henrietta brought him the sighting reports.

He sat down slowly. Like a man with his nerve screwed up to some unpleasant venture and told at the last minute that it was not on. Some ordinary seaman had scuttled Schiller. Relief. Disappointment? Whatever avenging nonsense old Tregarron was up to no longer had any purpose. That demented old man flailing his riding crop, spitting his hate, had been avenged.

Shepherd had been in at the beginning. He had decoded the original message and then the operation order. He had pleaded with Tregarron to demand some action. Until Alec Jervis, with the cynicism of an ex-submarine commander, said that they would do nothing because there was nothing that they could do. Now he felt deprived, his half-envisaged plan for a personal revenge stillborn. There was no satisfaction in retribution at an unknown place by an unknown hand. And he would never be allowed to say that he knew that it had happened. That 'the Poet' would never reply.

Soon after six Shepherd could keep his eyes open no longer. But it seemed as though he had barely stretched out on the camp bed at the back of the office when he was rudely awakened by Villers.

'You told me that your doctor had ordered a complete break,' Villers snapped.

23

Shepherd yawned and stretched as he stood up, wondering why the little squirt was snooping at this time of the night. Perhaps his Victorian soul was shocked that he was asleep in the same room as Henry.

'We're short-handed. I can hang on until Mr Tregarron clears up some personal business connected with the sinking.'

'Be quiet. Do you take me for a fool? I warn you, all of you, any more nonsense like this will be treated with the utmost severity. The Admiral has decided that there is no point in taking further proceedings against an elderly civilian like Tregarron. But you' – he tapped Shepherd lightly on the chest with his forefinger, and recoiled instantly as Shepherd doubled his fist – 'you are a different kettle of fish, Lieutenant. As an officer in His Majesty's Service the Admiral can put you in jail and throw away the key. Until such time as it may be possible to bring you to trial without jeopardizing the safety of the realm. I want no more of this nonsense. You will go on sick-leave as your doctor ordered. I shall require a certificate to say that you are unfit, and a chit to say when I can expect you to return. None of you, I warn you, will make a fool of me again.'

He slammed the door. Henrietta and Shepherd burst into hysterical laughter.

'I'm glad you find it funny,' Tregarron said from the doorway. He had a Gladstone bag in his hand and he wore tweeds. There was a heavy overcoat over one arm and a most un-English tweed hat on the side of his head. 'It is always funnier when an old man slips on the banana skin. But despite you and the Admiral and the despicable Villers, I think I could have pulled it off.'

'Pulled off what?' they chorused.

'I was going to shoot Kapitänleutnant Otto Schiller dead. And I see no reason to suppose that I would have failed … '

He had been preparing to kill Schiller ever since hearing about the death of Molly and the manner of her dying. There were people in Holland who would get him across the border and had an incentive to get him back alive. It had not been difficult to concoct a cover story to justify his presence on the coast. There were detailed records of the activities of the

U-boat crews ashore in Ostend and Zeebrugge in the Intelligence files. With his poacher's gun concealed in the back pocket of his Ulster he would shoot Schiller as he returned drunk to his shore billet. The body would go into the harbour. It would not need too much luck for him to be back in Amsterdam before the body was found. And a .22 made a very small hole.

But the spy scare started by the letter decoded by Shepherd had doubled the watch on passengers boarding boats sailing to the neutral countries. A Special Branch officer had spotted Tregarron and the game was up before it had started.

'Admiral Hall said that the Royal Navy did not believe in assassination as a weapon of war. And more to the point, killing one U-boat captain did not justify the risk of me telling them about OB14. The damned fool did not realize that that was the reason I took my revolver.' He slumped back into a chair, an exhausted old man. 'There is no fool like an old fool. It comes home to you when there is nothing you can do, not even with your own life, to revenge a personal injury.'

'It's a damned sight worse being an ineffectual young man,' Shepherd said. 'This time both of us have been robbed by some scruffy old fisherman. I have checked sighting reports for the days after the attack. A Q ship reported attacking a U-boat on the surface about 120 miles south-west of Folkestone. It was blowing half a gale with snow. They fired six shells and claimed three hits before a squall hid the U-boat. When the snow cleared there was nothing in sight. They did not claim a sinking. But look at those intercepts.' He waved his arm at the array of intercepts neatly laid out across the desk. 'It's deep water there. I think Schiller and his crew are still there. For all time. Some one beat us to them.'

Tregarron hauled himself wearily to his feet and leaned over the desk. He was grinning when he lifted his head.

'What the hell does it matter who killed the bastard? We got him. Before he got back to port to crow. Jerry knows. His friends know. Sooner or later Jerry will have to admit we got him.' He stood up ramrod-straight again. 'Henry, for God's sake find me some coffee and a sandwich.' A message container slid down the pneumatic tube and rattled into the basket. He grabbed it and slapped her bottom. 'Come on, woman, earn your keep. We are back in business again.'

The wind that screamed across the English Channel had been born up on the thousand-year-old mile-thick ice plateau lying on top of Greenland. In its passage past Iceland, down the funnel of the North Sea, through the Straits of Dover and into the Channel it had lost none of the icy bite inherited at birth. Wind, tides and conflicting currents raised a wild unpredictable chop that burst regularly over the men kneeling on the foredeck of the UC62. It was pitch dark apart from the yellow light from two storm lanterns. The fuel-oil tanks had been leaking for the past four days and now everything – the hull, the rigging, what was left of it, every handhole and lifeline – was coated with the slippery black mess. Like the men crouched on the foredeck, who were covered from head to feet.

One of them knelt on the deck-plating, with his face close to the huge patch riveted to the main ballast tank. With a shaving brush he splashed soapy water round the edges of the patch. He beckoned the lanterns nearer before grunting his satisfaction and banging on the deck with a hammer.

'Dry as an old maid,' he croaked. Some of the fuel oil had got into his throat. 'Wave the lantern at the bridge,' he ordered as he forced his cramped muscles to push him upright.

The wave came out of the darkness unseen and unheard above the noise of the screaming wind. The kneeling man pulled himself up with two hands on a buckled stanchion. A sailor holding a lantern leaned over to give him a hand as the wave struck. There was no purchase for the oiled feet on the greasy deck. The hastily grabbed lifeline slipped through his oily fingers. The lantern glittered under water for a few seconds before it was snuffed out.

'Man overboard,' someone croaked in an automatic reflex action. It was too late. Bootsmanns Maat Kurt Zeigler, aged nineteen years and eleven months, was lost at sea.

As the black water drained away the fore hatch opened,

illuminated by the light below. The remaining three men ran along the deck, leaping through the hatch with a dexterity born of long practice.

'Herr Kaleu'nt says to report to the control room, sir,' a seaman said, handing the engineer a towel to wipe off the oil and water.

Leitende Ingenieur Caspar Henne weaved through the confined space, shedding wet clothing as he strode along. He started to shudder, the strength leaking out of him at the knees. No matter how hard he towelled himself his flesh, puckered through exposure to the sea, seemed unable to generate any heat. He was naked as he passed the officers' wardroom, four bunks and a table behind a green curtain. He reached in, groping under a pillow for a bottle. His teeth chattered uncontrollably on the neck as he poured the schnapps down his throat.

He was a hairy man and the oil had made flattened patches that resembled the scabs of some loathsome disease. His crotch was a black smudge. The pain would come later when the heat of the engines drove off the numbness. He pulled a blanket off his bunk to wrap round his shoulders and paddled on, trying to scrub some of the oil off his testicles.

The IWO, the First Officer, Oberleutnant Hugo Wilhelm von Beibedecke, came out of the wireless room looking as though he was about to take his place on the quarterdeck of the battleship he had so recently left.

'Henne,' he snapped. 'You look ridiculous dressed like that in front of the crew. You cannot report to the Captain in that state. Get yourself properly dressed immediately.'

'Henne!' the Captain shouted from the control room. 'When you have finished gossiping with that gilded popinjay from the Kiel Regatta I'm waiting for your bloody report.'

Kapitänleutnant Otto Schiller was twenty-six but he looked years older as he leaned against the lowered periscope standard. Twelve hours' sleep in three days, unwashed and unshaven, he now had enough confidence that he could save his ship that he could afford to bait his First Officer again. Drops of spray pattered down the open hatch to the conning tower. Schiller ignored them. His officer's cap was jammed back to front on his unruly black hair. The opened oilskins showed his grubby white submariner's frock, rescued from a sinking British submarine.

'They're not perfect but them patches are watertight,' Henne said, his head cocked on one side to listen to the diesels. The boat's motion was easier with the revolutions up now that the foredeck was clear.

'She's safe to dive. You can do anything you want with her. Except more of those underwater charges. You'll need to blow the tanks now and then, but she'll get you home.'

'Hear that, Mr Beibedecke?' Schiller said. 'You have no need to worry about Tommi hanging you as a pirate. Henne says we can go home.'

'We are aware, sir, of how this submarine got its reputation,' Beibedecke said softly so that none of the men in the control room could hear him. 'I shall not boast about this patrol.'

'Because you are not used to leaving harbour, Mr Beibedecke. War is a nasty bloody business when you are at the sharp end. Something you can't learn in harbour. Damn it, your battleship couldn't sink. Her bottom is resting on bottles.'

'Which way, Henne? West by Ireland and Scotland with one wrecked and one doubtful diesel. Back to Zeebrugge through Tommi's impregnable Straits. Or we could run south, lay up in some Spanish harbour to make repairs, fix the second diesel. Or can you perform another miracle?'

Henne shook his head. 'Sir, there's a hole in the crankcase you could walk through without stooping. Two connecting rods gone. And the crankshaft ... And it's the wrong time o' the year to beat round the west coast with only one diesel.'

'Right. A Spanish harbour. We are nearer there than anywhere else. Mr Beibedecke can catch up on his laundry.'

The engineer shook his head. 'He'd need clean nappies when we put out to sea after twenty-four hours and found half the Royal Navy waiting for us.'

'All right. You start making a set of wings. Until then we go back the way we came, through Tommi's back garden. You hear, Beibedecke? Plot a course for home. Keep to the east. I want to be off Boulogne at midnight tomorrow.'

The boatswain appeared with two mates carrying coils of copper wire. Schiller turned to Henne. 'You lost a man. Who was he?'

'Young Zeigler. He didn't have a chance. Everything's coated with oil. It's as greasy as a pig's arse up there. And black as the pit ... '

'Jagow!' Schiller shouted to the boatswain. 'Rig fresh lifelines. It's your responsibility to see that each man is made fast to one at all times. Get that. We have enough trouble with Tommi without losing men to the sea. Go on, man, get on with it. I want that aerial rigged as soon as possible. Maybe we will find out what we have done to annoy Tommi.'

He blew into the speaking tube. Up on the conning tower, Leutnant Weiderer wiped the spray out of his eyes and ducked into the shelter of the casing. Schiller said, 'Jagow and two mates are coming up through the forrard hatch to rig a new aerial. Keep her heading into the sea and as slow as you can. I'll be in my bunk.'

He kicked his boots off and lay down, intending only to clear his mind and think about the coming passage through the Straits. It was not as difficult as Tommi thought, but it was never easy. Especially going north. There was too much traffic in and out of Calais and Boulogne, before you got to the nets, the hydrophones and the fixed minefields. There were marker buoys and mines along the nets and patrolling trawlers. You had two choices. Over the top, drawing as little as possible at full speed on a dark night. Or you dived deep and crawled under. He would be glad when they were through.

This trip had been an odd one ever since they had got that order to sink the destroyer coming out of Folkestone Roads. And it had turned out to be one of the big fleet minelayers. Why should a minelayer be carrying nurses? Tommi had reacted violently. Two near misses from the sharp bows of searching destroyers had kept them on the bottom all night. Two of those damned underwater charges had thrown them arse over tip, damaging a motor and some switchgear. They had surfaced into a snowstorm to sweeten the air and drift south-west making rough repairs. Then they had the luck to

29

meet a trawler with the best gun crew in the Channel. The second shell had taken out their deck gun. The next had punctured the ballast tank. The fuel-oil tank had sprung a leak, and a damaged battery had them coughing their guts up from chlorine gas. Only the squall had saved them.

Then, that night, one of the diesels blew up. Two connecting rods had smashed through the crankcase. Yes, it had been an eventful trip ...

The wireless operator woke him after two hours. Although he felt like the wrath of God he rubbed the sleep out of his eyes, bellowed for a mug of coffee and began decoding the message. If his First Officer had been anyone other than von Beibedecke he would have given him the job in exchange for another hour of sleep. But not Beibedecke. The man was senior to him in the Navy List. He had been on battleships throughout the war until he had volunteered for the U-boat service. He had dropped a rank while he did the patrols that would give him the experience to command his own boat. With his seniority and connections – there had been von Beibedeckes in the Imperial Navy since the days of the Hanseatic League – he would soon get a command.

He had already told Schiller what he was getting. One of the big Germania boats. For the Atlantic trade where the pickings were good. No ditch-crawling, among the sandbanks of the German ocean with a cargo of mines, for him. Schiller had other ideas. Beibedecke could have UC62.

> FROM KOMMODORE
> FLANDERS FLOTILLA.
> MOST IMMEDIATE.
> DER DICHTER. REPORT CIRCUMSTANCES YOUR SINKING FOLKESTONE DIEPPE PACKET BOAT NIGHT WEDNESDAY LAST. RETURN IMMEDIATELY QUICKEST ROUTE SUBJECT ONLY TO SAFETY OF SHIP. STUDY SILHOUETTES SHOWS GROSS SIMILARITY SUNK SHIP AND FLEET MINELAYER. ACKNOWLEDGE. FOLLOWING MAINTAIN WIRELESS SILENCE.
> KOMMODORE.

Schiller whistled silently through a gap in his front teeth. No wonder Tommi had reacted like an awakened bear. A packet boat. Of course, there would have to be an American on board. There was always a bloody Yankee with his missus and kids sailing through the middle of a war zone as if it was laid on for their entertainment. It served them right.

Now for the bloody report. But how could you condense a trip like this into two paragraphs.

They had made a disastrous start, stopping a Dutch schooner just after first light to collect the bags of coffee, hams and eggs and tins of Dutch cigars. He could smell them now. From up forrard where the torpedomen were playing skat. The gun crew were using her for target practice when two destroyers had attacked from the darkness of the western horizon. He had closed up to the hull of the schooner when the mainmast came down, shearing away the aerial, the jumping wire and killing two of the gun crew.

The new charges Tommi was using had given them a hard time. They exploded under water. Some sort of mine? It was like being hit by a piledriver. They had sat on the sand all day, creeping up at nightfall half-dead from the foul air.

But later that night as they closed on the Thames estuary they had come to life. That was when the patrol really started. When a broad hint became a fact. He could remember that young lad, Ziegler, the one washed overboard a few hours ago, singing as they reeved a new aerial ...

'Pipe down, that man. Quiet.' He picked up the speaking tube. 'Dead slow.'

UC62 rolled in a North Sea chop. Not a good start to this patrol. First night out, two dead gun crew and the wireless aerial adrift. He began to pace up and down chewing his unlit cigar, forcing himself not to look at the progress of the new aerial. If only those bastards knew how important it was to their captain. His *Pour le Merite*, his promotion and his transfer from these ditch-crawling minelayers on to a real U-boat in the Atlantic, America or the happy hunting grounds of the Mediterranean – all these things might be in jeopardy because of that damned aerial. Because of that damned Dutchman's coffee. They'd have his guts for garters if he fouled up this one just to feed his crew ... And the Kommodore, Flanders Flotilla.

And he could rely on his Magnificence, Hugo von Beibedecke, to make sure the story reached the right ears. Damn it, it was worse than sailing with a time-bomb aboard. Another couple of trips and he would get rid of him on to a Command course at the U-boat school. There were worse things than a summer in the Baltic.

Poor sod. He could imagine the pressures that had been brought to bear on his First Lieutenant. Because there was always a Beibedecke up near the top in Wilhelmshaven. Never right at the top, two paces back from the right hand of whoever was on top. You lasted longer there. He would bet on Beibedecke's progress. Two more trips in UC62, then the command course. Up a rank when he got a boat. One of the big U-81 class. Half a dozen trips to the Western Ocean. Up to Korvetten Kapitän and a desk in Flotilla HQ. There was always a need for good staff officers, and the undersea service needed a trained admiral.

Henne came on to the speaking tube. The aerial was fixed. It was 21.30. Afrikanisher, the wireless operator, was waiting for instructions.

'Right. Beibedecke, position report to the wireless room immediately. Then report to the bridge. Steer 180, half ahead both.'

He released the gun crew after Beibedecke arrived in the conning tower. And he put the look-outs on thirty-minute watches. Five-minute overlap.

'You are heading south,' Beibedecke said. Schiller pointed to the western horizon. The loom of a light could be seen despite the blackness and the rain.

'Outer Gabbard light,' he said. It was one of the lightships guiding the sweep of coastal traffic into the Thames estuary. 'Port ten. Steer 170.'

'We are too far south,' Beibedecke repeated. 'Our orders were to lay mines in the swept channel going north from Harwich.'

Schiller ignored him as he concentrated on the arithmetic in his head. The tide was in flood, the wind was from the north-west. The press of water through wind and tide was from the north, funnelling through the Straits. A high tide tonight. High enough to float a U-boat over the nets between the British and French coasts. If the message he was waiting for came it would do no harm to be a few miles south. 'Port five. Steer 165. Bring the revs up 100 on both.'

The wind picked up the spume from their wake and blew it in his face. He could smell ham frying below. It would do no harm. No one smelling fried ham would think of U-boats.

'At this rate,' Beibedecke said, 'We'll be tangled up in the nets across the Straits of Dover by midnight.'

Schiller leaned on the buckled handrail. 'Over them, Beibedecke, over them heading for green pastures.'

The speaking tube whistled. Weiderer reported that Flotilla HQ were transmitting. Schiller grinned into the darkness. His luck was still running. The hint the Kommodore had dropped before sailing was going to pay dividends. Maybe Beibedecke would get his command earlier than he expected.

'She's all yours while I go below to find out what is keeping our brass hats awake. Keep those look-outs on their toes: we are entering Tommi's private property. Call me if you see anything. You will log that until further orders we will take no offensive action except as may be necessary for the safety of the ship.'

A gust of rain splattered across the conning tower and UC62 rolled as an awkward chop hit her bows. The air was full of water and the unmistakable growl of the diesels. Spume and rain bit into the faces of the look-outs. Schiller rubbed his hands. It was a perfect night for running the gauntlet through Tommi's backyard and into the dining-room.

He went down the ladder like a cat, catching the gossip floating up from below. The draught created by running the diesels had sweetened the ship, sucked out the stench of gas, unwashed bodies, bilges and diesel oil. The mingled smells of cigars and coffee, the relief from the biting wind, made up for the cramped control room.

'Must be a general recall. We only left last night ... '

'Maybe the war's over ... '

'Shore leave ... '

'You haven't got the strength. The Kommodore wants us to entertain his young ladies ... '

'Special orders for Jonah ... '

As he dropped lightly on to the deck the gossip stopped. He felt their eyes on him as he walked past the officers' bunks, along the gangway past the galley to the wireless room. Jonah. That was a new one. Survivor, Lucky, Jammy, The Man who Walks on Water, Bubble Guts, Iron Fish; they were some of the polite names he had been called since he lost his last boat. The second one to go down under him. There were only three men aboard who had sailed with him before. And earlier than that, in the first weeks of the war, he had been the only survivor of a training boat rammed by a freighter in the Baltic.

He half-turned. 'That leave you were talking about, Ubshe,' he said to the helmsman, 'is cancelled. And it stays cancelled as long as you steer five degrees off course.'

Schiller was not the sort of captain who delegated anything; authority, responsibility, knowledge all stayed with him. But this message he had to share with Beibedecke. He had been in the U-boat service too long to share his crew's belief in his own immortality. So he sent Weiderer up to replace Beibedecke in the conning tower.

FROM KOMMODORE. FLANDERS FLOTILLA.

OPERATION ORDER 359. DER DICHTER ONLY.

THE FLANDERS FLOTILLA HAS BEEN ENTRUSTED WITH A TASK OF THE UTMOST IMPORTANCE IN MAINTAINING THE BLOCKADE OF THE ENEMY. YOU WILL PROCEED WITH ALL SPEED TO FOLKESTONE ROADS TO ATTACK AND SINK A FRENCH DESTROYER, NAME UNKNOWN. IT WILL SET SAIL AT 20.00 HOURS, WEDNESDAY, 16 FEBRUARY. IT IS LIKELY TO BE HEAVILY ESCORTED. THE ATTACK MUST NOT BE MADE UNTIL THE SHIP IS UNDER WAY FOR DIEPPE. EVERY EFFORT MUST BE MADE TO DISPERSE THE ESCORTS.

THIS OPERATION WILL TAKE PRIORITY OVER ANY ORDERS PREVIOUSLY ISSUED. UNDER NO CIRCUMSTANCES WILL ANY ACTION BE INITIATED WHILE ON COURSE FOR THIS OPERATION WHICH COULD IN ANY WAY JEOPARDIZE THE SUCCESS OF THE ATTACK, UNLESS THE SAFETY OF THE SHIP IS AT EXTREME RISK. MESSAGE ENDS. ACKNOWLEDGE. MAINTAIN WIRELESS SILENCE.

KOMMODORE. FLANDERS FLOTILLA.

Schiller's fingers lingered on the sentence about the escorts. It was nicely put, much nicer than saying, 'Do all you can to hinder rescue attempts. You are not sinking a ship but killing some passengers.'

Who was it? A top general like Kitchener killed by a mine? The way they were killing men on the Western Front he should have been ordered to escort them into either Dieppe or Boulogne.

The First Lieutenant smoothed the message flat with his elegant fingers. 'It will mean passing through the Straits of Dover. Nets, mines, trawler patrols firing starshells on nights like this ... '

'Brilliant. I'm amazed that your rust-bound battleship ever let such a mind escape. To reach Folkestone by 20.00 hours tomorrow we have to get through the barrage. You damned fool, there isn't a captain in the flotilla who hasn't done it. Luckily for us the Tommis have as many brains in Whitehall as we have in the Wilhelmstrasse. They never catch U-boats in the Dover barrage, therefore the barrage is impregnable. And when they do get one it shows how good the defences are.' He stabbed a finger on the chart. 'New course. Take us more to the east. There's not much chance with this wind and sea, but we would look idiots stuck on a sandbank. We stay on the surface through the night. All being well. Dive at dawn. I want to be there with at least four hours to spare. And fully charged batteries.'

He went back to the conning tower. The look-outs rotated, but he remained there braced by the crumpled handrail – eyes and ears alert as UC62, hull down, lurched south into the fierce wind.

Lucky Schiller they called him. Wet-arse Schiller. Old Herring Guts. The luck of the sea had lost him his first crew; a British torpedo the second. A Q ship had wiped out his gun crew and taken off the head of his First Lieutenant, minutes after he had left the bridge, and a mine, anybody's mine, had cost him his third crew. Tomorrow night he would redress the balance. Those old French destroyers, hit at speed, went down like a sack of potatoes. Time and place, that was all he needed.

Provided he got UC62 through the nets, the hydrophones and the Dover Patrol.

That piece of paper would get him his *Pour le Merite* and the next Atlantic boat. Goodbye minelaying. He had had a good run but he, more than anyone else, knew why the UC boats were called 'The Sisters of Sorrow'. He was the only survivor of his Captains' Course.

The wind and rain eased off soon after midnight as they came abreast of the Thames estuary. Schiller had got a fix on two lightships earlier and he was now confident of their exact position. The steward brought him a bowl of soup. He laced it with brandy from his hip-flask and drank it noisily. His lips were too numb to feel the heat.

'Stop engines. Diving stations,' he said. The noisy rumble of the diesels stopped. UC62 sank deeper. They had been running heavy holding her up on the hydroplanes. He switched to the silent running electric motors.

'Group up. Half ahead together. Silent running. I'll flog the first man to make a noise. Oberleutnant Beibedecke, when you have trimmed hull down report to the conning tower. Dressed for a wet night.'

Hull down, a bow wave streaming round the front of the conning tower. The sea foamed in round their feet through a shell hole. Beibedecke huddled deeper into his great-coat, waiting for his eyes to get used to the darkness. An icy spray hit them continuously. The cold burned his nostrils and seeped through the layers of clothing to clutch at his guts.

'Take a good look, Oberleutnant Baron von Beibedecke. Remember it next time your beloved Admiral is spouting about our naval might. Look around you. Remember when it was like this off Hamburg. What are your bloody battleships doing tonight, swinging about their anchor chains?'

As his vision cleared, Beibedecke saw half a dozen merchant ships between patches of mist. One of them, a 20,000 tonner, altered course to zigzag, passing only a few hundred metres ahead of their bows.

He flinched. 'They'll see us.'

Schiller was straining forward with his gloved hands

clenched tight on the handrail, as though he could project a torpedo by will power.

'Dead slow,' he said.

The rhythmic thump-thump of the triple expansion engines floated across to them as the steamer moved past into the mist. The lop of her wake boiled up around the conning tower. Someone below yelped as a dollop of icy seawater splashed down his neck.

'Belay that row,' Schiller snapped. He peered into the gloom. 'Half ahead together.' He pointed ahead. Destroyers on the hunt; one, two, three of them betrayed by the white foam curling from their bows. 'Down the hatch.'

The look-outs jumped down the hatchway. Beibedecke fumbled clumsily for the rungs. Schiller put a sea-boot into the small of his back and pushed. He ducked under the hatch and slammed it shut, swinging the locking clips into place in one swift movement.

'Dive, dive, dive.' The klaxon blared. 'Full ahead both.'

He dropped down on to the deck, rolling sideways like an acrobat in the dim shaded light. 'Take her down to thirty metres. Hold it there. Stand by for underwater explosions.'

The thrashing noise of the propellers grew nearer. One of them raced directly overhead. Now for it. Beibedecke hunched his head between his shoulders, waiting for the shattering explosion from the new mines that the British were using. Nobody was quite sure what they were, but when they exploded it was as if the boat had been hit by a gigantic hammer. The lights would go out and the cork insulation overhead flaked off like snow. But not this time. The noises faded away to the north-east.

Schiller grinned wolfishly as they came up to periscope depth. He twisted his cap back to front. 'Glamour boys. Forty knots, battle pennants flying and you can see the bow wave five kilometres away.'

But he swept the horizon before surfacing and restarting the diesel engines. In this traffic a little noise would not matter. Soon it began to rain again, a fine drizzle that soaked through everything. There were too many ships abroad. On two occasions, the first warning they had of something with a sharp bow passing in the night was the lurch and roll as the wake hit them.

'It's a risk,' Schiller admitted, shrugging his shoulders. 'Just being alive is to risk dying. Change the look-outs.'

Again and again they went to silent running to creep past ships that came and went into the night. They dived when the rain turned into driving rods that fogged the night glasses and bruised their exposed eyes. At four in the morning Schiller brought Beibedecke back into the conning tower for the run over the net barrage across the Straits.

'It's a shit or bust operation. You either go over the top at full speed and hope that you are not spotted or ... '

'And if you are spotted?'

Schiller looked at him. He would find out sooner or later the sort of courage needed to sit out attacks far worse than they had experienced that morning. About the marker buoys on the nets that betrayed you to the patrols, the contact mines that swung in towards you when a net was hooked, the hydrophones pinpointing your thrashing propellers for the benefit of fingers poised over the triggers of electrically detonated mines. But you got hung up on nets by being cautious; crossing was an operation that demanded a controlled foolhardiness.

'Blow all tanks; I want her lighter than a Zeppelin,' he said quietly. 'Silent running. Full ahead both. Or you can take her on to the bottom and feel your way between the sandbanks at forty metres. We don't have the time.'

There was no need to order silent running. Everyone knew where they were going and sat quietly waiting, men on watch and men off watch. The tension was like electricity in the air.

The top cable of the net rasped along the keel. The boat suddenly slewed through twenty degrees to port. A tin mug clattered on the deck as a man, caught off balance, fell. A petty officer put his boot on the man's chest to choke the cry as the hot coffee splashed over him.

Schiller looked aft. The top cable of the net was hooked on the port hydroplane. A couple of marker buoys bobbed up and down like agitated seagulls moving inwards towards their wake. Was there a mine alongside them?

'Stop motors. Full astern together. Flood aft tanks.'

The marker buoys bobbed and swayed, moving closer together. The look-outs were staring at them goggle-eyed, waiting for a mine to explode.

'Get back on watch,' Schiller snapped quietly. 'Staring at them won't help.'

UC62 slowed in a smother of foam and went astern. The buoys swung closer, bobbed up and down then separated. They were free.

'Stop motors. Full ahead together. Flood forrard tanks. Hull down. And watch that damned course.' He sensed Beibedecke's intake of breath. 'Change the look-outs. The silly buggers think it is all over. One bloody fishing boat could wreck everything. Aye, and sink the meal ticket of that bit of skirt you have tucked away in Ostend.' His teeth flashed as Beibedecke stiffened. 'You're not in your bloody battleship now, Herr Baron. In the U-boat service you shit and stink together. And everybody knows what you get up to ashore ... More if their imagination runs that way.'

He tried to hold himself in check. He was doing what he had accused the look-outs of doing. Suffering from reaction. Taking it out on the First Lieutenant. He bit his lip. In ten days' time, if the Kommodore kept his promise, and promises came easy to commanders sweating it out ashore, he would be rid of this damned coffin and its thirty-eight mines. Away from ditch-crawling between sandbanks, harassed by trawlers and airships and flying boats. After this trip they would have to give him the *Pour le Merite* and one of the Atlantic boats. Six tubes, a couple of deck guns and a free range round the Irish coast. No matter what Tommi did, his ships had to funnel through the north or south channels into the Irish sea. Maybe a trip to America where the pickings were even easier.

UC62 rolled and lurched. Spray broke over the conning tower. The sea was getting up. Somebody had been sick below. He could smell the stench in the updraught. The wake of an unseen ship lifted them, smacking the bows down in a splash of white water. These were busy waters. A look-out pointed. He caught the loom of a speeding ship against the horizon. Troop ships, leave ships, freighters, all carrying the sinews of war. His fingers itched but common sense and his orders restrained him. Even a few mines might raise a hornets' nest about his ears. Another thirty minutes and he would go back on to the diesels to charge the batteries for the long day ahead.

'Keep your eyes skinned, lads,' he growled. This was no time to spare the batteries. 'Half ahead both. New course. Starboard fifteen.'

Dawn came up on an empty sea with a smudge of land on the eastern horizon. And a long plume of greasy diesel exhaust smoke hanging low behind them. It was too much to risk in these waters. Henne would have to look at his injectors. He glanced wistfully at the red ball burning through the haze to the east. It was time they were out of sight.

'Look-outs below. Stop engines. Stand by to dive.' He slammed the hatch shut. 'Dive!'

UC62 slid under the surface to run slowly south-west down to Folkestone Roads, leaving the Channel to the next rainstorm, the fishing boats and the Channel packet boats. It was going to be a long, stifling day. But the end result would be worth the sweat and stink. Otto Schiller, son of a Rhineland pork butcher who had turned 'food processor' to get his son into the Navy's Officer Corps, thanks to dear Mama sleeping with that pig of a Deputy – he was going to join the aces.

The light was going when he came up to periscope depth, soaked up by the stormclouds driving low overhead. The French coast was mantled in gloom and there was no sign of the departed sun in the west. Half a gale, he thought, blowing up from the south-west. Dungeness Light flickered on the horizon. They were almost in position.

It had been a desperately frustrating day. These little minelayers were not big enough to sit on the bottom in comfort for a day. So he had let the tidal stream take him south away down towards Cherbourg. Around mid morning he had surfaced to sweeten the boat. He turned north, recharging his batteries, reasoning that if he were spotted he would be put down as a venturesome ace coming in from Ireland. Within fifteen minutes they had had to dive and watch two big ones steaming towards Cherbourg without an escort. No attack. Now the crew knew that this was no ordinary patrol. Their eyes followed him everywhere.

There were hunters about. Twice they had crash-dived at the sight of pennants of smoke, praying that they had not been spotted. Each time they had the agonizing wait for the attack to begin. Even when nothing happened the waiting did not get any easier.

Then in the early afternoon, Beibedecke was caught napping by a seaplane going like a bomb with the wind behind it. It was almost overhead before they dived with the First Lieutenant and the two look-outs sprawled on the control-room deck. There had been no sign that they had been spotted, but in the confusion UC62 got her bows down in an uncontrolled descent that finished with a thump on the sandy bottom. That disarranged some of the hastily repaired switchgear. It had taken the black gang 120 nail-biting minutes before Henne had reported to Beibedecke that UC62 was ready to be broken again. Schiller had slept. He knew he would get little chance later.

A solitary destroyer, pennant flying, brightwork glittering, spruce in new grey paint, appeared in the periscope, racing north for Dover with a bone in her teeth. Another new one, another Tommi to watch out for. They seemed to come in an unending stream. But the spring gales would take care of the new paint and the brightwork. And a few days of war off the Flanders coast would teach him not to stay on one course for so long.

Schiller dropped the periscope, checked the course and looked at his watch. Another five hours.

The hydrophone operator said, 'Propeller noises, red-zero-nine-zero. Approaching slowly.'

Schiller laid his forehead against the clammy metal surface of the periscope barrel. He could feel the crew listening, waiting. Beibedecke was doing his 'German officers have no fear' act, hands behind his back, pacing up and down behind the hydroplane men. All of them screwing up their nerves because some bastard had to go fishing. He glanced towards his watch and stopped himself looking at it. Then he walked slowly towards his bunk.

'Oberleutnant Beibedecke, you have the watch. Take her to the bottom. Call me in two hours. Absolute silence. Minimum power.'

He kicked off his boots, pulled the curtain across and forced himself to relax. High water would come at the appointed time no matter who or how many waited and watched for it.

The smell of coffee woke him. The steward was standing by his bunk with a mug of it steaming in the foul air. It took physical effort to breathe. Rolling off his bunk and pushing his feet into his boots had him panting like a dog. The crew on watch lolled about like dead men.

Beibedecke handed him the log. Damn the man, he still dressed as though he had the harbour watch on his battle-wagon. Half a dozen ships, two of them large single propeller jobs going slowly. Freighters and fishing boats. A busy street.

'Motors. Slow ahead together. Bring her up to periscope depth. Stand by to surface.'

They surfaced into a black night and an empty sea, their ears popping with the change in pressure blowing out the stench. There was no destroyer lying in the roads. Schiller had not expected one. Not after the weather they had had over the past days. He raised his night glasses. UC62 was two miles offshore. He could see the dimmed lighting along the promenade, the navigation lights on the end of the pier and a bright glare reflected from a plume of steam. The boat train? If the destroyer was alongside the quay, where was the escort?

It was the escort that bothered Schiller. Not for its offensive capability; he was confident that he could lose anything on a night like this, but it could stop him getting a clear shot at the target. With only two tubes he would need to be close and have luck running in his favour to hit a destroyer working up to thirty knots. So where were they? Fifteen minutes to high water.

'Sir, hydrophones report ships' propellers bearing green-zero-four-zero.'

A look-out pointed to starboard, at the harbour. 'Ships leaving harbour, sir. Trawlers, two of them.'

'Minesweepers,' Schiller said. This was getting interesting. Maybe Tommi had learned something from the Lord Kitchener affair. 'Hold your position, damn you,' he snapped at the look-outs as they edged nearer the hatch. His mind was racing. This order had to be based on information from a spy. Would a spy know the difference between minesweepers and a defensive screen? It was unlikely.

'Dismiss the gun crew. Get her trimmed hull down. Who the hell will see us at 400 metres on a night like this? Minelayers to stand by for dropping. Jump to it, man. We don't have all night.'

As UC62 crept along at minimum speed the minesweepers forged across their track, bucketing in the choppy sea, paravanes streamed to sweep. Schiller was grinning as the idea in his mind blossomed in its glorious simplicity.

'Group up, half ahead together. Port fifteen,' Schiller said quietly. He turned to the starboard look-out. 'Concentrate on that damned harbour. Your mate can look after the rest. The bearing will be changing as we move across the steamer track, so watch out. I want to know the moment the next ship moves. Get it. Miss it and I'll hang your balls on the jumping wire.'

He laughed at the expression on Beibedecke's face. 'Don't be so bloody po-faced. What are they doing, man? Why are they out there in the wind and rain instead of swinging at their anchors like your bloody battleships, eh? They're sweeping mines, damn it. Mines that we have not yet dropped. Get below. Take charge of the minelaying. Tell Meyer I want him to lay at a rate he has never managed before. Send Weiderer up with a chart to plot them. And a book of silhouettes. You have two minutes before we start.'

Boldly he turned to starboard, running parallel to the coast across the steamer lane. Weiderer reported.

'Stop-watch? Chart?' Weiderer nodded. 'Take a bearing on that light. Check that they are ready to lay.'

There was no time for the usual pattern. It would have to be a straight run across, and then turn to attack with the torpedoes from the south.

'Mr Beibedecke reports, ready to lay mines, sir,' Weiderer said.

'Start laying.' How quickly could they lay? Schiller glanced at the starboard look-out, but the man had his glasses fixed on the harbour.

The mine was in a chute. It had to be flooded so that the mine could be released to drop on to the sea-bed. Then a fusible link dissolved, allowing the mine tethered to the frame to rise to its pre-set depth just below the surface armed and ready to explode on impact. While that was happening the chute had to be drained, the hatch opened, 500 kilos of mine heaved into place, the hatch locked and the chute flooded. Drop.

Say four minutes. 200 metres between mines. It was too much. They were going too fast.

'Dead slow,' he said down the tube. He saw the look-outs stare at him. 'Keep your blasted eyes on your job.'

Dead slow. If the mine rose from the sea-bed before the U-boat had passed it, the explosion would split UC62 wide open. Depth of water? Before he could ask, a mine broke the surface beyond the stern before sinking to its moored depth.

'Three minutes fifteen seconds,' Weiderer said, taking a bearing and plotting it on the chart.

The sixth mine had been dropped when the starboard look-out said, 'Siren, sir.' Beyond his pointing finger Schiller saw a plume of steam, white against the black cliffs behind the town. The siren blew again.

'Stop laying. Hard aport. Reciprocal course. Steer zero-two-zero.'

It was a slow turn. At this speed they had bare steerage way. But it would take them east and clear of that row of mines. Once laid, mines were impersonal instruments of destruction, exploding no matter who hit them. The mine-layers were not known as 'The Sisters Of Sorrow' for nothing.

Weiderer began calling the bearings as UC62 came round on to her new course.

'Stand by to resume laying. Mark, Weiderer. Drop.'

'Ship is moving, sir,' the look-out said.

Schiller lifted his night glasses. He could see the masts

moving past the jib of a crane. But that was no destroyer. Of course, these gentlemen, whoever they were, could not be upset by putting out in this weather in a destroyer. It looked like one of Tommi's big fleet minelayers. She still had to get up speed. There was plenty of time. He had not laid the mines in the hope of hitting this ship. Minelaying was too chancy for that. But if some other ship hit one, Tommi might think of mines and not a U-boat firing torpedoes. The confusion might give them the vital few minutes they would need to get clear.

'Ship is clearing harbour, sir.'

'Stop laying. Secure mines. Mr Beibedecke to the bridge. Half ahead both. Stand by torpedoes.'

He picked her up as she swept past the pierhead, and tried to estimate her speed. He told Beibedecke to start the attack plot. It was a big minelayer all right.

'Course and speed,' he said to Weiderer.

'She's on course for Dieppe all right, sir. Ten knots, still picking up speed. She's got a bone in her teeth like a destroyer.'

Schiller grinned in the darkness and gripped the rail to still his trembling hands. So much depended on the next few minutes. A spray of rain hid the steamer.

'Dead slow both.'

Weiderer was calculating the angles he had to lay off. The ship was going to cross their bows about 300 metres away.

'Open bow caps.'

'Bow caps open.'

Only two miserable tubes. It would be easy to miss on a night like this. The big Atlantic boats had four forward tubes and two in the stern. He had to get this one right first time.

'Fire one. Start the stop watch. Fire two.'

Now the agonizing wait. So many things to go wrong. A defective gyro, the wrong depth-setting, pistols that did not work. God, if he missed this one the return trip round Ireland and Scotland would last a lifetime.

'Close up the gun crew.' If he missed he would sink her with the deck gun and risk being caught by some laggardly escort.

A plume of white water exploded upwards in the night like a jet of steam. One. As he lifted his glasses he heard the noise and felt the shock of the explosion. Another mound rearing up from the stern. She was still racing on, mortally wounded but unable to stop because of her inertia at that speed. It would tear the bulkheads out of her.

'Two hits,' the hydrophone operator reported. 'Noise of ship breaking up.'

The men down below would hear that. The torpedomen and the engine-room ratings, the men who never got on deck into the fresh air, who lived like sardines cheek by jowl with their mates and equipment from warping out to 'Finished with engines'. They would hear the noise of crumpling bulkheads, engine bedplates shearing, and the hammer-like thud as the boilers blew up.

They would know more than Schiller, because another gust of rain swept across and between him and the stricken ship.

Well, he had carried out his orders. The sentence about the escorts did not apply. He shuddered, remembering the hours he had spent clinging to a spar in the Bight after his second boat went down. It was not a good night for surviving. There was nothing to stop him taking a few prisoners to prove he had done as ordered. To confirm his assumptions.

'Slow ahead together. Come up on deck, Beibedecke, I'll need you to practise your English. Get half a dozen men on the foredeck. Rig a searchlight. I want all officers brought aboard for questioning.'

Slowly they slipped through the rain. Where the devil were the ship's lifeboats? And that searchlight. He could not see a thing. Somewhere ahead in the darkness the boilers exploded. Fragments pattered into the sea around the submarine. An arc spluttered as the searchlight lit up. A line of oil-skinned sailors came up through the forehatch. Schiller bit his lip. If there were destroyers coming out to investigate he might lose half those men. His men. Or the boat.

A lifeboat suddenly appeared out of the rain. The bows were almost on top of it before anyone saw it.

'Stop motors. Full astern both.'

It was too late. The bow sheared through a row of oars as a

wave lifted the lifeboat and slammed it down on the rounded foredeck. Gunwhale and side planking split as the boat tipped over, spilling bodies into the sea away from the outstretched hands of the sailors.

Schiller gaped as a woman in a white nightdress floated by, spreadeagled on the crest of a wave with her long blonde hair trailing like a pennant. As she opened her mouth to scream the wave broke over her face. Her body rolled, throwing one bare arm out of the sea before she disappeared.

The searchlight flitted from one patch of debris to another. Rainbows of oil floated between planks, gratings, an empty lifejacket, an evening dress obscenely filled and rippled by a wave, half a dozen partially clad bodies. Without steerage way the bows swung with the action of the waves, butting into a clump of bodies, sweeping a man off the grating he held under his chin. He screamed abuse and his clenched fist rose out of the water as a wave rolled his head under.

'Start motors. Slow ahead both.'

Another lifeboat surfing on the crest of a wave slid down on them. Schiller ordered the helm hard over, but at their speed it had little effect.

Half a dozen shirt-sleeved men tried to fend off with their oars. Two of them snapped, toppling the oarsmen into the water. Beibedecke ducked under the foredeck rail to reach a hand out to one of them. The submarine rolled and their outstretched hands missed. A flailing hand hit Beibedecke in the face. He reeled, throwing his arms out to keep his balance. His left arm struck the oarsman on the chest, pushing him away and under the pitching lifeboat. As the lifeboat swirled out of the searchlight beam a man shook his fist shouting, 'Murderer!'

Beibedecke picked himself off the deck. He walked stiffly to the conning tower, his white face turned up to glare at Schiller.

'I suppose you feel like God up there ... sir. Permission to report, sir. If you are trying to destroy all the lifeboats, there is one ten metres to starboard full of nurses. Are we taking prisoners or do you propose to kill all the survivors ... ?'

The deck shuddered as something exploded between UC62 and the shore. The mines had claimed their first victim.

Beibedecke was still babbling, ' ... cross-Channel boat with a hospital unit going to France. Fifty nurses and doctors. The rest were civilians.'

'Not in this war, Beibedecke. If they were going to France it was to do with the war. And they were warned. The Channel was declared a war zone back in '15.'

A gust of wind flicked a spray of spume and drizzle into his face. Automatically he licked the salt off his lips. God, it was cold. There would be no one left alive in the sea. Shock and exposure made a very effective humane killer. He had no appetite for lifting anyone out of a lifeboat. Neither had the men. Not in this sea, not after what had happened.

'Beibedecke, dismiss the men on the foredeck. Stow searchlight. All hands below. Stand by to dive.'

The searchlight went out. Now he could hear the hiss of rain beating on the sea, the wind soughing through the wireless aerial, the clang of metal on metal as the light was stowed. Out in the darkness a woman was sobbing. Red maroons were going up ashore. Calling out the lifeboat. The forehatch slammed shut.

'Half ahead together. Starboard helm. Come round on to one-eight-zero. Trim hull down. Relief look-outs to the bridge.'

As the water surged over the bows the bodies of a man and a woman clasped in each other's arms swept towards the conning tower. The jumping wire tore them apart. A khaki uniform shirt swirled by on the crest of the bow wave. Schiller leaned over and caught it. He squeezed out the water and stuffed it under his oilskin.

Why were they sneaking south in silence? He had done what he had been ordered to do. His knees were quivering, his whole body shook with cold and the reaction to the past twenty-four hours' strain on him. This was only the start of the patrol. There were four spare torpedoes, a hundred shells and twenty mines. And reports. A wireless message to the Kommodore.

'Beibedecke, relieve me on the bridge. Stop motors. Start engines. Cruising revolutions. Charge batteries.'

He would go west around Ireland. In this weather he might regret it but he would get his wish to have a crack at the Atlantic trade. And his report would put a crimp in the career of that ambitious First Lieutenant. No, the man had enough pull to get it squashed. Better to butter him up. A friend on the staff might be useful. Especially now he knew what it was like in the underseas service. It was different from the High Seas Fleet sailing into action, bugles calling, pennants flying, signal flags fluttering in the breeze, eager to burn and drown a few thousand sailors. What he had seen tonight was war as it had to be fought when a country with a harbour-locked Navy went to war with one that thought it owned the seas of the world.

He dropped on to the deck of the control room, his mind shaping the wireless message to the Kommodore. He saw Weiderer look at him, and above the stench of diesel oil and bilges he smelled perfume. The khaki uniform shirt had fallen from under his oilskins. He picked it up, fumbling in the breast pocket. A packet. The sodden paper tore as he pulled it out, spilling chips of fragrant lavender on to the deckplates.

'Propeller noises. Bearing 050 red. Approaching rapidly,' the hydrophone operator said. 'More propeller noises. Sounds like destroyers. Bearing 156 green. Closing rapidly.'

Beibedecke shouted from the conning tower. 'Destroyers. 300 metres.'

The look-outs jumped down the hatchway. Beibedecke's legs appeared. Schiller punched the klaxon. 'Dive, dive, dive, all hands stand by. Start motors. Full ahead both.'

The report would have to wait. The first thing was to survive.

CHAPTER TWO

Shepherd stayed on in the office, dozing on the camp bed, afraid to leave the familiar warmth of the office and its litter. No charwomen were allowed in the Department, they cleaned it up every blue moon; the thick atmosphere of Henrietta's cheroots and Tregarron's pipe, all these were more welcome than the clean sterility of his rooms.

Between cups of coffee Henrietta fed them the latest Departmental gossip. About the pressure to do something concerning the shipping losses. Two admirals were likely to be shunted into some backwater. Even the C-in-C might not escape a premature retirement. Lloyd George was pressing hard for convoys. Now. Unless they could stop the mounting losses it might be difficult to maintain the American supplies ...

The Diplomatic Section were cock-a-hoop over the telegram they had decoded from Zimmerman, the German Foreign Secretary, to their ambassador in Mexico City. Now they had to find a way to get it into the Americans' hands without compromising the work of OB14. There were ways ... And because of that, nobody except Villers was going to take much interest in the goings-on in the U-boat section for a few weeks.

Tregarron tossed a bulky file on to Shepherd's lap. 'Have a look before I take it back to Archie Grimble. He got the job of preparing the case against Schiller. As a war criminal. Now the bastard is dead we can close the file.'

It was a sickening document but Shepherd was unable to put it down.

'I'm not a professional seaman but I have kept a boat in the Solent for the past twenty years so I know a bit about the sea. It was deliberate murder. Our lifeboat was pulling clear, picking survivors out of the water, when he came at us out of the mist. He had a searchlight on and some men on the foredeck. He swung his bows at us and went along the side, smashing the oars. Then he tipped us over ...

I saw a woman in the water. No lifejacket, just a white nightdress. She was swimming towards the conning tower. The butcher stood in the tower watching her, and swept past without stretching a hand out to help her ...

There was a nasty sea runnin' an' it were dark. Rainin' in fits and starts. Mist. I seed the sub coming up towards me, so I paddles nearer. There's some sailors on deck and an officer. A chap toppled out of a lifeboat into the water. I think he was trying to climb on deck. It's sort of rounded. This officer leans over an' pushes the chap away under the water. So 'ard he nearly fell in himself ...

He was swinging the bows from side to side, ramming the boats. He hit us so hard that the planking split and she spun out of the light. Half full of water, leaking ...

I speak fluent German. Damn it, I went to college there. Used to do business with the swine. I am prepared to swear that what I say is the truth in any court in the land. This officer walked along the deck to the pulpit thing with the Captain in it. He said there was a boatload of nurses they could sink only ten metres to starboard. Then he asked whether they were to take any prisoners or could they kill all the survivors ...

There was a man and woman holding each other. He brought the wire between them ... '

Shepherd slammed the file shut. He would be sick if he r_ad any more. He was with Jennifer, in the rain, the darkness and the ice-cold sea. Had she worn a white nightdress? He would never know.

'I need a drink, several drinks,' he said. 'And a walk, a damned long walk. Coming?'

Tregarron glanced up from a pile of intercepts. 'It's raining but I subscribe to the general idea. As soon as these are done. See you in the club in about an hour. Order some sandwiches. Something elegant as a change from Henrietta's handiwork.'

It was not long before he regretted ignoring Tregarron's advice about a raincoat as the rain ran off his cap brim and dripped down his neck. The theatres were closing and every taxi was heading west. He was too miserable to care. Despite the weather Trafalgar Square was crowded. He bumped into a group of midshipmen holding each other up as they waved at taxis splashing by with their flags up.

'I say, sir, we have met before. At the club, lunchtime. Johnny Tatham was telling you all about blimps until Eddie told him to shut up.'

'Johnny Tatham's dead,' one of the others said. 'We're having a wake. For him and Eddie … '

'Shut up,' someone said as he captured a taxi. They were the airship pilots he had met in the bar. Tatham, they told him, had ignored Mr Carberry's orders that they were to wait for the wind to abate and fly up in the morning. The wind had dragged the envelope on to a projecting girder. The hot exhaust had ignited the hydrogen.

'I say, sir, you're jolly wet. Why don't you come along with us? The girls from the Gaiety are throwing us a super party.'

Ignoring his protests they bundled him into the taxi. It was easier to go than to argue. He could always slip off after they arrived.

She was the first woman he saw as she stood in the entrance slipping off her wet cape. Her dress was black and swirled round her ankles but the top was cut low, exposing white shoulders. A small gold locket nestled in the vee of her breasts. Until then Shepherd had always thought of black as something people wore at funerals.

'Richard,' she opened her arms to him. 'Darling, you look frightful. What have you been doing? And in uniform?'

'Hello, Elsa,' he said. 'You look absolutely stunning. Elsa Dolli, an old friend of mine,' he said to the astonished midshipmen.

'Richard Shepherd, do you want to catch pneumonia. You are soaked. We must get you into some dry clothes at once.'

'She nags,' he said to them as she rounded on the hall porter.

'Jenkins, a coat. At once. And a taxi.'

By the time Elsa had organized a greatcoat for him, Jenkins had performed his small miracle and was waiting with a large umbrella to escort them to the waiting cab.

'Where have you been, Elsa?' he said as she folded into his arms. 'No one has heard of you since '15. Remember. *Troops' Comforter.*'

She wrinkled her nose. 'That stinker. It died within a month. Thank God. Showing that the great British public had not abandoned all pretence of having good taste. I married Jack Cordle.'

'Jack Cordle? You left the theatre for him but you would not leave it for me.'

He was hurt and the words tumbled out without thought. His circle had impinged on the periphery of Cordle's. The Honourable Jack was heir to 5,000 acres of prime agricultural land and the royalties from a dozen coal-pits. They had been at Cambridge together but Cordle had gone for the society not a degree. From there he had been seduced into flying at a time when each flight cost half a dozen crashes. Not the marrying kind. Elsa had taken up with him after they had split up and she had got her chance in the West End. He could remember the pain. That Cordle should marry her was incredible. They had broken up after living together for six months. Because he had wanted to marry her. Being married to a young provincial solicitor was one thing, putative mistress of Cordle Hall another.

She sighed and put a finger to his lips. 'There were reasons, silly. Like a war and Jack being in the Flying Corps. He never had any doubts about the outcome. He would be either a major in twelve months or dead. Poor old Jack, he never saw his son. I couldn't stay in that dreadful play after he was killed. Now I want to get back and it's not that easy, darling. Two years is a long time in the Theatre. They sent me back from France four weeks ago. I have served my sentence, eighteen months hard. Driving ambulances until I couldn't sleep at night, when I thought how nice it would be to be deaf. I'm going back up north for a few weeks before they throw me out.'

He clamped his eyelids shut. The two women he had loved had to humiliate him. Was he the only man who sent his women to wage war by proxy?

Shutting his eyes was a mistake. The cab was warm. The heat of Elsa's body seeped through the wet uniform, and the

53

smell of the perfume in her hair teased back memories of their six-month idyll in a back street in York. He had rebelled against his father, refused to take his place in the office.

He was asleep before he remembered how complacently the society that he had rejected took him back after their final quarrel. Old Cecil Shepherd's son had sown his wild oats and come back to the fold. A good catch, a lad with prospects, now was the time to invite him back to the house. By the autumn of '14 he was engaged to Jennifer. He was in OB14 before Christmas. Caught.

He fell asleep again in the bath. Elsa pummelled him dry, poured brandy and milk into him and watched him sink back into an exhausted sleep.

Sometime before dawn he rolled over. It was like coming home. His hand felt the bare flesh of her belly, moved up to caress the hardening nipples before sweeping down to the thicket in her crotch. He was too fierce, too hasty in that first encounter. Wide awake and just as passionate the second time. He had not made love to a woman since their quarrel before the war.

She was gone when he awoke at midday, drugged with sleep and alone in the big bed. He stared around the strange bedroom, so obviously a woman's room – the littered dressing-table, the stockings and discarded clothing draped over the chintz-covered basket chair. The photographs were of strangers. Theatricals. Signed photographs. But on the table by the bed was a worn leather folder.

Elsa and Jack Cordle. Adjacent to them a picture of a baby. He felt like an intruder. Sleeping with another man's wife and in another woman's bed. Who did it belong to? Suppose she came back?

His uniform had been dried and pressed. Washed and dressed he had time to reflect on his infidelity to Jennifer. Richard Shepherd, who had been prepared to go to the ends of the earth to revenge himself on the murderer of his fiancée, had climbed into bed with another woman four days after her death. Two days after some fisherman in a converted trawler had done the job for him. So much for his undying love. He was the most contemptible man who had ever lived. Clerking in Whitehall was all he was fit for.

He found the note on the breakfast table.

Darling,
I have to go out for an audition. And then I have to go
north as my leave expires today. I shall be at a hospital in
Yorkshire for a few weeks until my release is through. For
old times' sake, forget what I said last night.
But do not forget me. Letters to Beach House, Cleveland
Bay (remember it), will be forwarded.
    Au revoir,
        Elsa.

Putting the letter in his pocket he walked leisurely back to
the office.

'Thank God you are back. I thought you had gone home to
York as the doctor ordered.' Henrietta was nearly in tears.
The office smelled like a distillery.

'What doctor? I haven't been to any doctor. What is the
trouble?'

'It's Mr Tregarron. I can't do anything with him.'

Bart was sprawled on the camp bed with his shoes off and
his tie askew, a blanket spread over him. An empty whisky
bottle lay beside his outstretched arm.

'He's drunk,' Shepherd said. 'It won't do him any harm. I
don't suppose he has had any more sleep than I have since it
happened.'

'That is the second bottle,' Henrietta said. She handed him
a transcript. 'That came in last night. He finished it at four
o'clock this morning.'

It was a report from a U-boat somewhere in the Channel,
reporting the sinking of a fleet minelayer leaving Folkestone
harbour last Wednesday. As ordered. Severe damage had
been made good and they were returning to port as ordered.
Der Dichter.

Otto Schiller, captain of UC62, the subject of that file, was
still alive. Probably off Ireland by now, heading for home.

Henrietta said, 'Mr Tregarron dealt with it before he
started drinking. They are putting on extra patrols round the
Lizard and out of Berehaven. They will get him.'

Shepherd shook his head. 'They don't have a hope. Unless

he does something stupid and I don't think Mr Schiller is built that way. So much for the Navy's impregnable Dover barrage. I wouldn't put it past the bastard to go home that way.'

He shook Bart lightly. 'Coffee, gallons of black coffee, Henry, as fast as you can boil a kettle. I know exactly what I have to do to kill Schiller, but I can only succeed with the help of you and Bart.'

'Kill Schiller? You're mad.' Tregarron sipped his mug of coffee and glared at Shepherd. He was angry at being awake with a splitting headache, angry at being drunk, angry at his impotence, at their impotence. 'The bloody Navy have every ship that will float combing the Western Approaches for him. Their only chance of finding him is by offering themselves as targets. And you say you can find and kill him. You're potty.'

'Bart, the most accurate information about the position of U-boats is in this office by midnight every night. Right?'

'And you know how much attention we get from our gallant sailor boys. Go on.'

'I am going to join the Royal Naval Air Service. The airship branch flying blimps.'

Tregarron hung his head in his hands. 'Damn you, Richard, I thought you had a scheme, something practical, or I would not have done you the courtesy of listening. You apply for a transfer every quarter — '

'Stop roaring like a wounded bull. I am not applying for anything. I am going to enlist.'

'And spend six months marching up and down a drill square playing with a rifle so that you can polish the brass on a barnacle-bound battleship on the wrong side of Scotland.'

'You don't know much about me, Bart, about my private dreams and ambitions ... '

'Don't be so stupid, Richard. You work in the most secret department in the Admiralty. There's a file on you a foot thick.' Tregarron yawned and said to Henrietta, 'More coffee. Some aspirin. Then beat up a couple of eggs in brandy with a dash of Worcester sauce.' He turned back to Shepherd. 'You wanted to be an engineer. Your father said you would be a lawyer. So you threw your cap over the moon after you got your degree and became the worst actor in provincial rep. You lived with the leading lady. Until she threw you out. Then you went back to the office. It's happened before, old boy, it happens all the time. Sons like rowing with their fathers and sleeping with experienced ladies old enough to be their mother's younger sister. Sorry ... '

Shepherd blushed an angry red but he stuck to his guns. 'I've seen the file and I know what it doesn't say. The uninteresting bits. That I had a modest success building wireless sets, that I am a licensed amateur operator. Ask Henry. When we go out to the triangulation stations the operators let me keep my hand in. And as for procedures, we use them day in, day out.'

'You can't enlist. You already have a commission.'

'Who will know if I don't tell them? I'll enlist as Peter Shepherd. Birth certificate. Here, sign this. Reference for P. Shepherd, clerk in the office of Jervis, Jervis, Chippendale and Jervis. And that one from the Reverend Charles Tewkesbury. He signs that many he won't notice one more.'

'The basic training will take months.'

'For a trained wireless operator? The little blimps have a two-man crew. Pilot and wireless operator. Alec Jervis says they can't get them fast enough. He did some of the spadework. For a cousin of mine. Keen but not too bright ... '

Henrietta returned with the pick-me-up and a brown manila file. 'I've done a quick resumé of the stuff we have on file. The more we know of the enemy the better. UC62 is a UC55-class minelayer built by the Danzig dockyard. We know the details. Captain, Kapitänleutnant Otto Schiller. First Lieutenant, Oberleutnant Hugo Wilhelm von Beibedecke. Schiller is a desperately ambitious younger son of a Rhineland pork butcher. Promoted himself to get young Otto into the Officer Corps with the aid of the local Reichstag deputy. With whom Mama was very friendly ... '

'Where on earth do we get dirt like that?' Tregarron asked.

'Beibedecke. Son of a naval family going back to the Dark Ages. Dropped a rank to get into the underseas service. Picked up a mistress in Ostend. Nice little girl. She regularly writes chatty little notes to her dear Aunt Mabel in Amsterdam. We pay her in Dutch guilders.'

'Do you know the penalty for the unauthorized use of those Intelligence files?' Tregarron asked.

'For use against a U-boat? And anyway, who is going to check up on the woman who looks after the girls who look — '

'That sort of feminine logic leaves me cold. There is one thing that must be said, Richard. You are more important than you think.'

'You flatter me.'

'I don't. You know too much. That is why you don't get a transfer to active service. I don't think it would worry Blinker Hall if you were killed, but he would wet his knickers – sorry, Henry – if you were taken prisoner. So do not go into this as though it was an undergraduate prank. Ten bob fine and a wigging when you are caught. As you will be. This has to be done quickly or not at all. Because they will go on looking for you. They have to. And God help you when they do catch you … '

It was late by the time they were ready. Tregarron took them out to dinner. One last meal to remember. They met Alec Jervis, happy as a sandboy that the medical board had approved his new job commanding a flotilla of minesweepers out of Whitby.

Tregarron started laying red herrings as soon as Alec suggested that Shepherd could look them up while he was on leave.

'Mr Shepherd is not going anywhere near York,' he said firmly. 'He's going to stay with a friend of mine down at Brixham. A month of good plain food and an appetite bred out of hauling in the nets on a Brixham trawler will set him up for the rest of the war.'

They saw him off at Euston. A pale-faced young man with a bloodshot black eye and a face discoloured with bruises. A smart young man, straight-backed in an expensive tweed suit, brown brogues with the deep gloss of hand-crafted leather and months of polishing. Two expensive pieces of luggage, and a brown-paper parcel. A new novel, John Buchan's latest, *Greenmantle.* Four men going east to fight a whisper. And like Shepherd, starting off in the opposite direction.

He read and dozed, watching the white steam racing past the windows as the train pounded into the night. But before they ran into Camberley he squeezed down the crowded corridor to check that the guard's van was still adjacent, examined the toilet compartment and went back to his seat. The corridor emptied at Basingstoke. He stayed there, listening to the engine panting and the echoes of the postmen loading mailbags in the empty early hours.

As the train pulled out of the station he took his luggage from the compartment to the end of the carriage. He darted into the toilet with his paper parcel. It took three minutes to change into a shiny-bottomed navy-blue suit, a dingy cracked wing-collar that did not quite match his shirt, and creased black shoes scuffed at the toe and worn down at the heel. He turned up the collar of his crumpled raincoat and pulled the brim of his cheap trilby over his eyes.

There was still no one about when he opened the door. He checked his pockets again. Tregarron had given him a thorough briefing. Third-class return back to London. Single, York to King's Cross. Gloves, one finger split, one darned. References. Quickly he stuffed the remains of Lieutenant Richard Shepherd with the brown paper into one of his suitcases. From the other he produced a cheap cardboard attaché case. Spare shirt, collars, vest and pants, Valet razor and strop, socks. Lock the big cases and tie the labels on. B. I. TREGARRON, KC. BRIXHAM. TO BE CALLED FOR. He hoisted them on to the canvas slings carrying the mailbags and walked slowly back through the train, looking for a third-class seat. He got off at Salisbury, crossed the footbridge to the 'up' platform and found a seat out of the wind and away from anyone.

Twenty minutes later he was falling asleep in the cold carriage of the stopping train back to London. He had plenty of time. The recruiting office in Chatham did not open until 9 o'clock.

He took the bus from Euston to King's Cross, getting off one stop before the station. Crossing the road he walked on to the station before catching another bus. Forty-five minutes, one revolting pork pie and a worse cup of coffee later he was in the carriage of an LS&T train on the way to Chatham. He was sure that no one was following him.

When he walked into the recruiting office he did not need to act the tired and hungry traveller. A red-haired civilian in a peaked cap and a blue reefer-jacket was leaning on the counter chatting to the Chief Petty Officer. Shepherd glanced at the certificates and the Merchant Navy discharge book. Someone else was joining.

' ... you're a bloody fool,' the CPO said. 'This time tomorrow you'll be wondering what made you take leave of your senses. But if that's what you want, sign the form. The doctor should be here in half an hour.'

He turned to Shepherd. 'Yes, mate, and what can we do for you?'

Shepherd told him. Unimpressed, the CPO rocked backwards and forwards on his heels, sucking on an empty tooth. 'Yerss, this is the right hole, mate. Royal Naval Air Service. Why should we make you a wireless operator? Birth certificate.'

Shepherd laid his envelope with his references and birth certificate on the counter. His hands were shaking. The red-haired civilian was watching him.

'You a Marconi man?' asked the CPO. All British Merchant Navy operators were trained and employed by the Marconi Company.

Shepherd shook his head. 'I've got my GPO licence and I am experienced.'

The CPO sniffed. 'Not enough to suit their Lordships, mate. Not if you was Mr Marconi hisself.'

'I want to go on to airships. The little ones. Blimps. I was told you were needing operators badly.'

'You name it, mate, we need them. Nah, mostly people like you want to get on aeroplanes. More glamour.'

'I want to go on airships. The little two-seater kind. I'm told you need operators in a hurry.'

'Don't push your luck, mate. Airships it is. Little or big is up to their Lordships. Ours not to reason why ... '

'What are the chances of being taken straightaway? Today.' Shepherd felt like a schoolboy asking a prefect if he could cut prep. The red-haired civilian had got up to stand alongside him. He saw the CPO's eyes flicker over him in one comprehensive glance.

'York,' he said glancing at the envelope. 'You come down lars night. And you're hungry ... an' skint. I don't see why not. The doctor will be here in a jiffy to see this gent.'

'I've changed me mind, Bert,' the red-haired man said. 'I'm going along with this gentleman. Put me down for airships.'

'For Christ sake, Shag, now I know you have gone bonkers. You'll never be more than an Air Mech. 1st Class if you stays in 'til Kingdom Come.'

The doctor announced himself and the civilian disappeared with him. The CPO slid a buzzer to Shepherd. 'Let's see what you can do with that. If you knows which end to hammer an' the doc says you are warm enough you are in, mate, an' you will have your dinner compliments of His Majesty this very day.'

He propped a piece of card with a typewritten message on it in front of the buzzer.

AAA 98764 52310 00000 12356 78654 AAA

THE QUICK BROWN FOX JUMPED OVER THE LAZY DOG. NOW IS THE TIME FOR ALL GOOD MEN TO COME TO THE AID OF THE PARTY.

ADMIRAL OF THE FLEET.

LORD NELSON.

Shepherd flexed his wrist, rattling off the alphabet to get the feel of the key. Then he sent the message, concentrating on not making mistakes rather than on high speed. About 30wpm, he thought. And not bad morse.

If Bert was impressed he did not show it. 'What about the lamp, ever used one?'

Shepherd nodded. 'I can do six words a minute.'

Bert nodded. He pulled the buzzer to him. 'See if you can catch this.'

The morse was a continuous scream like ripping cloth. Shepherd was concentrating so hard on getting the characters that he read out the message before he realized what he was saying. He blushed. 'That old brown fox was a silly old cunt.'

This time Bert did nod his approval. 'That weren't no trade test, understand. Just to show you wasn't telling lies. They'll make an operator out of you. Through there. Take your clothes off. It's ship's biscuit and weevils for you tonight.'

CHAPTER THREE

Shepherd had been on the airship station near Chatham for three days before he saw an airship. In that time he had marched up and down the drill square, washed greasy pots and pans, peeled potatoes, drilled with an old rifle, got inoculated against a host of diseases, washed more pots and pans and peeled more potatoes. His hair, trimmed once a week at a little place off Bond Street, was rudely cropped for sixpence by a one-legged pensioner who did not expect a tip. He had swept, scrubbed and polished the concrete floor of his squad's room in the barrack block, learned to sleep in a hammock and to wake up each morning to the asthmatical coughing of the cigarette smokers gasping on their first draw in the stink of the overcrowded room.

On the fourth day they got their uniforms and he saw an airship. Tregarron had warned him that the Navy saw nothing incongruous in appealing for more and more men while keeping those they had kicking their heels in depots for months on end. Shepherd, with the arrogance of innocence, had replied that in the Navy there was always a way to get things done. The first time he asked when they would get a posting he met a scornful stare and, 'When the bloody Navy wants you.' The second time he found himself volunteered for the kitchen again.

The airship, one of the twin-engined Coastals, was drifting across the aerodrome with both engines stopped, hotly pursued by fifty ground handlers.

'Stand fast,' the petty officer in charge of them roared, as some of the men dropped their kitbags to join in. 'Unless you aims to dangle on the end of a rope with a hundred-foot drop ... '

The gust of wind died away, giving the handling party time to grab the ropes dangling from the nacelle. Another gust caught the stern, sending a dozen men sprawling. It lifted, jerking a man aloft kicking and struggling with a rope looped round his wrist. The envelope suddenly creased, sagged in the middle as the pilot valved gas, lowering the stern. A petty officer with a megaphone bellowed some order into the handling party as they dragged the disabled airship across to the hangars.

'Cockney trippers on a Bank Holiday Monday outing to the bloody seaside,' their petty officer said. 'Let that be a lesson to you,' he shouted. 'Never put your foot in the bight of a rope, never twirl it round your bloody wrist, 'cos the guv'ment 'as enough trouble finding the cash to pay the pensions of sensible sailors.'

Now they had uniforms they had to be taught the Navy way of stowing their kit. The arrival of a Salvation Army mobile canteen broke that up.

Shepherd stayed behind, grateful for a moment of privacy. He needed to think but the only time for thinking was in bed, and he was so tired at the end of the day that he fell asleep immediately. He had to get out of here and on to an operational station. One on the East coast, in Norfolk or Yorkshire. Already he had wasted four days.

Tregarron had insisted that if he got stuck at this stage he was to give up. He had also said that the going rate for missing a draft was £5, but Shepherd had no idea who could perform such miracles. Or how to approach them.

'Police,' a warning voice hissed from the end of the room. 'The coppers are at the gate asking for you, mate. Scarper.'

He whirled round in alarm. Shag Miller, the red-haired little cockney who had enlisted the same day, claiming to be a wireless operator, came out of the shadows in the corner.

'On the run, are you?' he said quietly. 'Thought you was. Stands to sense, a toff like you 'listing in the ranks.'

'What the hell has it got to do with you?'

'Easy does it, mate. The Andrew is full of blokes running from something. Just wanted to make sure. Me being in the same boat.' He dragged a rolled hammock out and sat down. 'Take a pew, mate. We got to get outa here, you and me. But gawd, you've got a lot to learn. I 'eard you asking about how quick we might get a posting. Blimey, there's blokes been

63

here months. An' this is the first place the police will come alooking.'

He rolled a cigarette and squinted at Shepherd through a cloud of smoke. 'Whatcher do, get caught with your fingers in the till?'

'My girl — ' Shepherd began.

'Women, blimey they're more bloody trouble than the bleeding Germans. Didja do her in?' Shepherd shook his head but Miller was not looking.

'I did. It's a topping job if they catches up with me. They always takes the wife's side. I came back from a trip quicker than I thought. After three bleeding days in an open boat. Survivor's leave, that's a laugh. Caught her and her fancy man on the job. I wasn't going to do her any harm, well, nothing serious. Until the silly cow started yellin' her head off. Got any money?'

Shepherd shook his head. The three plotters had forgotten that in his new life money was the cash you had in your pocket. 'I can get some. I'll cash a — '

Miller cackled. 'Cash a cheque? Not bloody likely. Not unless you want the peelers down on you the mornin' after. Chuck us that fancy hip-flask.'

Mechanically Shepherd handed over his flask. Miller unscrewed the cap and sniffed before taking a long swallow. He screwed the cap on and turned the flask over in his hands, feeling the tooled leather, looking at the hallmark on the bottom.

He read the inscription. 'R. P. Shepherd. Blimey, mate, you were asking for trouble joining up under your own name. Or did you pinch this?'

'It's mine. How else could I join up? They wanted to see my birth certificate.'

Miller rolled his eyes. 'Jesus, mate, you've got a lot to learn. The Andrew ain't as particular as all that. You must have some bleeding money. Don't look at me like that, mate. It's you that needs the help. Now we got our uniforms it's time we cleared off.' Reluctantly Shepherd laid his store in front of him. Two pound notes and a ten-shilling note in his paybook. Nearly a pound in silver. He took off his money belt. Miller whistled as the ten sovereigns rolled out. Shepherd kept quiet about the two fivers folded at the bottom.

Miller took another sip from the flask. 'No money? You got a king's ransom there. An' this. That wasn't filled in no four ale bar.'

'Who gets the money?' Shepherd asked. He took the flask, wiped the rim and drank.

'That depends on what you are thinking of doing. It's one thing if you are going over the wall, another if you only wants to get out of sight … '

'A station flying blimps on anti U-boat patrols over the North Sea. Norfolk or Yorkshire. I don't mind which, but I'll take nothing less.'

'Blimey, you expects a lot for your money. There'll be nothing left of that lot when you leave. Not enough to buy you a set of papers.'

'That is what I intend to get. There's more money where that came from. Who does it go to?'

'It's like this. First we have to get out of the squad. Say, across to the wireless station. We could do relief watches. Now, that'll cost you ten bob to the killick an' your rum ration for the week. A quid to the PO. Then a couple of quid to the CPO at the station to soften him up to get you through your trade test. A present, that flask an' a fiver. Valuable, is a trade test. Once we've got a trade it gets easier, better let him have another sovereign. There'll be some paper to be fiddled. There'll need to be an accident with our joining papers. Something to move the date along a bit. That'll cost you another goldilocks for the Ship's Writer. An' one for old Bert in the recruiting office. He's a mate o' mine. Now we got a grade there's no reason why we shouldn't get posted. But it will cost another quid to get on the right draft, get it? And everything that's left to paper over the cracks.'

As he reached out for the money Shepherd poured it back into his money belt, leaving a pound note and a ten-shilling note. 'According to you that gets us out of the recruit squad. Get on with it. The rest will be there as and when we need it.'

Nine days after joining the Royal Naval Air Service, Air Mechanic 2nd Class, Shepherd, still self-conscious in his ill-fitting square-rig uniform, navy blue slacks and tunic, white shirt and black tie, stepped out of the stopping train on to the platform at Goole. He was dirty, hungry, had twelve shillings and sixpence in his pocket and was almost drunk with exhilaration. Despite Tregarron's pessimism and his own gloom he had done the impossible. He was a qualified wireless operator going on to an operational station flying airships against U-boats. It was not his first choice, he would have preferred a station in Norfolk, but Howden would do.

UC62 would have been repaired by now and ready for another patrol. He would be there, waiting for Otto Schiller.

It was raining again, a thin drizzle sweeping across the flat South Yorkshire plain. Shepherd wiped something out of his eye with a grubby handkerchief.

'Coal dust,' Miller said as he humped their cases on to the platform. 'They move it down the canal an' ship it out of Goole. That was a good choice you made, mate. This is a port. You're on the Humber. An' where there's ports ... '

'They should try keeping more of it in the ships,' Shepherd said, wiping the grit off his lips. 'You go to the RTO. Find out how we get to Howden. I want to make a telephone call.'

He had taken two strides when Miller grabbed his arm. 'Who the hell are you phoning at this time of the night – the police? 'Cos if you are, mate, I swear you'll go inside with me.'

The clutch at his arm, the stink of Miller's breath, squashed Shepherd's exhilaration flat. Suddenly this whining little man stood for everything that had been done to him since he joined; the bullying petty officers, the loss of his privacy, the regimented days and exhausted nights, the stink of greasy pots and the cold inhumanity of mass living, Miller stood for all those things. He whipped his arm out of the man's clutch, grabbed him by the lapels and slammed him against a peeling poster advertising 'Bovril, good for that sinking feeling'.

'Don't you ever do that to me again. Or I'll fix you the way you say you fixed your wife. Understand. I'll telephone anyone I want, where and when I want.'

Miller dropped on to his knees when he let go. As Shepherd

walked off he said over his shoulder, 'You dreamed the whole thing. I've read every newspaper for the past nine days. Nothing. And no matter how many thousands get killed in France every day, no yellow rag would miss two murders off the Mile End Road.'

He found a telephone by the booking office. He asked for trunks and gave the girl Henrietta's number. As he waited, piling pennies by the instrument, he began to tremble as he realized how near he had come to killing Miller. If he had got hold of him by the throat instead of the lapels ...

'I say, Miss Talbot, Richard here,' he said in his best silly-ass voice. 'Just a tinkle to let you know I'm on the loose, waitin' to have a crack at the old Boche, y'know ... '

'How nice of you to call. I must compliment your mother on your manners when I see her. But don't be a silly boy, you have better things to do than chat to old ladies. Even if I were free ... '

It did not sound like the Henrietta he knew. 'There is someone with you. Keep talking. I will ring later. Say yes if you will be at the office. I need money, a lot of money, urgently. OK?'

'Why, yes, dear boy. Call me whenever you like. It has been a pleasure hearing from you. Goodbye.'

Henrietta put the telephone down and turned to her guest, every one of the multitudinous panels of her silk dress shimmering and fluttering as she gestured. 'You must excuse that, Mr Villers. It's the curse of being a headmistress. One cannot fool oneself about the passage of time when the son of an old pupil invites one out to dinner.'

'You are too hard on yourself, Miss Talbot. I am sure that the office can manage without you for one night.'

'Certainly not, Mr Villers. Apart from the fact that the young man was only being polite I do not wish to be given special privileges because of my, er, sex. I shall be delighted to be on duty tonight.'

Suddenly she swooped on Villers, forcing the Secretary to sink back into the chintz-covered armchair. The huge sleeves of her dress fluttered dangerously near the photographs, ornaments and mementoes that littered the low mantelpiece.

'Mr Villers, so thoughtless of me, pressing sherry on you as though you were a visiting parent. Now a friend of mine gave me a bottle of this special whisky ... ' She poured a generous glass, turned to Villers and said, 'You were saying when we were interrupted?'

'Actually the reason I called, Miss Talbot, was to thank you for the, er, unofficial help you have given to the Department. We are well aware of the service you have rendered in the past. Not forgotten, y'know, Miss Talbot, not forgotten. And the fact is we need to trespass on your generosity again. Fact is we are just a little concerned about Mr Tregarron and young Mr Shepherd. Fine chaps but under great strain, y'know. And the Admiral was concerned about the way the young man went off on leave without, well, y'know, not naval fashion. Proper channels and all that. How was he? I believe you saw him off. Don't like to ask Tregarron. Makes it look formal, y'know. Can be misunderstood.'

Henrietta nodded. 'Of course. The dear boy was terribly upset by the death of his fiancée. And then he had to read those ghastly eyewitness accounts in the draft report. Most upsetting. And he really has not had any leave for over two years. I checked. We have his address and telephone number. I am sure that in two or three weeks he will be back roaring for work.'

Villers picked up his coat and rolled umbrella. 'Good show. I'll clear it with the Admiral. Leave it to me. But keep in touch, Miss Talbot, keep in touch with me. About the way things are going. Two vital men. We have to watch over them. Not only for their own health but also in the interest of the country's war effort.'

When he had gone Henrietta took his whisky glass between finger and thumb and dropped it in the wastebin. It bounced. She took a poker, hammered it into shards of splintered glass. It had been one of a prized set.

She changed out of her silks into tweeds and sensible shoes. As she pulled on a floppy brimmed hat and took a man-sized umbrella from the stand she felt like Joan of Arc going out to do battle.

UC62 had been in port eight days. Soon she would be

ready to go to sea. And they had to be ready now that Richard had got over the first hurdle. She had the utmost faith in her weapon. That young man had done what Tregarron said was impossible to do in less than six months. There was no reason why he should not have Kapitänleutnant War-Criminal Otto Schiller mouldering at the bottom of the North Sea within the week. Provided she fed him enough ammunition.

She put the sherry and the whisky away, slid the fireguard into position, straightened the lace centre on a table, tidied a couple of stray photographs, switched off the lights and carefully checked that the front door was locked.

Henrietta Victoria Talbot was going into action.

If Otto Schiller had been a cat he would have purred. He was warm, warm in a way that only someone who had spent ten hours on the bridge in the North Sea could appreciate. And he was clean, washed free of the eternal abrasive salt. The solitary pendant lamp lighting the wood-panelled bedroom did not move, the bed enveloped him without swaying and the scent of perfume replaced the stench of chlorine, diesel oil and unwashed bodies. As his finger tips lightly caressed the silken skin of the girl's back he closed his eyes, content, not knowing whether it was day or night. He was ashore.

The girl stirred in her sleep. His fingers stroked the soft skin at the base of her spine and curved over her buttocks. She was a big girl. The pot on the stove spat as it boiled and the fragrance of freshly made coffee filled the room. Schiller winced and his hands clenched round the soft flesh, his fingers digging in until the girl moaned with pain. He had been about to drink a mug of hot coffee the day that trawler came out of the murk.

That was the day he knew he had been at sea too long. He could see the muzzle of the gun swinging until it was centred on him, hear the clang of the breech as the gunner followed the shell, the words of command, foreign to him but the meaning understood. He had stood there paralysed, his throat muscles ignoring the brain's command to shout, 'Dive, dive, dive!'

69

But the gunlayer had kept the muzzle swinging to sight on the deck gun so Weiderer and three men died instead of him. It was an unfair world. Death should have come to the paralytic not to the quick. It was Fink toppling over the side with no head that brought him to his senses. Fink was one-third of his luck. Now there were only two men who had sailed with him on his previous ship. When they died he would die.

He pushed the girl away from him. Women were no use at times like this. He needed the company of men and drink. Men who knew why he drank.

'Be here when I get back,' he said, slapping the girl's bottom. 'Don't bother to get dressed.'

There were half a dozen fellow captains in the Officers' Club and all the signs of a party about to break out.

Von Bueller, whom he had served under in '15, called him over. He slid a bottle of schnapps into his hand. 'Well, Otto, time you got yourself out of the narrow seas and on to the Atlantic boats.'

'Chance would be a fine thing,' Schiller growled.

Von Bueller gripped his arm and winked. 'Don't make yourself so indispensable to your Kommodore.'

'That is not the situation at the moment. Not with the Tommis and the Yankees squealing about that damned Channel steamer.'

'No promotion. You were up for that and a medal months ago.'

'It is not considered good policy. We must not offend American public opinion. According to the Kommodore that's the message he got back from the pot-bellies in Berlin.'

Von Bueller laughed. 'You won't have to worry about that much longer.' He beckoned a waiter.

Schiller swallowed another glass of schnapps. And another. It was the only way to forget about that damned gun and those terrifying seconds of paralysis. He smiled at von Bueller. The Kapitän was visiting from the Heligoland Flotilla. Was he recruiting captains? There were rumours about a big increase in the number of long-range boats. But there were always rumours. God, he was sick of crawling about sandbanks and minelaying. One whisper about his vocal paralysis and he could forget about any kind of command. He would be lucky to get an appointment to the training school. He would be sailing a desk. The waiter was bringing a newspaper across to von Bueller and the Kommodore was waving his arms, bringing the others round him.

He spread the newspaper across the table, knocking a glass and the bottle on to the floor. Nobody bothered as they stared at a stained *New York Times*. It had been in salt water. The ink had run but the paper had been ironed and it was quite legible.

Von Bueller said, 'One of our boats brought it in last night. He took it off a Yankee oil tanker.'

'My English is not good,' Schiller said.

'You don't need to read English. It spells war. The Americans are bound to come in now.'

His finger traced the words in the big black headlines. 'ZIMMERMAN CARVES UP USA. Mexico and Japan invited to carve a piece off US. State Department today released the text of a telegram from the German Foreign Minister offering to cede US territory to Mexico and Japan in return for an alliance against England and France.'

Schiller heard the words as von Bueller went on reading but his mind was miles away. He had relations in America, he had stayed with them when he was a cadet in the Merchant Marine. Cousins. They still wrote. He could remember the letters, not the words, the sense. It would take more than a Channel steamer to turn them against Germany, against Cousin Otto. But the message was clear in every letter. They were no longer German, not even European. They were Americans. He could imagine their reaction if this stupid telegram was true. He picked up the bottle.

'I think I shall get happily drunk until I go back to sea.' He slapped the newspaper angrily. 'If this is true we have just lost a war.'

Von Bueller raised his glass in salute. 'Didn't you hear anything I said? There are 3,000 watery miles between America and France. Over there sinkings are easier than getting drunk on schnapps. Hartmann sank twelve ships in one day. Four in one hour. While we have been at war for four years they have learned nothing. Now we have a chance to show our importance. The U-boats can blockade America as the British blockade us. Better ... '

Schiller drained another schnapps. The alcohol was beginning to hit him. God, how long was it since he had last eaten?

He waggled a drunken finger at von Bueller. 'There's not many of us left from the pre-war service. Remember when we were not even a joke, just a dirty smell. And old, er, whatsisname, he said U-boats could never be as important as we said until they were big enough to be commanded by an admiral. Only battleships need admirals.' His finger poked von Bueller in the chest. 'We're short of steel, short of coal, short of men. We are building twenty-six U-boats but we're also building six bloody battleships. I like your idea, sir. We should have thought of it six months ago. The steel for those admirals' barges would have built the 200 U-boats we need for your blockade. We've lost the war.'

As he slid under the table von Bueller nodded at the others to take him away. He rose, leaving the young to look after their own.

'The big 'un, Mad Jack, says he's going to smash your face in,' Miller said to Shepherd with relish as the ring of sailors opened up to give them room.

Shepherd shook his head to clear the rum fumes. The tap room of the Dutchman's Leat swam in front of his eyes. Miller had persuaded him to wait here for the transport that was to take them out to the airship station at Howden. And four shillings had bought them a bottle of Navy rum.

'Why, what have I done to upset him?'

'You did tell him not to be so daft. The Navy's job, you said, was to get merchant ships safe to port. Obvious to anyone with a bit of sense, you said. He don't agree. An' he hates toffs more than he hates civvies. You talk like a civvy an' it was me that told him you was a toff.'

Somebody pushed him in the small of the back to send him reeling towards Mad Jack. Jack was three inches shorter, fifty pounds heavier, with shoulders like a tank, a longer reach and a pair of hands like mallets.

Shepherd had never enjoyed boxing but an elder brother and his school had hammered the rudiments into him. His hands automatically went up, fists clenched. As Shepherd reeled towards him Jack's right fist came up from floor level. It missed. Shepherd punched him on the nose with a hard left and skipped sideways.

Jack rushed him, brushing aside his classical defence with both fists pumping like pistons. Left, right, two hammer blows knocked the wind out of Shepherd. His left eye closed in company with the still-discoloured right one. His left stabbed Jack in the face as his right deflected Jack's left, but it was like shooting peas at a battleship. Another left jabbed his eye and a right cross knocked him down. As he got up, a size ten boot clamped down on his instep. Jack stepped inside his guard to smash left- and right-hand punches into his stomach.

They burst through the circle, knocking over a glass-laden table. Shepherd fell on his back. Jack's boot slammed into his ribs.

A police whistle shrilled outside. Somebody shouted, 'Police'. The encircling crowd stampeded for the nearest door.

Jack's face bent down to him. 'You all right, mate?' A hand slapped his face. 'Look alive, mate, it's the Shore Patrol.'

Shepherd stared blankly back at him, vaguely glad that the police had come to rescue him.

'Bloody civvies,' Jack growled, as he grabbed the lapels of Shepherd's jacket to pull him upright. With his other hand he threw a chair at the tap-room window. Shepherd's inert body followed. Jack jumped through a couple of minutes later, clutching their caps. He scooped some water from the gutter to toss into Shepherd's face. 'Now walk, you stupid sod. Walk in a straight line as far from here as you can.'

Miller held him up as they stood in the guardroom at the entrance to Howden Airship Station.

'What the hell happened to him?' the Master-at-Arms asked as Miller presented their papers.

'He got knocked down,' Miller said. 'Horse and cart, it was. Nigh on killed him. But he's all right.'

'Aye, a horse and cart in the Dutchman's Leat. You've made a bloody good start, the pair of you. The Captain doesn't have much time for airshipmen at the best but he just loves a drunken one.' Somebody in the shadows whispered in his ear. He grunted. 'Jesus, another bloody civvy come to teach Lord Nelson his business. Captain Botham will love you two. Take their names.'

The following morning Shepherd took a perverse sense of satisfaction in looking at his face as he gingerly guided his razor over the bruises. Two black eyes, a swollen lip twisting his face one way, a yellow swelling striped with graze-marks on the other side. Those, his short-back-and-sides haircut and his lowly rank should guarantee his anonymity if he met anyone who had known him in the Admiralty.

After parade the Flight Lieutenant stared at them with a noticeable lack of enthusiasm. 'So you are the chap who took on Mad Jack. Damned fool.' The Flight Lieutenant, with the Chief Petty Officer beside him, walked round Shepherd as if he was an exhibit in a slave market. The last of a bad bunch.

'I don't know what to do with them, Chief. We haven't indented for any wireless operators. Somebody in HQ has got his wires crossed. I think they do it to annoy me.'

'They're short-handed at the outstation, sir. Cleveland Hall. Mr Carberry's operator is in the sick-bay.' He sniffed. 'That's the third in four months. And if we sent the little 'un for Mr Dutton they'd have a spare.'

'Thank you, Mr Knowles, that is an excellent idea. Stop Carberry's complaint before he makes it.' The Flight Lieutenant turned to Shepherd with a face like thunder. 'You are lucky, Air Mechanic Shepherd, because our beloved commanding officer is in Whitehall conferring with their Lordships. Captain Botham, Shepherd, makes Mad Jack look like a spring chicken. He eats a wireless operator for breakfast every morning and he loves them drunk. You will never be so lucky again, Shepherd. Get out of my sight.' He turned to the Chief Petty Officer. 'Get them out of my sight, Mr Knowles. I don't care how you do it but get them off this station today. In the next hour if you can manage it.'

When he had gone, Mr Knowles looked at them for a

couple of minutes before he said mildly, 'Now you know where you stand, the pair of you. He is one of the nice officers. Stand to attention. Speak when you are told to. I think Mr Carberry is just the man to deal with a pair like you. He'll fly the arses off you. You, Shepherd, will report to the hangars in thirty minutes with all your kit. C27. She's off on a test flight. We will see whether you are better on the key than you are at brawling in public bars. The pilot will drop you at Cleveland Hall on the way back. Don't show your horrible face here until everybody has forgotten you. Don't stand there, man. Get on with it. Dismiss.'

C27 was one of the big non-rigid Coastal class with a long open car suspended under the envelope. There was an aeroplane engine at each end of the nacelle. The usual crew was four but there was room to spare for Shepherd, although the pilot did not look too pleased at his kitbag. He had little time to look about him. The engines were running when he arrived. By the time he had got himself seated by the wireless set they were airborne, setting course for the sea as they climbed to 1,000 feet. That was the trouble with Howden, the wireless operator told him. You had to spend the first hour of every patrol getting humped and bumped to blazes crossing the Yorkshire Wolds before you got the coast. Which was why the little blimps were being parked at places like Cleveland Hall right on the coast.

'Better you than me, chum,' the wireless operator said. 'Nissen huts, gas guard duty every three nights, no hangars, you can fly six days out of seven. Nearest pub going east is at the bottom of the cliff. 300 feet to come up afterwards. Going west you only have to walk five miles.'

He let out the wireless aerial, showing him how to brake the reel with the palm of his hand because the inertia of the lead weight on the end would snap the copper wire if it ran at full speed.

'Tune it in to base.'

Shepherd was lucky. Someone else was working Howden and he was able to twiddle the knobs until the signal was loud and clear.

'Send our call-sign to base. Wait for a reply. Don't panic

for a minute or so, there's no rush. Then send, "Call-sign, Charlie 27. Airborne 09.16. Armed air test. Course 090°. Altitude 1,000. ETA coast 09.54." '

He watched Shepherd send the message and log the replies. He raised his thumb. 'You'll do. Send them a position report every half-hour. Mr Perkins the navigator will tell where he hopes we are. Keep a listening watch on Howden. In case there's a recall. Change in the weather.'

He saw the blank look in Shepherd's face. 'An airship is a balloon with engines, right. Those tea kettles at each end break down every time someone sneezes. When they both stop you are in a balloon, and the prevailing wind is from the south-west, right. It's 400 bloody miles before you reach Germany, right. If you are lucky and stay up that long. Nobody has, so far. With one engine out and a 25mph headwind we stand still. Ground speed zero. But we are burning petrol so we get lighter, and we get higher where the wind speed is greater. So we listen to weather reports with great interest. Right?'

'Here.' He poked Shepherd in the ribs as he spun the tuning knob. 'That is the U-boat frequency. They usually chat at night but you hear them in daylight occasionally. It's in code so you don't know what they are saying even if you understand German, but it shows that there is a bastard about.'

He grinned sympathetically at Shepherd's battered face. 'What did you do to the Flight Loot, kick his dog? He's not a bad sort but you must have got on the wrong side of him to be shoved on to Carberry.'

'What is wrong with Carberry? Who is he?'

'Squadron Commander, CO of the outstation at Cleveland Hall. He's nuts. An old fool fighting a one-man war. He takes it as a personal insult if we lose a ship along here. God help the first pilot to lose a ship on a patrol. He does long trips. Wears out Sparks. And he is the worst airship pilot in the country. It's right. Four write-offs in nine months. Wrecked. His eyes are going and although he won't admit it his next job will be flying a desk.' He leant closer, pulling Shepherd's earphones aside so he could talk into his ear. 'Him and

Captain Botham hate each other's goolies. They were at Dartmouth together years ago. Carberry swallowed the anchor early on. Came back in '14. To airships. Botham lost his ship to a U-boat last year. Course straight as an arrow going south from the Forth at dusk. Boom. The Andrew has another thousand widows to support and Captain Botham sails an airship desk. He hates airships, Carberry and U-boats in that order. So watch your step.'

He left Shepherd on watch to go forward to help the mechanic prepare a large net. The coast came into sight. The navigator gave Shepherd a time and a new course and ETA to send back to Howden. But as they left the coast behind the forward engine suddenly started misfiring, shooting two-foot-long yellow flames from the silencer. The pilot switched it off. The mechanic draped an old pair of overalls over the radiator and started to change the sparking-plugs. The airship stayed on course out to sea with the wireless operator and the navigator peering over the side.

They altered course. Shepherd could not see anything so he kept quiet as they turned under the direction of the navigator, losing height down to 500 feet. The airship lurched as a depth-charge dropped into the empty sea. They went into a descending turn as Shepherd craned over the side looking for oil or traces of the U-boat. The net went over the side as they crawled along, barely ten feet above the wave-crests.

The pilot turned to him. 'Hey, you. Lend a hand with the net. And your mess can have herrings for tea.'

CHAPTER FOUR

Cleveland Hall was now only a name on the map and a memorial. It had been built in 1800 with the money from a dozen prizes taken in the French wars and the loot from ten years in India. Fifty years later the family who built it had disappeared as the money to maintain it was dissipated. Ten years later there was a fire. The local farmers gained a supply of dressed stone. Now, about a hundred years on, the RNAS reaped the benefit of the first owner's foresight. He had built the house looking south across Cleveland Bay, a bite out of the rugged Yorkshire coast three miles wide with a little fishing village below the 300-foot cliff. The new squire had cut the first road down to the beach, but most of all he needed shelter. So around the house he had planted a ring of trees, far enough away not to cramp the house, near enough to deflect the ice-cold north-easterlies. Oak, yew and birch – a hundred years of growth made a superb windscreen to shelter three of His Majesty's blimps, the establishment of the Cleveland Hall airship station.

A dozen trees had been felled to enlarge the opening that had been the drive. The stone floor of the Hall now held half a dozen ugly corrugated-iron Nissen huts – the flight offices, messes and sleeping quarters – and a sandbagged bomb store and a fuel dump had been cut into the undergrowth. Three blimps were tied down in the shelter of the trees, two of the new Zeros, SSZ 85 and SSZ 82, and one of the old original Submarine Scouts, SS 19. Now the blimps did not have to bounce over the Wolds for an hour and a half before starting their patrol. The sea was on their doorstep.

Shepherd thought SS 19 the most beautiful thing he had ever seen. This was the instrument that would undo Kapitän-leutnant Otto Schiller. It was huge. The Coastal that had brought him had been twice as large but he had had no time to look at it, too frightened of messing up his watch on the wireless set when he embarked. It had been as impersonal as a bus, a means of transport to take him to his destination. SS 19 was the destination.

The wind was getting up, the tops of the trees rustled and scraped, but on the ground it was calm. A weak sun shone through ragged strips of stratus. The silver envelope glittered, tugging mildly at the guy ropes looped through the Scrutton anchors which had been screwed three feet into the ground. It was bigger than a church, 143 feet long, 32 feet in diameter, 70,000 cubic feet of highly flammable hydrogen. The enlarged drive looked too small to allow it to pass on the way to the field used for taking off and landing.

The nacelle resting on the ground, suspended from the envelope by a cat's-cradle of suspension wires, control cables and guy ropes, looked incongruous under the sleek fat gasbag. It was a wingless aeroplane, a spindly fuselage of a BE2c with a 90-hp Curtiss OX5 engine in the nose driving a four-bladed propeller. It had two seats, the wireless operator in front in the shelter of the radiator with the pilot just behind him. Cables and more cables. Gas-valve cable, ballast-release cable, crabpot-valve cables, ripping-panel cable seized with red-coloured cord, elevator and rudder-control cables going back to the cruciform control planes on the tail of the envelope. The nacelle still retained its wheels and skids. With the fabric patched, puckered and faded it looked like a dragonfly stripped of its wings by some mischievous boy. Some romantic soul had painted Silver Cloud on the side, but the paint had faded and the rain had eroded most of the first word. Cloud Nineteen, his personal thundercloud, Shepherd thought. For abreast of the cockpit were the black metal bomb-racks. He ran his hands over them as he clambered into the cockpit.

'You must be Shepherd,' a voice said. Shepherd's heart went down into his boots. The man standing by the nacelle, flanked by his rigger and engine fitter, was Squadron Commander Carberry, the man he had met that fateful day in the club. The man who had so impressed those young midshipmen.

Hastily he scrambled out of the cockpit, but in the hurry to

79

salute he tripped and fell flat on his face in the muddy grass.

'Contrary to what you may have heard, Shepherd, I don't expect my bloody wireless operators to grovel at my feet,' Carberry said. 'And I do not expect them to trip over their own feet. You must be the man who took on Mad Jack. Wipe your face, man, you look like a nigger minstrel.' He stared at Shepherd as he wiped his face clean. 'We have met before. Where?' Shepherd shook his head, afraid to speak. 'Don't shake your bloody head at me. I can't stand intelligent donkeys. And I never forget a face. Do you have a brother in the Navy?'

'Nay, ah've no brother,' Shepherd said, affecting a broad Yorkshire accent. 'Got a cousin, though. He's got a cushy job in Whitehall.'

Carberry nodded after a moment's hesitation. 'I hope you are not looking for a cushy job, because if you are you have come to the wrong place. You will be flying with me so you can expect to get blisters on your arse. We will be doing the early morning patrol tomorrow. Their Lordships have come to their senses and are starting to organize the merchant ships into convoys. Know what I mean?' Shepherd nodded. 'Coal boats, dirty British coasters with salt-caked smokestacks beating down the Channel. They leave the Tyne on the tide, join up with some more off the Tees. Which is where we pick them up at daybreak. We take them south to the Humber.' His finger stabbed Shepherd in the chest. 'No ship has ever been lost while being escorted by a blimp. I do not intend to lose the first. The object of the exercise is not to sink U-boats; our job, never mind what the other silly buggers say, is to make sure we don't lose a ship tomorrow. We take off at 6 am, but you will be here long before then. You ought to spend the afternoon sitting in the nacelle until you can find everything blindfold. You pick up your Lewis gun and the spare drums from the armoury. If there is anything else you think you ought to know, ask. Today.'

As he walked away the petty officer, Bert Riggs, held out his hand. Shepherd took it. 'What's that in aid of?'

Harry Wragg, the engine fitter, laughed. 'Conscientious, is Bert. Likes to shake the condemned man's hand. Once. Have a good breakfast, Shep, you'll need it.'

He jerked a thumb over his shoulder at the two Zeros. The envelopes were the same as SS 19 but the varnished mahogany nacelles looked as though they had been designed for the job and not cobbled up out of some cast-off aeroplane oddments.

'That's a real airship with a real engine,' Wragg said. 'But Mr Carberry, he is the SNO, so why does he fly this old ragbag while his subs get the Zeros, tell me that? Because Mr Carberry uses them up the way he wears out Sparks. Five blimps and four wireless operators in fourteen months. An' our Captain Botham, he knows that sooner or later Mr Carberry is going to junk this one. She's the last SS ship on the station. Then it's Zeros all round. Get me.'

Shepherd gulped. 'Is there a telephone here?'

Riggs nodded, sucking at an empty tooth. 'All mod cons, mate. There's three in the office. Field telephone to Howden. Direct line to the SNO Humber and a direct line to the Admiralty. It's a fact, I tell you,' he added as Wragg snorted his disbelief. 'Direct lines, the Post Office fella told me when he put them in last week. Their Lordships is scared stiff that these convoys they're starting will only give Jerry a bigger target.' He turned back to Shepherd. 'Got a girl, 'ave you? For you, mate, there's one in the pub down on the beach.'

Wragg sniggered. 'Two mile, Shep. Downhill. Best pub in the world. You can get pissed up to the eyebrows but you'll be stone-cold sober afore you meets the Jaunty on the gate.'

The wind died as the sun went down. It began to rain, a fi.ie drizzle as though they were inside a cloud. There were fried herrings for tea.

Squadron Commander Carberry did his paperwork at night. Shepherd stood in the shadows outside the office, waiting for the chink of light showing through the curtains to go out. The hut was tee-shaped. The cross of the tee had at one end the officers' wardroom with their sleeping quarters at the other end. The leg of the tee had a couple of offices, a laboratory for gas testing, a chart store and, at the end, Carberry's office. Carberry and a petty officer sat by his paper-strewn desk until Shepherd could wait no longer. He slipped away to walk down the winding road to Cleveland Bay village and the Lobster Pot on the beach.

Three mechanics were standing shoulder to shoulder waiting to use the telephone. Shepherd mentally kicked himself for not sorting out the communication problem beforehand. Would the duty operator log any calls made to OB14? And what time would Henrietta be on duty?

He walked into an empty bar to drink a pint of cold flat beer. There was an evening paper on the counter. As he leafed through it the headline on an inside page leapt at him.

DOUBLE KILLING. GRISLY FIND IN GRAVESEND.
Following complaints by a neighbour, Mrs Elsie Purvis, police today broke into the flat of Mrs Pearl White. They discovered the bodies of Mrs White and an unknown man savagely beaten over the head. Interviewed by our local correspondent, Inspector Arkwright said that the partially-clad couple had been dead for some time. The police are anxious to communicate with Mr White, a wireless operator in the Merchant Navy. Mr White has been missing since he was released from hospital after being torpedoed off the Irish coast two weeks ago. The police, who think that Mr White may have lost his memory following his ordeal in an open boat, have issued the following description. 5′ 6″ in height, stocky build, red hair and sallow complexion, may be wearing a beard. When last seen he was wearing a Merchant Navy uniform and a dark blue reefer-jacket ...

He was not wearing a beard now. Shepherd folded the newspaper and slipped it into his pocket. It was not much of a description but if the police caught up with Shag Miller his own escapade was over.

He went back to the telephone. There was an hour's delay on calls to London. Did he know that there was a war on?

'Seen the paper, have you?' Miller said, startling Shepherd so that he banged his head on the underside of the staircase. 'For a fella on the run you're bloody keen on using the telephone. I watched you stuff that paper in your pocket. What's your game?'

'That's my business. Shove off.'

'I warned you, mate, if I goes down you goes with me. I'm as safe as houses here while I get things organized. Nobody is looking for Shag Miller. Give 'em another week and it'll be forgotten. Unless somebody talks outa turn.'

By the time he got through, Henrietta was on duty. She promised to send him money and to check whether incoming calls were logged. There was little on the chart. One minelayer, UC84, about fifty miles east of the War Channel, midway between Flamborough Head and Spurn Point.

'I am using the camp bed now and your sheets will in future be changed much more frequently. They were disgusting. Can you call early in the morning? The operators are half asleep. Say you are calling from T4.'

'What about the, er, Poet?'

'Nothing. But he should be out shortly. You know who, the Admiral's Admirable Crichton, was with me when you rang. He wants me to keep an eye on you and Mr T. If we could get a medical certificate for you I think we would be all right for two or three weeks. You will have to catch our man on his next patrol.'

By the time he got back to his bunk, wet through, he realized what Harry Wragg had meant. You had to be drunk to face the trudge back up the hill. He was pulling off his wet things before he remembered that Elsa Dolli had a cottage in the village. If there was no telephone it would have a fire.

A windborne spray of icy water splashed across the bridge. Schiller ducked, but his reactions were slow after the spell ashore. He swore and turned to watch the Mole sliding astern. UC62 was at sea again, free from that claustrophobic crawl along the canal. He hated it, sailing along dead slow with your hull full of those damned mines. If one of those bombers came along you were a dead duck. The new deck gun glittered dully in the starlight. A couple of dives in salt water would cure that.

This might be his last trip. A bloody fine thought to take out of harbour. This might be his last ditch-crawl in a minelayer. One more good one, the Kommodore had said.

Von Bueller had been with him, nodding his approval. It was a long time since he had first sailed with von Bueller. The Kommodore had been one of the little group dedicated to proving that the U-boat was something more than a toy for harbour defence. That was the year, 1913, when von Bueller upset a lot of fat-arses by torpedoing two battleships in fifteen minutes. In the summer exercises. Afterwards the All Highest, Kaiser Wilhelm himself, had inspected U8. Schiller smiled to himself. The All Highest had not been impressed. He believed that might was only mighty when it could be seen to be the mightiest.

Rumour had it, so von Bueller said, that Tommi was going to put his ships in convoy. Schiller had said that forty ships at eight knots made a better target than one at ten knots. By the time Tommi had regrouped after the first sinkings he would have his tubes reloaded for a second attack. But this was not his night on the bridge. As captain he had a duty to see that he was fit and rested when they reached the minefields guarding Tommi's War Channel. 'Leutnant Beibedecke, to the bridge,' he called down the speaking tube. 'I hope she didn't tire you too much, Beibedecke. It's a strain on older men, so I'm told. And an officer has a responsibility to be fit for duty, the most arduous duty on return from leave.'

Beibedecke nodded his agreement, standing to attention battleship-style.

'Set course for the Humber. Spurn Point. Call me when you sight the War Channel,' snapped Schiller.

He paused, standing on the cat ladder, too tired to bother. Beibedecke could do it. 'Get Afrikanisher to send the usual message. Slipped at whatever time it was. Departed Zee-brugge Mole ten minutes ago. Test dive starting. When you feel like it. You know, the usual guff ... '

Shepherd's teeth chattered as he stepped outside the hut, a towel tucked round his neck as though he was going to the ablution block. One hundred yards on a raw cold morning, with his breath floating ahead of him like a private cloud. The officers had a bathroom at the end of their hut. Carberry, he thought, was the sort who would wash and shave no matter what time the day began.

There was no one about as he slipped from the ablution block towards the office building. He had spied out the land earlier while talking to Carberry's batman. There was no one on guard at the entrance. A light shone from an open bedroom door and he could hear running water. Have a bath, Mr Carberry.

Over against the trees an engine coughed and spluttered into life on four cylinders, banging and misfiring until all the cylinders came in and the noise died away as it was throttled down to warm up. Harry Wragg was warming their engine. Shepherd slipped through the door into the corridor to tiptoe down to Carberry's office.

The door was unlocked. He went behind the desk, picked up the Admiralty telephone and sat on the floor with it. The operator replied after he had jiggled the hook half a dozen times.

'T4 here. Give me OB14, Room 156,' he said briskly, to hide the fact that he was whispering. He visualized four flight of stairs, a hundred yards of twisting corridor, more stairs, servants' stuff now, no carpet, the rooms at different levels to catch unwary feet and projecting beams to dent your forehead. Room 156 was tucked under the eaves, a small dirty window looking across the rooftops at a tracery of bare boughs screening the park. At this time it would be shuttered, the smoke from an indifferent coalfire competing with Henrietta's cheroots.

'Duty Officer.'

'Henry? You were alseep. We are off at dawn. Convoy patrol Tees south to the Humber. Any news? Make it quick.'

'You-know-who is out. Usual departure signal at 21.50. Try listening out for him. The code is unchanged. Good hunting. I have sent you some money.'

He carefully replaced the telephone and then crept on his hands and knees to the door. No one. He slipped through and walked quietly towards the entrance.

'Here, you. What the hell d'ye think you are doing in 'ere?' It was Carberry's batman with a cup of tea in his hand.

'I wanted to see Mr Carberry about the trip. But he is in

the bathroom. I'll see him out at the ship. There is plenty of time.'

'What sort of bloody Navy do you think you're in? This ain't the Savoy. The lower deck's not allowed in 'ere. An' take a tip, mate, if you are flying with Mr Carberry you never have plenty of time. Get out!'

It was cold and dark around SS 19. Torches moved in and out of the trees like glow-worms. A stepladder by the side of the nacelle led up to the petrol tanks slung halfway below the envelope. Wragg stood on the steps, holding the big funnel in place with a chammy leather inside it to strain the fuel. Shepherd carried it up to him. Thirty gallons each side in two-gallon tins at ten pounds a gallon. Water ballast, more two-gallon tins. Two 100lb bombs. Shepherd watched Carberry check that they were secure on the racks. Safety-pins through the nose-fuse and the withdrawal wire clipped in place. Bomb-release toggles checked.

Shepherd collected a Lewis gun and three double drums of ammunition from the armoury. The armourer said, 'You've signed for that, mate. It's on your charge. Bring it back. Don't get yourself killed before you do. 'Cos we don't take that as an excuse.'

Carberry had a standard Lee Enfield clipped in a scabbard between the cockpits. Shepherd nodded when he was asked whether he could shoot.

'Good, we'll see who wins when we sight our first mine. I think the rifle is better for potting mines. And it doesn't need 180 rounds, if the man using it knows what he is doing.'

PO Riggs had lashed extra bags of sand to the skids before he unhooked the fore and after guys from the anchors. A dozen men, the handling party, took the guys. More men, three a side, held the nacelle. Shepherd climbed into his cockpit. Carberry handed him a couple of flimsies. 'Weather forecast. Not bad for March. You'll be bloody cold. Recognition signals. A couple of two-star red flares, one after the other, or plumes of water from the vents. British submarines. We do have some. None reported in our area but you never know.'

Carberry climbed in. It was still dark. His torch flickered

over the instruments, followed the line of the gas-valve cable and the ripping cable. 'Petrol on. Switch off. Suck in.'

The nacelle wobbled as Wragg pulled the propeller round. Up and down went the push-rods. Tappets like cast-iron fingers opened and closed the valves. The engine sounded like a drunk soaking up whisky after a month on the wagon. Petrol fumes bathed Shepherd in the front cockpit. He sat watching, frozen into immobility despite his long john underwear, shirt, two sweaters, a long submariner's frock, scarf and leather coat. He could feel the sweat cooling, chilling his body. He tried to move and flew into a panic when he found he was jammed as tight as a cork in a bottle. Slowly, puffing at the effort, he extricated his right hand and laid it by the key. And where was the aerial reel? He knocked the clipboard on to the floor. Chart, weather report, recognition signals. Oh God, he had made a cock of it already.

'Switch on.'

'Switch on. Contact.'

Wragg was poised in front with his outstretched hands reaching up for the propeller blade. He flung his weight down. The undercarriages swayed, stretching the bungee rubber-binding holding the axle on to the vees. The warm engine coughed, spat yellow flame from the silencer at the grass and rattled into life. The nacelle quivered with life like a jelly, and the petrol pipe in front of the cockpit vibrated into a blur.

Carberry hit him on the shoulder. Wriggle, twist, turn round somehow. Carberry raised an enquiring thumb. Shepherd jammed his clipboard behind the set and raised a thumb in reply.

The rattle of the engine died away until it was ticking over so slowly that the individual blades could be seen. Carberry lifted his right arm, his fist clenched. A warrant officer standing in front of them and a few yards to the left lifted a megaphone to his lips.

'Forrard guys, aft guys, stand by.'

Riggs knelt by the sandbags lashed to the skids.

'Away two bags,' Carberry said. As Riggs removed the bags he stretched his arms upwards with the palms inward. 'Hands off.'

The men holding the nacelle let go and took one pace away. Carberry shook his head, lowering his arms.

'Hands on.'

The men stepped forward one pace and again held the nacelle.

'Off one bag.'

Riggs unlashed another bag of sand.

'Hands off.' Carberry raised his arms again and the men released the nacelle, stepping clear. The nacelle quivered and stayed firmly on the grass. Carberry waited for a minute before lowering his arms. The men took hold again.

'Off one bag.' Riggs removed another sandbag. There were only two now, both of them lashed to the sides of the cockpit within reach of Carberry. And there was a tank of water ballast.

'Hands off.' Again his arms went up in the air. As the handlers released the nacelle SS 19 moved slowly upwards, shuffled sideways a few inches and settled back on the grass. Carberry lowered his arms and then raised his thumb. As the handlers took hold of the nacelle Riggs waved a salute and stepped back out of the way.

The warrant officer lifted his megaphone. 'Guy ropes stand to. Forward march.'

Carberry eased on a trickle of power. The wheels crunched through the grass as, guided by the forward and aft guy ropes, SS 19 headed for the opening in the trees. It was no more than a greyness in the surrounding blackness. Shepherd held his breath, unable to believe that the monstrous gasbag above him would fit into that aperture. One projecting branch, one spark, and they would make a fine torch.

He knew the mechanics of what Carberry had done, but he was still bewildered by the drill-like execution. Carberry had slowly discarded weight by removing sandbags until SS 19 was only slightly heavier than the air it displaced. Once outside he would take off like an aeroplane, running the wheels along the ground to get up speed, then lifting the nose to generate enough lift from the envelope to get them in the air. It was a way of conserving gas and ballast. Ballast was as important to the airship pilot as fuel was to the engine.

Without it there was no way to arrest their descent on landing.

The trees closed in on them. Sitting in the nacelle it was impossible to see how close the branches came. A word of command. The aft guy party moved diagonally, pulling the tail over. The grey blur became a tunnel of tree-trunks, black undergrowth. One branch – Shepherd saw white wood where one of them had been lopped recently – one branch catching that taut fabric and the whole contrivance would be a pricked balloon. 70,000 cubic feet of hydrogen spilling over a hot engine and eight red-hot sparking-plugs. There was no more than a breath of wind. He shuddered, thinking about going along that tunnel in a breeze.

They came out of the wood and he could see the sky, a grey slab lightening in the east superimposed on the black landscape. Puddles of mist hugged folds in the ground and curled about the hedges.

Slowly the nose was turned into wind. The engine rattled up to full power, sprinkling Shepherd's face with oily freckles. The noise died away. Carberry had been burning oil off the plugs while the nacelle was held.

Now the pilot lifted his arms into the air again. 'Ease off the guys ... Hands off ... Let go, all,' roared the megaphone.

The men on the guy ropes let go and stepped back, followed by the men holding the nacelle. Carberry lowered his arms and opened the throttle.

SS 19 trundled sedately over the bumpy grass, slowly gathering speed. The pilot wound back the elevator wheel. The nose lifted. A final bounce, a sink until the wheels were just kissing the grass, and SS 19 went up out of the field like a lift. Carberry eased back the throttle as he started a gentle turn back over the field on to a northerly heading. The sea, cold, wrinkled like an old woman, appeared to starboard.

Carberry thumped Shepherd on the shoulder. 'Let out the aerial. When we get to 500 feet report to Howden. Airborne 05.59. Let me know if you can't raise them. We may have to climb higher. The Wolds.'

By the time they reached 500 feet Shepherd was too stupefied to do anything, what with the ceaseless battering from the slipstream, gusts of hot air from the engine, and draughts from under the floor that turned his feet, despite the fur-lined boots, into blocks of ice. The miniscule windscreen was soon smeared with oil, but it did nothing to stop splashes from catching his goggles. The strap holding them across his helmet was not tight enough. As he bent over the side to release the aerial the slipstream plucked them from over his eyes, bounced them on the bridge of his nose and flicked them behind his head. The strap on the back of his helmet held them, bobbing about, twisting, hitting the back of his neck. As he groped behind him for them a blob of hot oil flew into his tear-streaked eyes.

Carberry's fist thumped his shoulder. 'Have you got that airborne report off yet?'

At last Shepherd retrieved them. Holding them in place with one hand he released the brake on the aerial reel. The aerial was 250 feet of copper wire with a streamlined lead weight on the end to hold it away from the nacelle. As the brake went off, the weight took charge. The reel spun round smartly, rapping him on the wrist so hard that he thought it was broken. By the time he found that it was not, there was no aerial on the reel.

Carberry thumped him on the shoulder again. He eased back the throttle and lifted the earflap of his helmet. Shepherd copied him.

'It never fails. Don't they teach you anything in the training school apart from how to salute? Everybody does it the first time, you damned fool. Don't let it happen again. Put the spare on. Use your hand on the rim as a brake.'

They were at 1,000 feet, flying straight and level over a featureless sea, before he got the message through. It was dawn, the sun bounding over the horizon and flushing pink a few scattered strips of stratus. Shepherd stamped his feet on the floorboards and banged them together to induce some feeling in them. This was the moment he had dreamt about. Now that he had contacted base he would listen in to the U-boat waveband. He would pick up UC62 boasting about his latest escapade and lead Carberry to the scene. Two bombs should be enough but to be on the safe side he would wireless up some escort vessels, a couple of lean destroyers to make sure of the kill and to collect the evidence.

Carberry had other ideas. He pointed ahead. It took Shepherd a long time to see the line of red can-shaped buoys stretching north and south. They were almost overhead before he recognized them, and at the same time he thought he saw the other line of them two miles to the east. This was the War Channel, protected on the flanks by British mine-fields which had been kept clear of German mines by the minesweepers' daily round. Carberry flew over the inner line, turning north-west.

'Start searching,' Carberry shouted, pointing to the binoculars. He grinned. 'Ten bob for your first U-boat, half a crown for a mine.'

Shepherd realized that he had more to do than listen to the wireless. Carberry was working like a one-armed paper-hanger, watching the engine instruments, altimeter, gas-pressure gauges and compass, logging changes of course and juggling with the control of the crabpot valves. As the sun rose the heated gas in the envelope expanded, giving them more lift. Now Shepherd could appreciate why they had taken off 'heavy'. SS19 with her nose down was still climbing. Carberry struggled to hold it on the elevators, trimming the blimp nose down with varying amounts of air admitted into the fore and aft ballonnets through the crabpot valves. But eventually he had to valve off hydrogen through the gas-valve in the top of the envelope.

Shepherd turned to searching an empty sea. In the next hour he found five periscopes. Four of them were porpoises. The fifth was an empty bottle. The next was a trick of shadow and windblown spume from a breaking wave-crest. The next sighting was a certainty, a straight line in the jumbled waste of sea. A slender spike sticking up in the water, betrayed by a feather of foam behind it. He focused and refocused the glasses on it before pointing it out to Carberry.

This time the pilot scanned it carefully through his own glasses before steering for it. But as they swept overhead they could see that there was a drift net attached to it. The feather was caused by the current racing by. There was no sign of a fishing boat, but a few miles north, just as the smoke on the horizon signalled the approach of their convoy, they flew over a litter of broken planking, a lifejacket and an oar.

The minesweepers came first, three converted trawlers, paravanes spread to catch the mooring ropes of the mines and bring them to the surface. A light flickered at them from the bridge of the leader. Shepherd watched, fascinated by the sight of the three sweepers and, ten miles behind them, twelve ships coming out of the Tees to join the fifteen southbound from the Tyne.

Carberry hit his shoulder again. 'That light, they're signalling to us, you bloody fool. What are they saying?'

Shepherd gawped at him. It had never occurred to him that the flickering light was conveying a message to them.

'Send "Say again slowly" when they stop,' Carberry shouted. 'The silly buggers always do that. Some regular Navy flag-waggler showing off.'

Shepherd unhooked the Aldis lamp, plugged it in and slowly clattered out his request as the pilot took SS19 into a wide circle. The message came back noticeably slower.

Good morning. Thought you had got lost. Three stray mines lifted and destroyed. U-boat reports. 02.00, U-boat reported on surface five miles east-north-east Seaton Sluice. Saw nothing. 02.46, destroyers report chasing surfaced U-boat heading west-south-west from Dogger. 04.00, coast-guard reported one surfaced proceeding slowly north, two miles due east Flamborough Head. Did you see anything? Message ends.

Carberry took the message slip. 'One of them might be right. Every black shadow is a U-boat at night. Nearly as many as porpoises. Tell him about the wreckage ahead. We will take up station between them and the convoy.'

Now for the first time Shepherd realized how vast the sea was as they slowly circled round and round the convoy. The ships were in three columns sailing down the west side of the War Channel, a block of shipping five miles long. An old four-stack destroyer led the way, with four converted trawlers on the flanks weaving in and around like sheepdogs as they chased the strays back into line and admonished the smoky coal-burners.

If he had not been so busy Shepherd would have been disheartened at their chance of finding one particular U-boat in this waste of water. Three times they raced from one side of the convoy to the other to investigate something suspicious. They found barrels, pieces of timber, net buoys, porpoises, a chest of drawers, an ominous patch of floating coke half a mile across and the waterlogged remains of a lifeboat. But no U-boats.

They had been airborne for four and a half hours, and Shepherd was half stupefied with fatigue and cold when he spotted the mine. It was floating in the middle of the Channel almost submerged, a black sphere with copper horns. Remembering his past mistakes Shepherd said nothing at first. It disappeared under the nose as the blimp swung on to another leg of a zigzag. He looked for it again. It was not there and he put it down to another porpoise. But he swept the binoculars round to look behind them and saw the glint of the horns as it rolled in the trough of a wave. The sweepers were miles ahead. The convoy was five miles away, heading for the mine.

'Mine! Mine!' he shouted, pointing aft. Carberry swung the airship round, keeping it to one side so that it remained in sight.

'Wireless the destroyer. Quickly. Mine report. Five miles dead ahead port column. Break out the Lewis. After you've sent the message, I'll have a pot at it with the rifle.'

He wound the elevator wheel forward, pushing SS19 into a gentle dive aiming for the mine, crabbing sideways to allow for the wind. It was noticeably stronger, he thought. Coming from the south-west. As they flew slowly over the mine he dropped a smoke-float. It fell about fifty yards away. Good enough as a warning, he thought, but useless if he had been trying to bomb a U-boat. He broke out the rifle, checked the magazine and took aim.

Crack. The noise of the rifle a foot from his ear made Shepherd jump with fright. Carberry fired a ten-round clip as SS 19 circled like a baby elephant in a circus ring.

He was reloading as Shepherd clipped the Lewis gun on to a spigot sticking out from the side of the nacelle. He fitted a drum of ammunitition, cocked the gun and waited for a clear shot as Carberry brought them round for another run.

'Watch the propeller!' yelled the pilot. 'Wait until we are well abeam.'

There was no sight on the gun. He looked along the barrel and fired. The splashes showed he was short and behind. Straining to hold the juddering gun, firing five-round bursts and correcting from the splashes, he lashed the water round the mine into foam. Nothing happened.

Carberry swung the blimp around again. He shouted as Shepherd squinted along the barrel, 'Cease firing!'

The destroyer was coming up on them like a greyhound after a rabbit. Straining its pre-war boilers, smoke trailing behind like a pennant, a clean white bow wave flared up and out from the stem. Half a dozen seamen armed with rifles lined the rails.

Carberry eased the throttle right back, letting SS 19 drift slowly back towards the convoy. Shepherd turned to the pilot, grinning with excitement. A plume of white water lifted and fell as the mine exploded. Carberry scowled at his obvious enthusiasm.

'Bloody fools. His job is to guard that convoy. The mine might have been dumped by a U-boat just to distract the escort. Stop admiring the pretty picture and get on with your job.'

The mine episode gave Shepherd a second wind, it justified their being up here floating over the ships slogging south at five knots. He found that he could tune the wireless set and watch the sea.

It was over two hours later when he heard it, the typically harsh note of a Telefunken transmitter. A U-boat transmitter. He told Carberry.

The pilot eyed him curiously. 'How do you know it is a U-boat? All right, this is the wrong place to argue. I'll take your word for it. Give me a bearing and distance to run. I'm not interested in general knowledge.'

There was nothing he could say in reply. There was a

U-boat. Something they both expected to be there. For different reasons. But he could not say where it lay. And without his code-books he had no way of deciphering the message. It was a long time since he had felt so helpless. His grand scheme had come unstuck. The glimmer of an idea nagged at the back of his mind but he was too tired by the cold and the perpetual slipstream tugging at his helmet, plucking at his goggles as he leant over the side, to bring the thought into focus. Soon afterwards Howden passed a message. Their relief was on the way. The Zero was in sight before he had copied the signal.

He flickered a farewell message to the convoy commander. Carberry eased himself out of the cockpit to walk stiffly along the skids to pour a spare quart of oil into the sump, as SS 19 crabbed against the rising wind on course for Cleveland Hall.

Carberry slapped Shepherd on the shoulder as they climbed stiffly from the nacelle. They had been flying for nearly nine hours. His joints seemed to have set permanently in one place, his head still heard the engine noise and he needed matches to keep his eyelids open. Carberry was in high spirits. His new wireless operator was a good joss, a harbinger of good flying and luck. That was the first time, he declared, that that engine had run for more than a couple of hours without giving trouble.

Shepherd had planned to call Henrietta but he dozed off in the middle of tea. He lay in his bunk trying to collect his thoughts and think of something positive to do on the next trip. The cold woke him in the early hours of the morning. Someone had taken off his shoes and draped a blanket over him. It seemed as though he had just got back to sleep again when the guard came round to wake him for the morning patrol.

He had to sneak into Carberry's office again to ring Henrietta. She was furious with him. They had just deciphered a long angry tirade from Kapitänleutnant Schiller about his day-long shadowing of a convoy. About the need to sneak away, surface in broad daylight to race south at full speed so as to submerge and creep in again without being able to get close enought to attack because of the escorts and a damned airship.

'You were there circling over him, Richard. Why didn't you go for him? You do carry bombs, I suppose. This game cannot go on for ever. If you let chances like this slip by we will never get the man before he gets his posting on to one of the Atlantic boats. Then we will never find him. You really must keep your eyes open ... '

The ingratitude of it cut him to the quick. For a moment he was speechless. Then he heard footsteps. Carberry. The thump of his heels hitting the floor, the long stride, were unmistakable.

'Somebody coming,' he hissed. 'At least we know he is there ... '

'Richard, measure the distance between the minesweepers and the convoy. I think Schiller stumbled on something that even he does not realize the importance—'

He put the receiver back on the hook, replaced the instrument on the desk and cowered under it as the door was whipped open. The beam of a torch traversed the room, bouncing from the floor over the desk and across to a table littered with flying gear, charts and official publications waiting to be amended. Shepherd held his breath. He could see Carberry's feet. A white towel fell to the floor. As Carberry bent to pick it up the beam wavered towards Shepherd's hiding-place. But it went out as he grunted, picked up the towel and left, slamming the door behind him.

Shepherd waited, listening to the footsteps. Then he went along the corridor, turning left for the bathroom. The door was unlocked. He stood for a moment with it cracked open, but he could hear nothing. Somehow he had to find a safer way of talking to Henrietta. And what the devil was she so interested in the gap between the convoy and the minesweepers for?

The weather had changed. A blustering west wind blew a thin drizzle in their faces as they went out to SS 19. It was not ready. Harry Wragg had taken off one bank of the V8 engine to replace warped exhaust valves. Working without a break he had refitted the block, but now he had to cure all the leaking water connections. And test it. Half an hour at least.

Carberry took Shepherd back to the Flight Office while he

96

got the latest information from the SNO Humber. There had been a dozen U-boat sightings which Carberry dismissed with a wave of his hand.

'Imagination, most of them. A fisherman lights his pipe and some old woman reports that a U-boat is signalling to a spy ashore. We know that they are there but the only thing you can be sure of is that where they are reported is where they ain't.'

Shepherd swallowed the retort on his lips. He remembered the care taken to log each U-boat transmission and plot the bearing on the chart. But the sighting reports did not differentiate between their reports and some coast-watcher's imagination. But the reports that really hurt Carberry were the sinking reports. Four of them, none in convoy and none escorted by blimps.

As they left the office an engine stuttered into life and settled down to a smooth tick-over as it slowly warmed up. As they approached, Harry Wragg slowly opened it up to full power with a dozen men hanging on to the nacelle. Carberry was nodding his head when the engine backfired like a runaway machine-gun. Yellow flames spitting out of the silencer bathed the underside of the envelope in a golden glow. From ten yards away they could see the engine-mounting twisting under the intermittent loads.

The engine-fitter was almost weeping tears of frustration as he throttled back. 'It's not on, sir. I told you she needed all the valves replacing. I wouldn't trust it to fly across the Bay.'

Carberry nodded. 'My fault, penny wise pound foolish.' He shouted for Riggs. 'How soon can you have Mr Dutton's Zero ready, fifteen minutes?'

The petty officer made a face. 'She had a gas-check yesterday and we refuelled her last night. But we have to change the bombs over and I'd like a quick check. Thirty minutes ... '

'That'll give me time to have a wash and a sandwich,' Wragg said. 'And get a clean pair of overalls.'

The Zeros had three seats, one behind the pilot for a mechanic and one in front for the wireless operator. Carberry stared at Wragg.

'When did you last go to bed?' he asked. 'You don't have to tell me. Sorry, Wragg, looking at the sea for a speck of a periscope is no job for a man tired out before he starts. I'd rather you took the engine out. Send it back to Howden for overhaul. Then get some sleep. Riggs, see that he does as he is told.' He saw the disappointment on the fitter's face and slapped him across the shoulders. 'Don't be so damned impatient, Wragg. It's going to be a long war. Shepherd and I will soon write off this old cow and that abominable Yankee coffee-grinder. Then we'll all have Zeros and you will be complaining about the blisters on your backside.'

Shepherd approved of the Zero. His cockpit was in the bows of the boat-shaped nacelle with a pleasant smell of wood and newly applied varnish. The view was better, as the engine was mounted at the rear driving a pusher airscrew. There was no radiator to block his view, and the air inlet to the ballonnets was away aft behind the propeller. And soon after take-off he appreciated the windscreen and the absence of the battering slipstream.

At 500 feet the top of the envelope seemed to be in the cloud base when they picked up the northbound convoy off Flamborough Head. Condensation ran off the envelope to slap him in the face. Below, the escorts were working hard in a choppy sea to get the convoy closed up after the usual night-time straggling. It was only after he had got his routine search established, position reports made and a quick check on the U-boat band that Shepherd had the chance to think about Henrietta's odd request.

He knew that all submarines, British and German, were not what they pretended to be. Submarines. They were surface ships that had the capability to dive under the water and stay there for a limited time. A very limited time. Alec Jervis had told him that five hours was comfortable, twelve hell, and twenty-four hours a miserable death. Like their mobility. Twelve knots on the surface in reasonable weather. Fast enough to catch most merchant ships and manoeuvre into position for an attack with gun or torpedo. But under water, UC62 would be lucky to hold six knots and that for a short time. Within the hour the batteries that powered the electric motors would be hot and gassing, the overstrained plates buckling. Four knots was a reasonable speed under water. Too slow to catch anything.

That explained Schiller's fury. Seeing all those ships go by out of torpedo range and unable to close by surfacing because of the escort. Especially the airship. For at sea there were no natural straight lines. Nothing. Until a periscope emerged, drawing its tell-tale feather behind.

'Periscope!' Carberry shouted, his arm pointing abeam beyond the buoys marking the Channel. 'Are you blind or asleep? Signal the destroyer.'

He pulled the Zero round in a tight turn to cut across the track of the U-boat. As he swung right to align the blimp with the course shown by the periscope, his fingers plucked the safety-pins out of the bombs. Shepherd got no reply from the escort leader but he saw one of the trawlers on the flank head towards them. He left the key to use the Aldis lamp to flash a message. The skipper did not wait to reply. Plumes of steam jetted from his whistle on the funnel as the trawler altered course to intercept the U-boat.

Now they were overhauling the periscope hand over fist. With the engine flat out and every cable throbbing, the airship sounded like a gigantic orchestra. Carberry made a guess that they were over the U-boat and dropped the first bomb. As if in reply, two streaks of bubbles appeared in front of them heading for the distant convoy.

'Torpedoes!' Carberry shouted. 'Flash that trawler. Then try to sink them with the Lewis.'

He valved some gas. The Zero fell out of the sky in a steep dive as he went hell for leather after the two torpedoes. It was a cheeky long-range shot from over 2,000 yards, but running towards the convoy from the flank it looked as though at least one of them must hit something. Every ship was sounding the alarm on its whistles.

Shepherd took aim with the Lewis in the port socket as they slowly overhauled the torpedo tracks. If there were air bubbles on the surface the engine producing them must be some distance ahead under the water, he reasoned, as he altered his aim to fire ahead of the leading track. Short bursts. Five rounds. Correct from the splashes. The line was good but short. Up a bit. The range was closing as they overhauled the torpedo. It was barely fifteen yards away and as they came level with it he could see its shape under the water. He fired a long burst into the nose. The stream of bubbles stopped. As he looked for the second one the sea rose up in a solid wall of white water to engulf the Zero. His torpedo had exploded.

The sea came through the windscreen like a mass of concrete knocking him into the bottom of the nacelle. He swallowed seawater in gulps and wondered whether it was possible to drown while flying in an airship. As he pulled himself up out of the water filling the cockpit he saw the second torpedo somersault through the air. As it hit the sea it exploded. A hole appeared in the front of the nacelle. Something whizzed between him and Carberry, ripping away the coaming covering the nacelle. A broken cable ripped a long gash in the sleeve of his leather coat.

The Zero came through the wall of water like a ship emerging from a hurricane. The windscreens had gone, and the Lewis gun, and water poured out of the holes in the nacelle. The engine had stopped and the wave-crests were licking at the keel.

The blimp moved soggily, reluctant to stay in the air, but as the water drained away it rose slowly. Shepherd looked for Carberry, heaving a sigh of relief as the pilot's head rose from his cockpit. He was bare-headed and water plastered his black hair against his scalp. Shepherd felt his own head. His helmet had gone.

Carberry pushed the safety-pin back into the fuse of the remaining bomb and pulled the release toggle. The Zero lurched upwards as the hundred-pounder dropped away.

Shepherd could only think about having Schiller directly underneath them as they discarded the bomb. Henrietta would never forgive him. 'That was our last bomb. That U-boat will get away. We don't even have an ammunition drum to throw at it.'

Carberry's seat had broken. He was standing up in his cockpit, untangling the lanyard holding his revolver and holster. He threw them overboard.

'Don't be such a damned fool, Shepherd. The Navy will have to take care of your U-boat. Our concern is to get ourselves home. Take a look around you.'

It was a frightening sight. A couple of suspension cables had parted, and the nacelle with its dead engine hung drunkenly from the envelope fifty feet above a very unfriendly sea. There was nothing there. He had forgotten about the west wind. It still blew. With a dead engine they were nothing but a holed free balloon drifting towards a distant Germany, protected from the drizzle by the overhang of the envelope. Away to the west he heard the double boom of exploding depth-charges, but he could see no sign of the convoy or its escort.

'You can forget about them,' Carberry said. 'They have the convoy to look after. When they get the time they might remember to send a message reporting where we went down. It'll be too late. We have to get ourselves out of this one. See if you can fix the wireless set while I look at the engine. Don't waste any time on anything fancy. We're losing gas and I don't care for the prospect of swimming home.'

Carberry climbed out of his cockpit on to the rails fixed along the bottom of the car. He said, 'After you have looked at the wireless, make a pile of everything we can throw overboard. And that will include everything you are wearing except your long johns.'

He shuffled aft to start drying out the ignition system of the Rolls-Royce Hawk engine. Shepherd looked at the wireless set. It was wrecked.

'Throw it overboard. Cut the battery loose and heave that over the side. And the bomb-racks.'

As he heaved the broken bits overboard Shepherd felt something wet drip on to his hand. Petrol. He shouted to Carberry, pointing to the broken petrol pipe and the fuel pouring out. The pilot shrugged his shoulders and told him not to smoke.

Once Shepherd had thrown all the debris overboard there was nothing to occupy him. He was suddenly aware of the silence by the little noises usually unheard. The background noise of the sea below, the creaking of the cables and an

101

ominous rustling from the envelope. The gasbag was beginning to lose its sleek fatness and there were creases in the ballonnets, because without the engine and the slipstream from the propeller there was no pressure to fill them.

Carberry called to him. 'Come back here into the engineer's cockpit. You will have to turn over the engine.'

Gingerly Shepherd swung his leg out of the cockpit and felt for the rail. A piece of plywood splintered in his hand as he took his first tentative step. He froze, staring down beyond his feet at the sea. It looked a lot nearer.

'Steady, man. Don't look down. Look at me. Shuffle, one foot at a time. Reach your hand out to me.'

With the pilot's help he shuffled the ten feet along the rail and scrambled into the engineer's cockpit. It was directly under the radiator. A crank handle like that of a car projected through the bottom from the engine.

Carberry climbed on to the cylinder heads of the engine. Steadying himself with one hand on a suspension rope he wound his silk scarf into a ball and soaked it in the petrol pouring out of the broken pipe. Bending down he pushed the sodden fabric into the carburretor air intake. Then he stood up to patch the pipe with a bandage and a roll of insulating tape.

The Zero twirled in a gust and sagged downwards. The lift they had gained from jettisoning the debris had gone. Carberry doubled up over the engine, retching from the petrol fumes that had soaked him. He recovered to drop back on to the skids by the engine.

'Crank the engine over half a dozen times,' he said.

Shepherd heaved at the crank. His hands were greasy. The propeller blades rotated through half a turn and then the compression ripped the handle out of his hands. He took a stronger grip, braced his legs against the sides of the cockpit and started to swing the engine again. Slowly the propeller turned through six revolutions, sucking neat petrol into the cylinders. Carberry pulled the rag out of the intake.

'Save your strength,' he said, patting Shepherd lightly on the shoulder as he shuffled along the rail back to the pilot's cockpit. 'When I shout "Contact", swing that crank as though your life depended on it. Because it does.' He switched on the ignition. 'Contact.' He wound the handle of the starting magneto.

Shepherd threw his weight on to the crank, pulling the propeller through two turns quickly before he was forced to slow. The engine spat, ripping the handle out of his grasp. A trickle of blood appeared between his fingers as he grasped it again. One cylinder fired, then a second, four of them, misfiring, crackling like a machine-gun but running. As the engine warmed up, the last two cylinders fired and it ran more smoothly – after a fashion, because the propeller was out of balance and the crankshaft had bent. The nacelle quivered like a disintegrating jelly but the ballonnets were suddenly firm again. Carberry turned west. The Zero had changed from being a cripple to one of the walking wounded.

'Find something to jettison,' Carberry said. He pointed to the petrol tanks slung between the nacelle and the envelope. 'Get up there and cut the right-hand one away. A full tank will be no use if we have to swim. Then heave the tools overboard. Dump the trail rope. And take that leather coat off.'

It took them an hour, sixty everlasting minutes, before they saw the cliffs ahead. Cliffs running up to 300 feet high while they were lurching along barely fifty feet up. There was nothing left that could be thrown overboard. Carberry was running the engine flat out, trying to hold the heavy airship in the air with dynamic lift, but the vibration was breaking up the nacelle and the petrol feed-pipe vibrated loose twice.

Shepherd knelt on the floor of the nacelle, trying to watch the breakers at the foot of the cliff instead of a seam of stitched mahogany that was steadily opening up under the pounding from the out-of-balance engine. There was less turbulence and the sea seemed to slide past quicker as they came within the shelter of the cliffs about two miles away. Carberry turned south.

'Eight minutes to Cleveland Bay!' he shouted. 'We'll go in on to the beach. Take your boots off and your uniform. Keep your leather coat until the last minute. Everything else overboard. Pull my fug boots off. Over with them. Quickly ... '

UC62 was at periscope depth crawling along at two knots with a jammed rudder and the aft hydroplanes buckled. The underwater charges had crippled her. The emergency lights were on and there was a whiff of chlorine in the air. Soon they would have no choice but an ignominious surrender. Schiller gestured for the periscope.

The cliffs were closer. He swung the periscope to view the horizon and slammed the instrument down. There was a damned airship cutting across their track at less than twenty metres. He waited for the inevitable explosion. This one would be certain to finish them. He counted in his head. Nothing happened. He turned to Beibedecke. 'We have an airship escorting us. But they are asleep. They didn't see us. But you had better tell Henne that if we don't have rudder control in fifteen minutes we'll be boring a hole in one of Tommi's cliffs.'

'Tell him yourself,' Henne said, reeling into the control room. He retched and broke into an uncontrollable fit of coughing. 'You have rudder control, two mechanics in the sick-bay and a dose of chlorine on the way.'

His long legs buckled under him as he slid to the floor with his back to a panel. His chest moved painfully in and out as he struggled for breath.

Schiller stared at the oil-blackened figure of his engineer. The man had saved them again. He snapped to the helmsman, 'Full right rudder. Steer due east. Half ahead together.'

They were not going to break up on the English rocks. But that would have been an easier end than choking on the chlorine gas given off when seawater and the acid in their batteries met. He knelt by the engineer, slapped his face. 'Henne, did you cure the leak.' The engineer stared back at him, nodded, and started coughing again.

Schiller snapped his fingers. 'Get him to the sick-bay. Up periscope. Quickly. That airship had a funny look to it. Maybe they have their own problems.'

Beibedecke shrugged his shoulders. 'We must be leaking oil. At this depth he'll see us.'

But Schiller was chuckling as he gazed through the lens. The hydrophone operators wrapping wet cloths across their mouths gaped at him.

'Damn it, I told you they're in a worse state than we are. That looked like their uniforms they were throwing overboard. Stand by to surface. Gun crew at the ready. This will have to be a quick job. Surface. Blow main vents.'

He was laughing as another one of the crew reeled into the control room coughing. This would be a report to remember. Something to wipe out the thought of those damned convoys. Nobody in the flotilla had ever shot down an airship.

'Weiderer ... ' He stopped. Weiderer was dead, cut in two by that damned Tommi trawler. What the hell was the new midshipman's name. Caspar. The poor sod was having no luck on this cruise. He had taken twenty shells to sink an old schooner. 'Beibedecke, take charge of that deck gun. A quick job. We are in sight of shore. I want that airship shot down.'

Beibedecke gaped at him. 'You cannot shoot down an airship with our gun. It will not elevate high enough. And we have not got the right sort of anti—'

'Don't argue with your captain, Beibedecke. I have seen the airship, you have not. It is only flying on faith and will power. Just put four big holes in the envelope before it reaches a beach. The sea will do the rest.'

As UC62 surfaced, the excitement was sweeter than the fresh air. Schiller ranged the sea with his glasses. Nothing, not even a fishing boat. Just as well there was barely enough water for them to dive. Once past that headland the airship would count itself saved.

'Start engines. Half ahead together. Starboard twenty. Gun crew on deck. Leave the forrard hatch open, Mr Beibedecke. The boat needs sweetening. See if Mr Henne is fit enough to look at the aft hydroplanes.'

The bay was opening up in front of them – a strip of yellow sand; tumbled rock knitted together with grass and bushes; the cliff-face seamed by old falls. Two trees growing out sideways halfway up. A road switchbacking up to the top. A flag of some sort. Yellow? God, it was a wind indicator. The airship was heading for its base.

Beibedecke called out the range. Cottages clustered together beyond the beach and up along the road under the trees. Fishing boats hauled up above the high-water mark. The airship was in real trouble. That looked like a coat being thrown overboard.

'Fire when ready, Mr Beibedecke.'

He watched critically. His First Lieutenant was a man who did not believe the evidence of his eyes. The target was an airship so the gun had to be elevated. A flash in the cliff-face showed where the shell landed. Again. The windows of a white-painted cottage glowed red as a shell burst inside. Damn the fellow. The U-boat was rolling heavily now and the airship was almost end-on to them.

A chimney disappeared from a cottage. A fishing boat lifted into the air and fell broken-backed across its neighbour. A hit. The starboard tailplane fluttered like a flag before breaking loose. A kite as big as a barn door dragged along by one cable. The tail of the airship sagged down. A yellow flame blossomed in the air below it and raced forward into the envelope. Two bodies leapt out of the nacelle as the nacelle kissed the wave-tops. It was down. The nacelle stopped suddenly and the huge bulk of the envelope settled on top of it. Just when it seemed that the fire was out a ripple of flame leapt along the top of the bag, turning it into a ball of flame. Schiller shuddered. Tongues of flame were sailing up to cliff-top level.

'New target. Starboard, cliff top. Put ten rounds searching fire in the woods at the top of the cliff.' He turned to the speaking tube. 'Hard a-port on to south by east.'

Henne reported as they turned away from the bay heading for deeper water. Schiller was laughing. The engineer shook his head gloomily. 'Two hours work, at least. On the surface ... '

Schiller grinned. This patrol was not so bad after all. He swept his arms around. 'Take your time. There's nobody here to bother us.'

Beibedecke was looking back at him, his ten rounds fired. He levelled his glasses at the cliff. Something was burning up there, smoke rising above the trees until it was flattened by the wind. It would look good in the report. One airship shot down and damage to the airship's base by shellfire. An attack on Tommi's homeland. If the High Seas Fleet could boast about the Battle of Scarborough, Otto Schiller would claim the honours in the Battle of Cleveland Bay.

'Cease fire. Dismiss gun crew. Henne, you have the deck for repairs. Don't waste any time ... '

Shepherd, huddled in a foetal ball on the peeling floor of the nacelle, was too immersed in his misery – he was now wearing only his long johns underwear and they were soaked in drizzle and condensation dripping from the envelope – to realize that they were being shelled.

He heard Carberry shout as he switched off the engine, felt the Zero sag downwards as their speed died, but the words meant nothing. Nothing that could happen could make him more miserable. It was so damned undignified. Being wounded in the service of your country, even killed, was something one lived with. The Sacrifice of War. But not freezing to death clad only in wet woollen underwear.

He looked behind. Carberry had twisted round to stare at something on the sea. The starboard tailplane fluttered away, trailing a bracing wire carrying a pennant of torn envelope. Suddenly the air between the sagging envelope and the engine was ablaze. And beyond, half a mile away, a U-boat cruised on the surface taking pot-shots at them.

Carberry was yelling at him. He threw a glove at him. It should have been thrown overboard. Water squirted up through cracks in the floor of the splintered nacelle but he sat there too bemused to move.

'Jump, you bloody fool.' Carberry stood up to poke Shepherd in the ribs. A tongue of flame snaked along the underside of the envelope. His hair started to burn. Beating out the flames with one hand he dragged Shepherd to his feet with the other.

There was no air. Shepherd thought his lungs would burst as the burning hydrogen swallowed up all the oxygen. Carberry fell back exhausted. Now it was Shepherd's turn. He threw himself across the shattered cockpit coaming, linked his arms under the pilot's shoulders and rolled over the side dragging Carberry with him.

The water was like ice killing all feeling, stupefying the mind. He hit the bottom with his head long before he expected it. Carberry was torn from his grip. Desperately holding his breath he groped for him on hands and knees. He had to get him away from the black shadow settling above them, the burning envelope.

The shadow drifted away. His bursting lungs forced him to the surface. The water was no more than five feet deep, reflecting the heat from the burning hydrogen. His knees buckled under him and he went down again.

A pair of arms reached down to grab him. His head came up gulping air. He fell back unconscious with his left arm still round Carberry's body.

He came-to lying on his back on the floor of the public bar in the Lobster Pot. Somebody was trying to pull his wet underpants over his hips. Automatically his hand grabbed hold of the cloth as he tried to hold them on. He opened his eyes.

Elsa Dolli was standing over him dragging his pants off. 'You never struggled before,' she said ripping the wet clothing away. 'Here,' she threw a large towel over his middle. 'Scrub yourself dry with that. And drink this.' She held a glass of rum to his lips. Her fingers lightly touched the swollen bruises on his face. 'Your poor face. Anyone would think you had been fighting.'

There was no strength in his arms as he tried to rub himself dry. Elsa took another towel while he sipped the rum.

'What are you doing here?' he asked.

'Rubbing you dry, you damned fool. I live here, remember. I told you that I had kept the cottage for the boy. For that matter I could say the same to you. You are a long way from Whitehall. Joyriding, were you? And got more than you expected.'

The rum and the warmth of the towelling drugged him. He could hardly keep his eyes open as she bundled him up mummy fashion in a couple of blankets.

'The pilot, Mr Carberry, is he all right … '

'He is now, after we pumped half the North Sea out of him. You're both all right. Go to sleep, love.'

Draining the last of the rum he rolled over. Carberry was watching them. His lips twitched into a fleeting smile, 'Thank you, Shepherd. I believe you saved my neck. The girl seems to have got you confused with your cousin. You know, the one with the cushy job in Whitehall.'

The Base Doctor released them late the following day, unable to find anything wrong with them. Carberry stated that neither of them were to claim survivor's leave. They were back at Cleveland Hall for tea. Carberry looked a bit lopsided because a patch of hair had been burned off, but the salt water had done some good to Shepherd's bruises.

Miller brought Shepherd up to date with all the gossip as though he had been away two months. Sub-Lieutenant Dutton was thinking about making a formal complaint about Carberry taking his Zero. And then wrecking it. Jerry had got a new secret weapon. A mine with a delay on the mooring-cable release so that the mine floated up after the Channel had been swept.

'When did this happen?' Shepherd asked.

'Yesterday morning, mate, while you was tucked up in your little white cot. We had nothing up on account of you wiping out Dutton's ship, the base mechanics were pissing about with that Yankee coffee-grinder an' the other Zero was at Howden having a gas-check. One of the Coastals from Howden was on patrol but they picked the wrong convoy to look after. It was the northbound out of the Humber as got hit. One of them new sloops got her bows blown off. *Buttercup.* Then a ship in the centre column lost her fo'c'sle. And another two collided, dodging mines. You've never seen such a pig's breakfast. Ships steaming every which way. Jerry had a field day. 'Course there was a U-boat hangin' about. Well, there's always one, ain't there? While they were trying to sort themselves out the pigboat slips a torpedo into a grain boat an' just misses another. An' then damn me if she don't surface an' put half a dozen shells into one of the trawler escorts. They got them all into port but there hasn't

109

been a ship up or down the War Channel since it happened.'

'What makes them think it is a new mine?'

'Well, it stands to sense, don't it? There weren't no mines there when the sweepers come by.'

Shepherd shook his head. Henrietta had been smarter than any of them. She had seen how clever Schiller had been at Folkestone. The minesweepers had sailed on time but the boat train had been late. A ship had been mined in a swept channel. Now he knew why she had asked him to time the interval between the convoy and the minesweepers. He grunted with disgust at the fog in his mind and squirmed on his straw palliasse. That idea at the back of his mind, Henrietta had got half of it but there was some sort of a corollary to it. Something that would solve their problem with Schiller. If only he could remember.

'Don't take it so hard, mate,' Miller said. 'It weren't nothing to do with us. There was no airship there. The scuttlebutt says that the skippers are refusing to sail without an airship overhead ... ' He looked at Shepherd suspiciously. 'An' there's a letter for you. If you're on the run how come somebody knows where you are?'

Shepherd grinned. He already had the letter in his pocket. It held a Post Office savings book with £100 in it and a curt note from Henry saying that this was a loan and was it not time he started doing something to earn it?

'An' that bird, the one that rubbed your tum dry, was asking after you. Smashing bit o' stuff. Is there a Mr Dolli?'

'You've got it wrong. Her name is Mrs Cordle.'

'Have it your own way, mate. The locals call her Mrs Dolli. She's got a cottage just up from the beach. Her kid lives there with a nurse.'

Petty Officer Riggs put his head round the door. 'You've had a christening,' he said. 'You are a damned sight worse than he is, so it's Jonah's Apprentice from now on. And it serves you right, you are on tomorrow morning. Early call, 4 am. For gawd's sake keep him out all day. He's driving everybody mad. On account of him taking this new mine of Jerry's as a personal insult. And bring the ship back in one piece.'

110

Shepherd went to bed early. It was the only way to get any privacy in an environment that equated thinking with brooding, which was a bad thing not to be tolerated.

He had seen the bastard. It was etched permanently on his mind. The weeping clouds, the U-boat arrogantly cruising in their water, the deck gun spitting flame, and in the conning tower, binoculars in hand, Kapitänleutnant Otto Schiller. He moved, gestured with his arms, telling the gun crew to change their aiming-point, to leave the crippled blimp and lob shells blind into the camp on top of the cliff. Two mechanics wounded and the evening meal ruined. He breathed, moved and had won that round. Otto Schiller, the Poet, was no longer a devil incarnate, a figure in the night crushing boats, killing. Otto Schiller was a man and Richard Shepherd had been within yards of him, had come close to killing him. And close to being killed. There had to be a way of doing it again from some position of advantage. He fell asleep.

CHAPTER FIVE

Elsa Dolli was running just fast enough to elude his out-stretched hands, the wind moulding her thin silk nightdress around her body. At last his hands closed round her waist but his trousers fell down, tripping him.

Otto Schiller had a thigh-boot planted on his chest. He was striking matches, trying to set his hair alight. The air was afire, starving his pumping lungs of oxygen. The heat scorched his face.

Henrietta brushed Schiller aside with the tip of her umbrella, ordering him to stay where he was, to be dealt with later. She prodded Shepherd with a sensible brown brogue, sending him rolling downhill into an ice-cold sea that froze him into immobility. He was a block of ice frozen solid except for his red heart pumping heat into a greedy sea. He screamed.

'Steady on, mate. Pipe down or they'll all want to go with you,' the guard said, pushing the early-call book into his hands for a signature. 'You want to tuck your blanket in tighter, mate, else you'll be getting pneumonia for sure. An' gawd help you, it's blowin' half a gale outside, special delivery, all the way from Iceland.'

The walk to the office was like something he had been doing all his life. Was this only the third time? Wait by the door let your eyes get used to the darkness. God, the wind is like a knife. The noise. Tree branches rustling and scraping. Wind screaming through the trees, fluting over a dozen stove-pipes. A door aimlessly banging. Walk across to the office block. Flat against the wall. Wait. No lights, no guard. Open the door, into the shadow of the stile. Wait. There is no need to hold your breath. Down the corridor, into the office. Now you can breathe. Quietly.

He picked up the telephone and sat on the floor waiting for his breathing to get back to normal.

112

'Morning, chum, T4 here. Give me the Duty Officer, OB14, Room 156.'

Hurry up, man, I have not got all night. At last. 'Hello, Henry, did I wake you up.'

Click. The light in the office was switched on. Carberry was standing in the doorway holding a revolver with a barrel as big as a small cannon.

'Ringing up your cousin, I suppose. The one with the cushy job in Whitehall. That telephone has a bell in my bedroom. It rings once when ever someone picks up the receiver. Damned nuisance, I've been trying to get it fixed for months. This is the third time I have heard it, the third time since you joined us. What are you up to?'

Shepherd replaced the telephone, moved to the front of the desk and stood to attention as Carberry took his seat. The revolver still pointed at him.

'I am sorry, sir. I know I have done wrong but I've got a girl on the exchange at the Admiralty. It's the only chance I get to talk to her.'

Carberry laughed. 'Stop acting the bloody fool, Shepherd, or whatever your name is. You may think you sound like Gerald du Maurier but I wouldn't give you a part in the camp concert party.' He put the gun on the desk, keeping his hand close to the butt. 'You don't know how deep in trouble you are, Air Mechanic Shepherd. Our Captain Botham is a hater. He hates everybody above the rank of captain, he is suspicious of his peers and he despises anybody below him. I doubt whether he considers the lower deck part of the human race. Most of all he hates admirals and the Admiralty. More than he hates the Germans. He is going to love you. It will be a gift from the gods when I tell him that I have on my ship, which is under his command, a lieutenant from some skull-and-crossbones attic in the Admiralty masquerading as a wireless operator. He'll be so pleased that he will be polite to me ... for a day or so. But you, he'll skewer you to the wall of his office and keep you there for target practice. And God help your boss. Now, what the hell is going on?'

'Well, like I said, sir. My girl—'

'Sit down, Shepherd. Stop playing silly buggers. The game

113

is up. You were not aware of it but it was coming to an end anyway. Your antics the other day, hauling me out of the cockpit, keeping me away from the fire, put the kibosh on whatever you are up to. Captain Botham signalled for some details about you as all your documents are not here. You might have got a medal. He thought it was a hell of a joke. "Another cock-up by some stupid chairborne officebound wallah in Whitehall. Damn fool reckons we have two wireless operators who have not been in the Navy long enough to know how to salute. I told him what I thought about him and his bloody records. Haw, haw." I shudder to think what he will say when he learns the truth ... '

Shepherd remained standing to attention while alternative stories raced through his mind. Somehow he had to keep going.

Carberry was yelling at him. 'Sit down, damn you. Oh, for God's sake, man, say something. Damn it, I'm on your side.'

'In that case I would prefer to see you working for the opposition ... '

Carberry hammered his fists on the desk. 'Progress. Thank God, you have dropped that ghastly fake accent. Look, forget what I said about Captain Botham. He is an old man before his time, marooned among a crowd of youngsters messing about with things he is ignorant of and despises anyway while his contemporaries romp ahead in rank and experience. But even he is doing what he thinks is right to finish the war. We all try to do our bit. That is why I am on your side. Temporarily. I do not believe you cloak-and-dagger people would go to all this trouble to put you on my ship without good cause. If you tell me the problem I will see if I can help.'

'Without going back to the Admiralty?'

'Sorry, that is out of the question. I'll do what I can for you but I cannot protect your boss. Make no bones about it, Botham will have his guts for garters. Well?'

Shepherd stared at him trying not to smile. Carberry might think he was different but he had been formed in the same mould. They could not believe that he had got so far without any official backing. How could they believe in the infallibility of all those bits of paper? People handled the bits, men the system said were incapable of thinking and had to have an officer to do it for them. He wondered if Carberry would believe the truth.

'I want to kill a German U-boat captain, Kapitänleutnant Otto Schiller. You saw him the other day on the bridge of the UC62. He shot us down but before that he murdered my fiancée ... '

When he had finished Carberry waved the revolver at him before putting it in one of the desk drawers. 'After listening to that I should hit you over the head and send for the doctor. Or hit myself over the head for listening. But it is so incredible that some of it must be true. Which bit and how much?' He scratched his head angrily. 'It is so damned naïve, such a typically civilian attitude, that it must be true. If I hand you over to Captain Botham he would never stand the shock.' He rubbed his eyes. 'You are a confidence trickster. I don't believe any of it,' he roared, pushing his chair back so violently that it toppled over. He leant over the desk, lowering his head like a charging bull. 'Nine days in the Navy and you got a trade test and a posting ... '

'It cost me £10,' Shepherd said. 'But I am a competent wireless operator.'

'Balls, Mr Shepherd. You know the form, you can bash a key, but a wireless operator ... never in a million years.' He stilled Shepherd's objections with a wave. 'All right. I will believe that, for the moment. Now, you look like a normal reasonably intelligent young man. Tell me, the entire resources of the Royal Navy are being deployed to destroy U-boats, any U-boats. Without success. How are you, the nine-day wonder, going to find and destroy one particular one?'

Shepherd said, 'You don't believe that story yourself, sir. U-boats are an irritant diverting effort away from the battle the Navy wants to fight. The second Jutland.'

Carberry grinned. 'You talk like a lawyer. But I expect you to answer that question before you leave. If you are not some sort of Whitehall spy where does this other chap, Miller, come in?'

'Just a means to an end. Nothing to do with me. There is a way I can prove my story. May I?'

115

Carberry's eyes opened as he asked for OB14, Room 156. While the operator was putting them through, Shepherd took a deep breath and went in to attack.

'I am not the only one in this, I could not do what I have to do alone. The others have suffered at the hands of Schiller. You do realize that you are one of us. What did Captain Botham say when you reported the loss of the Zero? Shot down by a U-boat ... '

Carberry's face burned an angry red. He thumped his chair back in place. 'You really lead with your chin, Shepherd. It's a good job I was not holding my revolver. Captain Botham made some very personal remarks. It does not make things any better remembering what he said about you. How would you like your picture in the newspapers?'

Shepherd shook his head. 'Henry? Don't argue or ask questions. Did Schiller report in. Good, I thought the gentleman would be unable to resist the temptation. I want you to tell Squadron Commander Carberry exactly what he reported. Both reports, shooting down the airship and his activities yesterday.'

He handed the receiver to Carberry, crossed his fingers and waited, watching the changing expressions flit over the squadron commander's face. Finally Carberry handed him the telephone. He said, 'Henry, if I do not call you back inside an hour pack your bags and take a trip to Timbuktu. Take Bart with you.' He rang off and turned to face Carberry.

'Cocky bastard, your Herr Schiller,' Carberry said through taut lips. He drummed his fingers on the desk, realized what he was doing and rubbed his eyes. He was angry. 'You are talking to the wrong man, and you know it. One of the reasons Captain Botham and I fight like Kilkenny cats is because I once expounded my theory that it was more important to stop U-boats from sinking ships than it was to sink U-boats.' He rubbed his eyes again, exhaling loudly. 'I'm going out of my mind but reluctantly I believe you. Although you have yet to explain how you intended to sink Schiller. Nor do I approve of your quest. We are at war. The purpose of a war is to kill so many of your opponents that they give up. So people get killed. Just like the poor devils caught by this new mine Schiller was using the other day.'

Shepherd felt his heart thump. The man was talking exactly like the three conspirators. 'What makes you think it was a new mine?'

'You may be a code-breaking expert and an authority on U-boats but believe me I know our minesweeper skippers. If they say a channel has been swept clean, it has.'

'It was. Until Schiller has watched the sweepers pass. Then he goes across the Channel laying his mines. They don't have to be anything special. We think this is something he has worked out since Folkestone. And we think he is keeping it to himself. To make up for the convoys putting a crimp in his wheel. So we have to get him before he makes a big killing and it becomes general practice. That is how we are going to get him.' He looked at his watch. 'Aren't we going to be late for our appointment with a convoy off the Humber?'

'Don't show your ignorance, Shepherd. Listen to the wind. There is a gale on the way. The patrol was cancelled hours ago. I said nothing so that I could find out what you are up to. I wish I had left well alone ... '

He went to the window. It was light outside as he swept the blackout curtains aside. The wind was pouring over the tree-tops like a river. A dozen men were wrestling with a plunging Zero, taking up the guy ropes to haul the envelope nearer the ground. SS 19 in the centre of the windbreak was unaffected.

'How many mines does this U-boat carry?'

'UC62? Thirty-eight. She's only been out for a few days so she will have some left. Schiller is desperately keen to get on to the big Atlantic boats. It's not just ambition. Minelaying is a risky business. If he could break a convoy ... '

Carberry picked up the telephone, rang Howden. He put his hand over the receiver. 'How long can you keep up this charade?'

'If I can get a medical certificate, at least for three or four weeks. After that the Department will probably put me up for a medical board. *Kaput*!'

'I know men who have spent the past two years on regular

bone-crushing patrols without seeing a U-boat. You expect to sink a particular one inside four weeks … '

'I got here inside two weeks. Starting from scratch.'

Carberry put the telephone down. He walked back to the window, picking up his helmet on the way. 'That was the seaweed expert. Weatherman. According to them the gale is coming through slower than they expected. After lunch. Patrols are still cancelled.'

Shepherd felt his guts tightening up inside him. His bones still ached from that last flight. 'Schiller could get half a dozen ships. And he could give the Admiralty what half their experts are forecasting, a broken convoy giving the U-boats a bigger target.'

Carberry looked grim. He had to carry the can, it was his decision. He squinted out of the window again. 'Get your gear. SS 19 needs an engine test. Take an extra couple of drums for the Lewis. Take-off in thirty minutes, if we can get out without ripping the envelope.'

Carberry roused the camp for the take-off. Every one of the fifty men on the camp was dragged in, including the armed guard who normally protected them from invasion by the fishwives from the village walking the three miles to Cleveland Halt on the railway line from Whitby.

He needed all of them. The envelope of SS 19 had been hauled down out of reach of the torrent pouring over the trees. Once released, the airship fought the handling party like a newly-trapped wild animal. After half an hour Carberry had to give up. Twice they got the airship safely along the narrow cut, but the moment the bow poked out from the shelter of the trees the wind took command. Each time, the handling party had to fight tooth-and-nail to hold the taut fabric away from the branches. Shepherd had his eyes shut. He had seen what could happen when a gasbag punctured.

Back in the clearing Carberry took the blimp as far back from the sheltering trees as possible. He ballasted up until the airship was light, weighing off until the blimp floated up when the nacelle men took their hands off. Then he dropped a full bag of sand. After the command, 'Brace,' the nacelle men dug their heels in as he opened the engine up to full power.

He lifted his arms to shoulder level. The megaphone bellowed, 'Forrard, aft guys, let go.' The men on the nacelle stiffened like a defeated tug-of-war team as the blimp strained forwards.

Carberry lifted his arms into the air above his head. The nacelle men stepped smartly backwards. Light and at full power SS 19 went up like a rocket. It had some forward speed before the full force of the wind hit them. Then it was pandemonium. A gust wrenched the rudder bar away from Carberry's feet. The envelope was blown over as they swung sideways on to the storm. Carberry got hold of the rudder, standing on it to straighten them as the blimp twirled over the downwind hedge of trees towards the sea.

There was less turbulence over the sea but the wind was as strong, flattening the wave-crests into long ragged lines. Carberry came round into wind at 300 feet, inching his way forward until he could sight over the top of the exhaust pipe on to a rocky outcrop of the headland. Slowly he manoeuvred the blimp until it was dead into wind hanging motionless over the rock.

As he swung the nose south-east, crabbing sideways into the west wind, he shouted to Shepherd, 'Log the wind, 275° at twenty-five knots. I'll check it again when we sight the convoy. Then every hour.'

As Shepherd scribbled the information in his log he glanced at the chart. If SS 19 had still been fitted with her original 75-hp Renault engine her top speed would have been five knots faster than the wind speed; if she had been capable of reaching her top speed after two years' work; and if the Renault had been able to run at full throttle long enough for her to have got up to top speed. The 90-hp Curtiss OX5 made her that much faster but it was supposed to be more unreliable. And if the engine failed ... Shepherd's finger traversed the chart. 450 miles, nothing but the North Sea turning into the German ocean. They would never make it as a free balloon, not in this weather with the turbulence pumping the gas-valve.

Carberry poked his shoulder. He wiped the oil flecks off his goggles and began to search while his hands retuned the

119

wireless set to the U-boat band. Nothing. He returned to Howden to send a signal reporting them airborne on an armed-engine test. Ignoring their recall signals he repeated his message three times, asking if they were receiving him before going back to the U-boats. He automatically crossed his fingers, critically watching the engine, the vibrating push rods, the blurred rocker arms, the colour of the exhaust. There were no water leaks, none that he could see, no steam puffing from the vent pipe. Yet.

They had done some inspired guessing about the timing of Schiller's minelaying before they left. Now it was surprising that no one had tried it before.

The sweepers had to leave before the convoy and had to steam at a minimum speed to stream the paravanes. They guessed ten knots. But the convoy was unlikely to get away dead on time. Merchant Navy skippers did not double into column of line like privates in the army. And the speed of the convoy was that of the slowest. Five to six knots, no more than eight. So the sweepers were pulling ahead of the convoy at two or three knots. After three hours there would be more than an hour's steaming between the two. That, they thought, was the earliest time Schiller would need to lay mines between the two.

Shepherd picked up the minesweepers first. There was smoke on the horizon. Trawlers always made smoke. Just as there was always someone in the convoy doing it. UC62 would have no difficulty in measuring the gap.

The wind was veering round to the north, increasing their speed over the ground. They were soon over the sweepers, the broad arrow wake of the paravanes spreading out behind. There were four of them today, three trawlers and a paddle steamer giving a large overlap on the sweep. Shepherd gulped in sympathy as the paddle steamer plunged into a wave taking green water over the bows.

He started the stop watch, waiting for the smoke of the convoy to appear on the horizon. This was about where UC62 ought to be. Carberry started to zigzag across the swept channel. Even on a day like this they ought to be able to see the mines hanging under water. Provided you were directly over them. With your eyes focused on the right place. And no oil splatter on the lens of your goggles. With the sides of the nacelle vibrating, ruining your vision through the binoculars if you rested your arm. Anyone could see them if they were still alert after looking at the sea for four hours.

Shepherd saw the oil streak soon after the smudge of smoke on the horizon heralded the convoy. A thin iridescent line running roughly east and west across the Channel, broken in places by the action of wind and wave.

Carberry turned west, reasoning that if a ship hit a mine the look-outs would look east towards Germany expecting to see a U-boat. So a U-boat captain with brains would be lying in wait to the west.

They moved agonizingly slowly into the head wind. There were no mines. The wind had freshened as it moved round to the north. At full throttle they were making across the sea no more than five knots. And still no mines. There had to be mines, why else should a U-boat cut across the track of a convoy?

Shepherd looked up at the approaching convoy. It was no longer a patch of smoke; now he could resolve it into three ragged columns. The inevitable scruffy tramp that could not stay in line. 200 yards out of position. A sloop leading. Trawlers on the flank. Carberry shouting. There were red can buoys below. They had reached the west side of the War Channel. There was no oil streak now. It had spread, been broken up into a hundred fading patches. This was where the U-boat had lain in wait. They had turned the wrong way. And the convoy was bearing down on them and somewhere ahead of it was a line of mines.

Shepherd looked north, wondering whether it was time they sank their pride and called the sweepers back. Looking down sun he caught the glitter of iridescence. He focused the binoculars and saw the copper horn of a mine roll through the trough of a wave. Carberry's reasoning had been right. He had got the timing wrong. The U-boat had gone out across the Channel but had laid the mines on the return. The mines were 400 yards north.

Urged on by Shepherd, Carberry punched their way up to

the second oil streak. Half a mile inshore of the War hannel the tell-tale streak stopped. UC62 lay underneath them. But today they had only two 65lb bombs with impact fuses. They should be enough if dropped in the middle of that puddle of oil.

Carberry dropped a smoke-float. 'Raise the Escort Commander,' he shouted. 'U-boat under smoke-float. Mines in the swept channel ahead of you. Do not let the convoy scatter while we deal with the mines. Message ends. Get on with it ... '

He pulled the blimp round in a tight turn, following the oil streak east. Shepherd pointed down, his face contorted with anger. 'That is Schiller down there. I know it is. You will let him get away again.'

Carberry snatched the Very pistol out of its holster and pointed it at Shepherd's forehead. It was three feet away. He could see the cardboard disc on the end of the cartridge identifying the colour. Two-star red. It would burn a hole in his skull one inch in diameter.

'Let him stay there. I don't want British sailors there with him, on the outside of the pressure hull. Get weaving on that lamp. And then use the wireless to bring the sweepers back.'

The convoy that had seemed so slow was now too fast for them as it bore down. And they had still not seen a mine.

It was the oil streak, knowing where to look, that saved them. Without it they would not have had the time. A plume of steam from the sloop's whistle, she had got the message. Carberry thumped Shepherd's shoulder. They were coming up on the first mine.

But Carberry knew he was asking the escort to do the impossible. No merchant ship was going to sit there motionless with a U-boat in the offing. Already one of the bigger ships, guessing what the smoke-float and whistling meant, was accelerating, pulling out of line. Exactly what Schiller had in mind.

'Get on the Lewis, Dead-Eye Dick,' Carberry shouted to bring Shepherd away from the wireless set. 'We don't have the time. It's too late to stop the convoy.'

Twenty-five ships, little more than half a mile away. They

couldn't stop even if they wished to. In fifteen minutes that orderly array would be scattered across the sea. Schiller would get his chance.

The Lewis chattered. Shepherd's aim was improving. The first mine blew up in a mountain of white water. Another, and another. One of the trawlers was racing up the flank to start at the eastern end of the line. Another one. It was a tighter pattern than they had expected. About every 150 yards. He must have had plenty of time. The trawler had scored. The big green and white Swede was working up to speed, moving ahead of the others. Damned fool. The sloop was racing for the smoke-float.

Shepherd fired and missed. No explosion. But he might have sunk the mine. Carberry looked back as Shepherd switched his aim. The mine floated to the surface. The bullets had cut the mooring cable. Now the golden horns glinted in the sun as it rolled with a wave. And that bloody Swede was heading straight for it. There was no one in the bows looking for mines. The men out on the wings of the bridge were looking for torpedo tracks. Knowing that he had the faster vessel the Swede was interested only in the lurking U-boat. But while he was concentrating on evading the non-existent torpedoes he was going to run straight into half a ton of high explosive.

The Lewis jammed. Shepherd bashed at the cocking lever, trying to extract a split case.

Carberry wound the elevators hard down. But the blimp was lighter now than on take-off. They had burned petrol for the last two hours, dropped a smoke-float and fired two drums of ammunition. He valved gas until SS 19 was diving at full throttle for the sea. For the sea and at the bows of the big Swede. Even those men straining to pick up torpedo tracks could not fail to see SS 19, the size of a small church, bearing down on them. But the big ship kept ploughing on, picking up speed, ignoring the escort. The blimp's wheels spun as they flicked through the crest of a wave. Captain Botham would have a fit reading this week's report, Carberry thought. Shot down by a U-boat last week, collided with a neutral ship this week. Blast that skipper. He was waving his cap. Did he imagine that they would be playing games with a bloody U-boat about. There was only one way to make him move.

The blimp bounded up a hundred feet as Carberry eased the elevator wheel back. 300 yards on the beam Carberry pulled the nose round until he was aimed just forward of the Swede's bridge. He dropped one of the 65lb bombs. Still with the safety-pin in the fuse.

The Swede did not know that. His reaction was instantaneous. A plume of steam from the whistle and the bows swung to starboard under full rudder and one screw stopping.

The men on the bridge were shaking their fists as SS 19 swept by, but Carberry was too intent on giving Shepherd a shot at the mine to notice. He got it with the first burst. Spray from the foam lashed the bridge as the Swede swept by, only yards from the explosion. There was no time to watch as Carberry turned to follow the oil slick out to where the U-boat had turned for his minelaying run. Between the blimp and a trawler they got the mines dealt with minutes before the first ship crossed the line. Then there was nothing to do but wait as the ships ploughed by, whistling their thanks.

Shepherd was so intent on watching the convoy steam safely by that he was shocked to see the buoy marking the eastern edge of the War Channel drift past. It was time they were backing up the sloop depth-charging the oil slick to the west.

He was suddenly aware of a different note in the roar of the engine, a change in the vibration rattling the nacelle. Again, it was worse this time, a distinct miss in the even roar. Then a backfire that shook everything as the unburned charge exploded in the silencer. He turned to Carberry to point at the steam blowing out of the radiator vent-pipe. Carberry passed him a message slip. 'Send that to the Escort Commander. We are in trouble. "HMAS SS 19. Need assistance urgently. Engine losing power. Unable to make any westing. Can one of your trawlers tow us into port? Any port in the coming storm. Message ends." '

They waited through long minutes for an answer. Shepherd remembered the nail-biting agony of that last flight

124

as they threw out everything to stay in the air. Had he to go through that again? They were drifting east now as Carberry eased back the throttle to keep the water temperature below boiling.

' "Escort Commander to HMAS SS 19. Negative. Orders are to keep convoy escort intact. Thank you for your assistance. We are sorry that we have been forbidden to help. Assistance on the way. Can be expected in approximately one hour. Should be with you before the forecast force 8 gale catches you. Good luck." ' Carberry shook his head as he read the message. 'See if you can raise Howden,' he bellowed. But at 300 feet they were probably too low for an inland station to pick them up.

Shepherd shook his head. 'I'll use the U-boat band. The triangulation stations will pick us up and plot our position.'

'Hurry. Once you have made contact tell them we will go down to ride on a sea anchor. I might be able to fix the engine.'

The sea anchors were canvas buckets at the end of fifty feet of grapnel rope. Two of them. Carberry checked their drift by timing chips of wood floating the length of the nacelle. Then he removed and replaced the sparking-plugs in the engine. It was always worth cleaning OX5 spark-plugs. But there was nothing he could do about the broken valve-springs in number four cylinder.

SS 19 hung above the waves, just high enough to miss the crests. The wind tugged at the envelope, the tide tried to sweep the sea anchors south. In the troughs the tide won, but as they rose on a crest it was the wind's turn. The nacelle pitched up and down and spun round and round like a manic horse on a merry-go-round.

Shepherd was sick until he thought he had lost his stomach. Spitting blood. Cold and wet. Windblown rain, cold rain. Blown spume that was even colder.

Carberry was screwing in the last sparking-plug when one of the drogues parted. Like a circus elephant ridiculous in a pretty apron, SS 19 curtseyed and slowly spun around the remaining anchor.

'You will have to swing it,' Carberry said. 'You know

125

the drill. Do you good, having something to do. Takes your mind off it. Can you manage?'

Shepherd nodded. He could not trust himself to speak. Now the sea was turning round and round, on top of the pitching up and down and the sideways squiggle of the nacelle and a lurch as one wheel caught a wave. He leaned on the propeller blade retching a foul bile that the wind blew back into his face.

'We'll have to haul in the drogue,' Carberry shouted. 'Take a turn round the bomb-rack. We daren't lose it and if it touches the propeller we are done for.'

It took the combined strength of the two of them to haul it in eventually. They were both cold and wet. But Carberry was not trying to be sick.

'Hot coffee once we are airborne under power.' SS 19 was drifting downwind now at wind speed. 'Take a good grip. One hand for the ship, one hand for yourself. Petrol on, switch off, suck in.'

The stink of petrol. His handkerchief soaked in the stuff stuck in the carburretor air inlet. Petrol and vomit. He raised his thumb, unable to open his mouth to reply to Carberry's litany. Swing his weight on the blade. It moved, hung on the compression, flicked through without firing. He slipped, and his hand slid down the strut until he hung horizontally looking down on the sea, his body projecting halfway through the plane of rotation of the propeller.

He liked the phrase, imagining it in Carberry's report on his decapitation as he swung the propeller again.

'Switch on. Contact. Remember, Shepherd, if you slip, Schiller has won, game set and match.'

The spasm of anger spun the propeller round so quickly that it caught first time. He braced himself in time, feeling the blast of air from the propeller as the blades whirled by inches from his nose. Slowly he inched his way along the skid back to his own cockpit.

Carberry opened the throttle as the engine warmed. SS 19 was alive again and fighting. Already the nose was into wind and the motion was easier. But he had to go out on to the skid again to stow the drogue properly. And to measure their backward drift. He eased the throttle back to shout, 'I'm going up to 500 feet. Wireless your friends. Tell them I am going to run the engines on full power, such as it is. We might make some headway. Petrol for about two hours if the engine lasts. And this buffeting is losing us gas. Tell them to get a move on. When you have done that we'll get as low as possible.'

After twenty minutes of fighting their way west the cooling water was boiling again. Carberry nudged the throttle back a shade, but soon after a hose burst spraying them with boiling water. They were so busy trying to fix it that the trawler was underneath them before they realized it.

The trawlermen had just time to take their drogue before the engine stopped. Then they reeved a three-inch grass line through the vee of the undercarriage. Only then would Carberry allow them to transfer to the deck of the trawler. They were none too soon. Without the engine feeding air into the ballonnets the gas-pressure dropped. Shepherd and Carberry had only been on the deck a few minutes when the envelope buckled in the middle, twisting the nacelle on to its side. A couple of suspension cables snapped, letting the tail dangle like a dead dragonfly. The trawler, with the still buoyant envelope bobbing up and down on the stern, had a motion that was indescribable. As Shepherd fought to keep his stomach under control he bumped into the skipper.

'Did the Escort Commander get that U-boat?' he asked. 'Last time I saw him he was peppering the spot marked X with depth-charges.'

The skipper shook his head. 'Tricky things. I don't trust them. The sloop dropped one when he was going too slow. Jammed the rudder and his screw. I was supposed to tow him into port until we got your message. The U-boat got away.'

Shepherd bolted for the rail. He wished he was dead, knowing that he did not mean it. Now he was convinced that UC62 was being saved for him.

CHAPTER SIX

Shepherd was in such a state when they landed that he was sent to the local cottage hospital and kept there overnight. It was late afternoon on the following day before the old doctor in charge would let him go, and then only on the condition that he went back to Cleveland Hall by ambulance. SS 19 had been flown back in the morning, after the patched envelope was topped up with gas.

Carberry had left a note.

Your friend Henry(?) rang you up for a change. She sounds impatient. There is talk about you having a medical board. A chap called Villers is gunning for you.

The U-boat got away. If it was your friend, O.S., he has a charmed life. He is on his way home badly damaged. I think your caper is coming to an end but in view of the resource you have shown so far I am deferring any action on my part.

Shepherd lay on his bed fully dressed, waiting for the ambulance. His body felt as though it had been trampled by a herd of elephants, and a little man was hammering bamboo shoots under each fingernail. It would be so much simpler to settle for what they had done and go back to the office. But then he would have to explain his injuries. Falling off his bicycle?

And what had they achieved? Schiller had won every round. And according to Carberry yesterday's mines were now firmly thought to be of the 'new delay action' type. An expert from Mount Vernon was on his way north to investigate them.

'Well, my boy, how do you feel?' the old doctor said. 'You know, you need a fortnight in bed. Here, not in your barracks. I know what the Services are like. You'll be on fatigues in a couple of days. Well, I've said my piece. The ambulance is on the way. I want to dress those fingers before you go.'

Shepherd sighed realistically. 'I wouldn't mind going on leave but it is not easy the way things are at the minute ... '

The doctor snorted. 'Rubbish, you youngsters have no sense of proportion. It's either shirkers doing nothing or young fellas like yourself trying to win the war on your own. Look at yourself.' He pushed a mirror in front of him.

Seeing himself shocked Shepherd. The bruises he had got in the fight with Mad Jack had turned yellow, there were black rings round eyes that seemed to have sunk into his head, a patch of hair by his left ear had been burned off and a line of dried blood traced a cut along the line of his jaw. He looked down at his hands and had to avert his eyes. Two fingernails on the left had been ripped off and the others were either split or blackened.

The doctor nodded at his discomfort. He was old, his formal clothes creased and stained, and a pair of glasses hung on a silver chain from his lapels. He would have been retired but for the war, Shepherd thought. Perhaps he preferred it this way. He took Shepherd's left hand.

'We'll tidy these up before you go. It's only my opinion but I think you need a rest. It's ridiculous to think of flying in your state.'

'It's not as easy as that. I mean, you can't say losing a fingernail is like being wounded. My CO would laugh at me. But I am so damned tired.' He hesitated and firmly sat on the feeling of being a fraud. 'If you could give me a medical certificate saying something like "Nervous exhaustion following severe emotional strain". Next to actually being wounded that's the sort of thing that will get me a few days' leave.'

The doctor turned to the nurse. 'Dress those two fingers.' He sat down at his desk to write out a certificate. 'Here. And if that does not do the trick, my boy, you telephone me at this number. Twenty-eight days. My God, you make me ashamed to call myself a doctor. The next time I see that fellow from Howden he'll get a piece of my mind.' He raised a hand at Shepherd's protest. 'Have no fear, my boy, your name will not come into it. But by God, in future that man will think twice about his moral responsibilities as a doctor as well as his duty to the Navy.'

They made Shepherd a sling for his left arm now it was really painful and did what they could to the split nails and burst blisters on his right hand. By the time they had strapped his bruised ribs Shepherd was ready to stay in the hospital. He did not feel so guilty as two porters old enough to be his grandfather carried him on a stretcher into the ambulance. He was halfway to Cleveland Hall before he took out the certificate and began to chuckle, imagining the shock that was coming to the portly red-faced Surgeon Commander in charge of the sick-bay at Howden. Now all he had to do was to get a letter with a York postmark off to Bart Tregarron with the certificate. And to warn Henry.

He glanced at his watch as the ambulance jolted over some rough ground and stopped. They could not be at Cleveland Hall. The rear door opened. Elsa Dolli climbed in, her lips taut with anger.

'Now that you have some clothes on and I can see who you are supposed to be, there are a few questions you have to answer, Richard Shepherd. Do I call you Lieutenant Shepherd or are we Air Mechanic Peter Shepherd today? Complete with comic Yorkshire accent. Damn you, Richard, I don't know what you are up to but I have spent too long behind that wheel trying to shut my ears to the screams of men who know what war is really like to have any time for men who want to play at it.'

She was leaning forward as he had seen her so many times before, tensed, delivering a passionate performance. Her breasts strained at the smooth khaki barathea. He kissed her. For a fraction of a second he felt her respond but then she pulled herself away.

'You are improving,' she said. 'You did that of your own free will. Not because of an old association, not to put your father's nose out of joint or to spite your mother. For your own—'

'Reasons. It seemed the natural thing to do—'

'To avoid answering awkward questions. One day a Whitehall warrior; the next, Honest Jack, a matelot rescued from the waves. And how the hell did you get old Dr McArdle so steamed up on your behalf. He really does think you are a hero. But I checked. Some knight in shining armour, you damned fraud. You were up with that man Carberry. A joyride. Engine-test, they called it. The boy from the Front Office having a look at the men at work. You make me sick.'

He racked his brains for something sensible to say. She had not changed. That had been one of her attractions for him, a passion for the underdog that sent her charging in where angels, and occasionally some sensible people, feared to tread. She was quite capable of writing to someone in Whitehall. Then the fat would be in the fire.

'That was a shocking business about Jennifer,' she said quietly. 'We did not have much in common. I don't think we liked each other, and once I could have scratched her eyes out. But that was a terrible way for a girl to die.'

He nodded. 'You are too hard on yourself. She told me once how much she envied and admired you. For your independent mind ... '

'How cosy. I can remember her mother saying, "My dear, how courageous of you." It seems only yesterday that everyone assumed that any woman on the stage was a whore. I suppose you joined up because of her death.'

Shepherd nodded. Thank God, she was going to accept him as another avenging recruit. He *was* one. But suppose she met his mother in York. His mother would not speak to Elsa. But she might now, if her story was true. It was one thing to cut the ex-leading lady of the repertory company. You could not do that to the widow of poor young Cordle. The Cordles had been clients for a hundred and fifty years. Suppose she thought it a suitable story for the Cordles' dinner table ...

The ambulance rocked in a passing gust. It was getting dark. He was reminded of the rooms they had shared looking down on to the main line to the north. It shook like that every time an express rushed by. His pathetic six-month rebellion. The happiest six months of his life. No money, the agony of walking on stage each night, playing one part, learning another, walking home with Elsa ...

She slapped his face. Hard, it was meant to hurt.

131

'You damned liar. My God, Richard, you have changed. Before you were Mama's darling and terrified of your Pa, but you did not tell lies. And you never took me for a fool.'

He fell back on to the stretcher to avoid her probing finger hitting his ribs again.

'Don't you remember a fortnight ago Lieutenant Shepherd was patronizing the ambulance driver, the little woman he used to knock up twice nightly? You can't become a rating once you are an officer and you don't get onto active service two weeks after joining. You are talking to someone who has seen some service. What are you up to?'

He caught hold of her wrists, yelping with the pain as he stubbed his fingers. For a moment he thought he would faint but something hard under the stretcher stabbed his bruised ribs. What the hell was he to do with her? She was quite capable of trying to march into the office.

'But that's where you are wrong. I did both,' he snapped. Then he groaned. This was to have been a secret known only to him and Henrietta and Bart. Now Miller knew a bit, Carberry knew it all and he was going to have to tell Elsa.

'My hands are killing me. Have you got any brandy? Thanks. I warn you, it's a long story ... '

Otto Schiller stubbornly ignored the pain in his throbbing fingers and pulled himself up the cat ladder on to the conning tower of UC62. His head ached, his shoulder throbbed and the pain in his hand made him want to cut the fingers off. He was not surprised. The tenth of Tommi's underwater charges had fallen so close that it had wrecked the electric motors. He had been thrown across the control room and knocked himself out, cutting his forehead, dislocating his shoulder and breaking four fingers. While he was unconscious Petersen, the machinist's mate who doubled as the sick-bay attendant, had stitched and bandaged his forehead, put his shoulder back and crudely splinted his fingers together. Now he was in a foul temper and he was going to enjoy venting it on Bei-bedecke. Automatically he scanned the horizon, the weather and the boat's trim. It was a dark night with enough wind from the west to make the U-boat wallow in a following sea. He dismissed the two look-outs and ordered Beibedecke to the bridge.

He let Beibedecke stand behind him waiting while he leant on the rail trying to control his temper. The state of UC62 when he woke from his drugged sleep still rankled. With both electric motors and one diesel out of action UC62 was limping home on the surface half an hour before sunset. Four men had been killed in the attack and a dozen injured. Beibedecke had one squad tending the injured while another got the dead ready for burial.

Schiller had soon put a stop to that nonsense. The dead were still unburied, while everyone who could stand was with the black gang sweating with wedges and crowbars to realign the electric motors.

'What are the responsibilities of a U-boat captain, Oberleutnant von Beibedecke?'

'To carry out to the best of his ability those orders given him by those placed in command of his flotilla by the All Highest ... '

'Stow that crap. What does a captain do apart from sinking whatever he is ordered to sink?'

'He is responsible for the health and well-being of his officers and crew, for the safety of his ship ... '

'The safety of the ship, Beibedecke. There is no point in being concerned with the well-being of a dead crew. Who gave you the authority to order Maschinist Maat Petersen to inject me with morphia?'

'Your shoulder was dislocated, you were bleeding extensively and you had four broken fingers.'

'Did I cry out, give any indication of being in unbearable pain? After you had rendered me unconscious you then took no positive action against the ships attacking you.'

'What did you expect me to do ... sir? Both motors were out of action, there were no lights and the boat was leaking like a sieve.'

'Just one more charge exploding that close and you were finished. You could have surfaced to fight it out ... Heroic but daft. Or to surrender. Not to be recommended but it would have saved the lives of your crew. Or you could have

133

dumped some oil and fired your dead men through a tube.'

'That would be sacrilege. Those men died in the service of their country.'

'That would have been their final and finest sacrifice for their comrades. You surfaced in daylight. Why was there no gun crew on deck, no work in hand on the motors, no effort made to get the boat in a fit state to dive? You know that our only defence is our ability to dive.'

'Half the crew were injured. The gangway was blocked by the dead and injured and the repairs were too serious for anything but a yard.'

'Balls! You have to tell engineers what has got to be done. Henne says that he will have one motor running in a couple of hours. When we can dive, Beibedecke, we have a chance to survive. Your sick and wounded would rather reach Zeebrugge all blood and muck than drown in the German ocean neatly splinted and bandaged. Because of this and other incidents I am giving you an adverse report, Oberleutnant. I do not consider you to be a fit person to command a U-boat.'

Schiller lifted the binoculars. There was something out there, behind them, breaking the western horizon. A ship. He caught the glint of white from her bows.

'Return the look-outs to the bridge. Gun crew to stand by. Steamer approaching from astern.'

He watched the gun layer trying to track the ship despite a wounded arm. Angrily he left the conning tower, ran along the deck and nudged the man aside. This was one that would not get away, although common sense told him that this was stupid in their crippled state. The ship did not have to be one of Tommi's Q ships; any aggressive merchant ship could put them under. So it had to be a shit-or-bust surprise attack. All over in the first few seconds.

Apparently unsuspecting the steamer was overhauling them on a converging course. There had been no sign of a zigzag.

Schiller's eye twitched as he stared through the sight. Either the crew of the steamer were complacent half-blind idiots or they were, like him, calculating the closing range between the two of them, getting ready to open fire or alter course to ram.

'700 metres.' Voigt started calling out the range. '600.' Schiller controlled his impatience. Another 200 metres. He remembered his first gunnery instructor, a foul-mouthed petty officer. 'Make sure your first shot misses ahead. One behind scares nobody. One ahead and they shit their britches or think you are giving them a warning.' His hand stroked the traversing wheel.

'Fire.'

The first shot was ten metres ahead of the bows. So much for gunnery instructor's advice. The next one hit the fo'c'sle. The gun crew were working like demons. A hit amidships. Some deck cargo caught fire. Was she turning to ram them? That's what he would do. Another hit amidships. And another. Fanned by the ship's speed the fire grew, but he went on firing until the boiler exploded and there was nothing left to aim at.

'Cease fire. Clear up this mess.' Kicking aside a couple of empty shell cases he strode back to the conning tower.

'Bridge here. Log, one fully-laden cargo ship sunk with all hands; log the position. Sunk while proceeding back to base with both motors out of action and only one diesel working. Wireless HQ, tell them to send out a seaplane tomorrow. They can look for survivors and escort us in if we have more trouble.' He waited, bent over the speaking tube. 'One motor only, thank you, Mr Henne. Keep working on the other.'

He turned to Beibedecke, picking up their conversation as though nothing had happened. 'I am not doing this lightly, Oberleutnant. I had you picked to take over my command when I get the Atlantic boat they have promised me. But I have no choice. Have you anything to say in your defence?' He wiped the lens of the binoculars, scanned the horizon. 'You may as well say something. Do you want to go back to your battleships?'

Beibedecke sprang to attention, the click of his heels emphasizing the formality of his address. 'With respect, Kapitänleutnant Schiller, there are three comments I would like to make. Not necessarily in my defence.

'One. I do not agree with your views on my actions this day. And I submit that your behaviour in the past few minutes demonstrates that you are prepared to hazard your command in the interests of your own ambitions. The steamer, of negligible importance, had only to alter course a few degrees and we would have been unable to prevent her from cutting us in two.

'Two. My position on the UC62 is open to another interpretation. I am senior to you in the Navy List. Perhaps my appointment was to give me the undersea experience needed to prepare me for command of one of the Atlantic boats. Your invaluable minelaying experience would be of little value out there.

'Third. Your conduct in command has debased the honour of the German Navy and the flag it flies. You have been responsible for civilian casualties which were not necessary, of no military value and a positive hindrance to the efforts of our Diplomatic Corps to keep other nations, such as America, from entering the war against us.'

Schiller laughed. He spat over the side. 'Horsecock. You have never been to America, you can't imagine what it is like to be an American. To you they are just good Germans living in the sticks somewhere west of the Friesians.'

He turned to poke Beibedecke with a hard forefinger. 'I've got cousins there. I've been, I've lived with them. Up a pig's arse with your Diplomatic Corps! You go talk to my cousin Emil in Milwaukee. He makes beer, good beer, German beer. Do you think he cares if I sink a few civilians off for a weekend in Paris? He knows what goes on in Paris. He knows it is my neck or theirs. And he knows me ... '

Carefully he unfolded the headline he had cut from *The New York Times* announcing the discovery of the Zimmermann Telegram. 'But when he reads this in the *Chicago Herald*, how your stuffed shirts are giving away bits of his country to Mexico, to Japan, he stops being a German. He is an American. You and your friends have lost this war. Damn it, you couldn't even keep your stupid idea a secret. And when you lose this war, Oberleutnant Hugo Wilhelm von Beibedecke, you will have lost everything. I am still putting in an adverse report.'

He turned sharply to stare out into the darkness on the port beam, 'What was that, a flare?'

136

It was more like a flame than a flare, a spark waving up and down against the black water. It was a flame. For a moment as the binoculars came into focus, Schiller thought he saw the pink blur of a man's face lit by a burning brand. The flame suddenly shrank, fluttered in the air, disappeared. The darkness rushed back with an animal force as though it had sucked in and swallowed the light.

Beibedecke had not seen it. Had it been a flame, a signal or someone carelessly lighting his pipe? Or phosphorescence on a breaking wave? You start seeing things that are not there when you begin to lose your marbles.

'Helm to port, easy does it. Bring her round to zero-one-zero. Look-outs to the bridge. Deck gun crew to stand by. Rig the Maxim.'

UC62 wallowed round across wind and sea. A breaking wave drenched the conning tower with spray. She rolled like a drunken pig.

Schiller stared into the darkness. There was something there, that flame had not been his imagination. There had to be something, but not necessarily German. Maybe that steamer's escort waiting for revenge. Maybe one of Tommi's submarines. They each waged a savage war on each other. Maybe the 'old man' was seeing things. There was nothing there now.

He saw the white blurs that were the faces of the gun crew turned up to look at him in mute enquiry, as he and Beibedecke moved out of the way to let the Maxim crew lug their clumsy gun with its cans of ammunition into place. The cocking handle clattered as the gunner engaged the cartridge belt.

'Maxim ready, sir.' The gunner was asking for something to aim at.

Automatically Schiller looked at his watch. It was a useless thing, he thought. It took longer to get into action than the 3.5-cm deck gun. There were no volunteers for that post. Too many had been left behind to swim home.

He swept the horizon again. Nothing. 'Voight. Load. One round starshell. Dead ahead. Maximum elevation. Stand by.'

Nothing. It was quiet on deck with only one diesel running

137

half speed. And half the crew wondering if the Captain was seeing things. He heard the clang of metal as the gunners changed shells.

Machine guns. It sounded like a roll of thunder. A line of tracer sparkling up into the night from the port beam. Ten rounds, straight up into the sky. A signal for help.

'Illuminate machine-gun position. Fire starshell.'

It was barely a hundred metres away but they would have passed it in the darkness if it had not been for the gunfire. A Friedrichshafen seaplane, all struts and wires, one crumpled wing dipping into the sea, silver dope and black cross on the other one glittering under the light from the starshell. The observer was out on the wing-tip of the good wing, fastened to a strut to keep the damaged wing out of the sea. Schiller held a flask of schnapps to his lips while they cut him out of the sodden straps.

The seaplane crew had had no hope of lasting out the night until they saw the flash of the U-boat's guns. The floats were breaking up after two days' buffetting. The pilot had found enough petrol to burn his shirt, and then he had crawled into the rear cockpit to fire the machine-gun.

Willing hands hauled the seaplane closer. The exhausted pilot was sprawled over the rear cockpit still clutching the trigger of the machine-gun. Schiller stepped on to the float. It dipped soggily under his weight, and seawater licked at his ankles. He handed the schnapps to the pilot, staring curiously at the gun clipped to a ring round the cockpit. It was a Lewis gun captured from one of Tommi's aeroplanes.

'We are in trouble ourselves,' he said to the pilot, staring at the Lewis gun. 'We won't be able to tow you in. Not in this sea.'

'Not in this broken-down applecart,' the pilot muttered. 'Another two hours and we were done for.'

While a couple of men helped the pilot into the U-boat Schiller inspected the gun and the mounting. It was so light and convenient. No big cans of bulky belts. And there were spare drums of ammunition. Put this on a simple pipe-rail round the conning tower and there would be no need to lug that bloody Maxim about.

'Meyer,' he called to the torpedo artificer. 'You have five minutes to unship that machine-gun and its mounting. You can use the Maxim to pry it off if you want.'

Meyer gave an understanding grin. He and Henne were the last of Schiller's luck. Three survivors.

A few minutes later, Schiller and Beibedecke stood in the conning tower watching the stem of UC62 crush the starboard float and struts. The seaplane rolled over, the heavy engine taking it down like a stone. Schiller grinned exultantly. A ship sunk and a seaplane crew rescued, let Beibedecke make something out of that.

As they turned back on to course for home the horizon rippled with light reflected from the low cloud. Minutes later they heard the rumble of the guns. It was not a quiet night on the Western Front.

Schiller turned to Beibedecke. 'You have the watch. Dismiss the gun crews. Post look-outs. Keep them on their toes. Wireless base about the rescue. Notify them that we will now enter harbour at 10.45. We definitely expect that seaplane escort from first light onwards.'

Licking the salt off his swollen lips he shivered with anticipation, imagining the froth from the first glass of beer ringing his lips. God, he was going to drink the club dry.

CHAPTER SEVEN

Shepherd licked his swollen lips. Fighting people like Mad Jack and making love to Elsa were incompatible pastimes. He moved slightly; his left arm was dead from the shoulder to the fingertips, two bolts on the ambulance floor were boring through the folded blankets into his backside but he was reluctant to disturb the girl cradled in his arms. His neck muscles ached and he had cramp in his shoulder-blades as he stared up at the whirling ventilator in the roof.

He had really put his foot in it this time. Since parting in January '14 he had seen Elsa twice and each time they had finished in bed. On the floor of an ambulance, he corrected himself, wearing nothing but a grubby army blanket. There was no doubt about the way ahead. He had to purge his guilt for the death of Jennifer by killing Schiller.

'Richard.' Elsa pecked his cheek and sat up tucking the ends of the blanket under her arms. A locket on a gold chain hung in the vee of her breasts. 'I know why you are gazing up at the heavens. You are listing all the crimes you have committed in the past three weeks. Desertion; enlisting under false pretences; suborning officers of the Royal Navy; improper use of the country's Intelligence files; concealing evidence from the police; bribery and corruption of His Majesty's servicemen; misuse of service equipment; obtaining a medical certificate by lies and deceit to back up more lies; using one of His Majesty's ambulances for immoral purposes; and seducing while on duty one of his drivers. Any three should be enough to get you shot.'

He reached for her but she pushed him aside lightly. 'They check on how long it takes lady ambulance drivers to move wounded heroes. Especially lightly wounded ones. Shut your eyes.'

She pulled the blanket over his head.

'I'm going to marry you, Mrs Cordle,' he said.

She tweaked the blanket over his eyes again as she wriggled into her petticoat. 'We'll see about that when the time comes. Declarations of intent do not justify peeping.'

'What are you going to do next? About this U-boat captain.' She slapped his hand away. 'Behave yourself. You are a wounded hero. With no strength, remember, due to nervous exhaustion. Dr McArdle should see you now.'

'I had to get that medical certificate. It gives us a breathing space. And an excuse to get Henry and Tregarron up here for a council of war. UC62 will not be on patrol for over a week. We have to be ready for him next time.'

'Really, Miss Talbot, some of these doctors have no idea of the difficulties they cause us. Twenty-eight days, that is a bit stiff. He has had a fortnight's sick-leave already. Our boys in the trenches are lucky to get fourteen days,' Villers said, flattening the certificate on the desk.

'It is a medical certificate of illness, not a leave-pass,' Henrietta said tartly. 'You could have a word with the doctor.'

'I have, Miss Talbot, indeed I have. The SNO at Whitby thinks very highly of the chap. Another one of these damned Scots who think shouting to be a substitute for the King's English. Damn it, at one point in our conversation he was referring to me as though I was Shepherd's commanding officer. Ridiculous feller. Made me out to be some sort of slavemaster. Damn funny place for Shepherd to go to at this time of the year.'

'It's not that far from York. Pretty place,' Henrietta said, guessing that Villers' knowledge of Yorkshire would be that it was one of the bigger lumps between the Home Counties and the Scottish grouse-moors. 'I think Mr Tregarron and I ought to visit him … '

'Certainly not,' Villers snapped. 'Not the pair of you. Not Tregarron. Can't have the pair of you missing, y'know. The war still goes on. But you go. It's a very proper sentiment.'

He unlocked a drawer for the certificate. 'We'll keep that to ourselves, I think. No point in bothering the Admiral.'

He scribbled a few words on a sheet of notepaper, folded it

and slipped it into an envelope. He sealed it. 'Give him that. Just a few words to show that he is not forgotten.'

Carberry was less impressed by fading bruises than Dr McArdle. They went on patrol the following morning. Shepherd sweated with fear despite the bitterly cold wind as Carberry took SS 19 out of the centre of the clearing again. As the tail wind blew them over a white-capped sea, he watched the vibrating water-pipes from the engine to the radiator and listened intently to the steady roar of the engine. Then the pain of operating the key with blackened fingernails drove the fear out of his mind.

It was a dull patrol, a reversion to the old practice of looking for U-boats and escorting individual ships. They saw nothing. Two schools of porpoises, wreckage east of Flamborough Head, and they destroyed a floating mine outside the War Channel. When they blew it up half a dozen British moored mines exploded in sympathy. The people who had to replace them would not be amused. Towards the end they found a Schneider seaplane with a seasick pilot and a dead engine. The lifeboat they summoned got there minutes before a float strut buckled and the seaplane sank in three feet of water on a sandbank.

The wind had got up again. It took them two hours to reach the coast. To stop himself from chewing his fingernails Shepherd tuned in to the U-boat band. One of them was transmitting. It only added to his humiliation, not being able to do anything about it. Until he had his idea.

He leaned over the side and began to haul in the wireless aerial, hand over hand, until he had the lead weight at the end in his grease-covered hands. Below the nacelle the aerial now hung in a huge flattened loop. He had remembered that the movable aerials used by the triangulation stations were loops. A bit more complex than this but a loop just the same. Now he had to swing the aerial through the signal. He passed a note to Carberry asking him to turn to the right. It worked. The noise of the morse increased and then began to fade as the turn took the loop across the transmission. He got Carberry to turn left and got the same result. Back to the right again. He used his hands like a policeman on point duty to signal more or less turn, until he had the airship flying along the bearing to or from the transmitter. He asked for the compass bearing.

'Zero-six-three,' Carberry shouted. 'Do you mind giving me an idea of what you are up to. We are now two miles further from the coast than we were when you started. I thought you didn't like trawlers.'

The transmission stopped. Shepherd let the aerial slide through his gloves to trail in the normal way. 'Along that bearing there is a U-boat on the surface. It is either between us and the coast, which is unlikely, or between us and the Friesians, or just possibly off the Irish coast.'

Carberry ruddered them back on course for the coast. 'God preserve us when you get back to Whitehall. The rubbish you produce is still rubbish but it is produced with confidence.'

The wind had eased the following day and the handling party got them through the trees on to the aerodrome. Carberry celebrated by taking two depth-charges. The wind dropped to a zephyr and they brought the bombs back after seven hours. They spotted either two periscopes or one periscope twice. The escorts depth-charged with enthusiasm without any visible result but dead fish that they were too tired to collect. However, as Carberry said, all the ships reached port and there was always a chance that the U-boat skippers would die of frustration.

There was a telegram waiting for Shepherd from Henrietta.

DOCTOR'S CERTIFICATE ACCEPTED. GRUDGINGLY. I ARRIVE YORK AM TOMORROW TO VIEW PATIENT. T. NOT ALLOWED OUT. WHEN AND WHERE. HENRY.

'Tomorrow morning. As early as possible,' Carberry said. 'I've been thinking about that stunt you pulled this afternoon with the wireless aerial. It might be worth going out some night with a moon to try it on the dog.'

'There is a three-quarter moon tonight,' Shepherd said.

'Yes, and the forecast is a 500-feet cloud base with heavy rain. Have some sense. Why do we have to have your girlfriend at this meeting?'

143

'Her father owns trawlers. Most of them have been requisitioned for minesweeping, with their skippers. Elsa knows them all. I have an idea how we can put the kibosh on Schiller. He is bound to try that trick again. And to make my counter-trick work we will need help from the trawlermen.'

Carberry nodded. And he agreed without smirking that as Shepherd's home was in York it would be better for him to go tonight rather than in broad daylight the next day. Elsa would put him up. Carberry agreed that she might.

Shepherd was feeling lighter than any blimp as he left the Flight Office. Everything, every little thing, was dropping into place, coming together at last. He had a breathing space. He knew how he could get UC62 and Schiller. He danced a little jig as he walked into the hut to collect the Post Office book Henrietta had sent him.

The hut was in darkness. Everyone had gone off to the cookhouse for tea. The blackout shutters were not in place and there was enough light for him to find his bed and the bank book. But as he slipped it into his pocket an arm curled round his neck and dragged him backwards.

'What's your bleedin' game, mate?' Miller said. 'I've had all I can take watching you licking up to that bloody barmy flight commander. Gettin' ready to make a dash for it, are you?'

A sickening punch in the kidneys sent him reeling on his knees. Miller hit him in the face with a right and a left, then put him down with a thump on the jaw. When he got up Miller had the book in his hand.

'One hundred bloody quid. You bloody bastard. I knew you were up to some fiddle.'

'It's no use to you. Nobody will give you that sort of money without seeing your identity card. And it will take you a week to get a draft for £100 approved. Not that you will get far. You are on guard duty tonight ... '

Miller pushed the book into his pocket. 'You're too bloody stupid to be true, mate, there's blokes I know as'll work miracles with this. An' I can wait 'til tomorrow. No hard feelings, mate, you did right to start running. I told you we had to keep moving. The peelers have been to see all recruiting offices round the Smoke looking for wireless operators joining up in a hurry.'

He slapped his hand over the pocket holding the book. 'This is as good as a set of papers and a ship to Aussie to me. And in this 'ard world you has to pay for information received. So long, mate.'

Despite the scrimmage with Miller that had refreshed the fading colour of his bruises Shepherd had recovered his exhilaration as he waited for Elsa in York station. He had one frightening moment when he almost bumped into Jennifer's father. He had sidestepped quickly behind a pillar as the old man followed the crowd on to the mainline platform. There was a hospital train due in from France. While the crowd milled round the panting locomotive and the carriages standing by the long curved platform, Shepherd skipped lightly down some steps to a side platform as the country train wheezed in, draped in a cloud of steam from a dozen leaking joints.

Arm in arm Shepherd and Elsa joined the crowd – the happy, the disappointed and the curious – jostling over the footbridge towards the exit.

'What do your mother and father think of your latest escapade?'

'I am not the damned fool I was four years ago. This has nothing to do with them. They don't even know I'm here.'

Elsa laughed. 'You have not changed that much. I'll bet you a month's pay they will know before tomorrow night.' She shivered as a spray of rain licked over them. 'I'm frozen to the marrow.'

He squeezed her arm, pulling her close to him so that he could peck her nose. 'I have some ideas on how to cure that.'

The following morning Carberry collected Henrietta off the night train, and gave her breakfast at the Station Hotel before bringing her back to Elsa's flat. Shepherd knew they had arrived when he heard Elsa giggle.

Henrietta believed in travelling in comfort. She was wearing a tweed costume of a vaguely purple shade, a matching travelling cape big enough to make a small bell-tent, and her round fur hat. She was smoking a cheroot. Beside her, Carberry in his best uniform looked like a grade C3 reject made up to play in musical comedy.

Shepherd made the introductions. 'Elsa Dolli, sorry, Cordle. We shall need her father's help. He owns trawlers. Elsa has a grudge against Jerry like the rest of us. She lost her husband when the Fokker monoplanes were making mincemeat out of the old BE —'

'You have all the understanding and tact of a drunken cattle drover,' Henrietta snapped, seeing the colour rise in Elsa's cheeks. She patted her arm.

Elsa smiled back at her. 'I know him of old. Just a boisterous puppy at heart. A St Bernard puppy, all paws and tail wrecking everything not bolted down.'

It was Henrietta's meeting. From one of the two suitcases she had brought on the journey she disgorged a mass of information. A chart of the North Sea with the routes of each of UC62's patrols over the past twelve months; decoded intercepts from recent patrols; a dossier on Schiller and another on Beibedecke. Details of the UC-class of minelayers and abstracts from the Intelligence file on the Flanders Flotilla.

At her suggestion they spent an hour looking and reading through the material. But she would not allow anyone to make notes. Elsa's mood had changed. When she offered to make coffee and Shepherd got up to help he got a hefty kick on the shins for his good intentions.

Henrietta, at the head of the table like the chairman of the board, was about to open the meeting when the doorbell rang.

'If that is the police,' she said looking at the paper-strewn table, 'I'm afraid we all face a long period in gaol.'

'It's your mother,' Elsa said to Shepherd. 'I told you she would find out. You should have worn a beard and a wig last night.'

'Go into the kitchen, Richard,' Henrietta said, making for the door like a galleon in full sail. 'No matter what you hear you are not here. Is that understood? I will deal with this. Squadron Commander Carberry, kindly hover in the back-

146

ground. Close enough for Mrs Shepherd to get a good look at your uniform. Thank you.'

Henrietta opened the door. 'Good morning,' she said, taking the cheroot out of her mouth.

'Good morning, I have come to see my son.'

'Of course, come in. You must be Mrs Carberry. How on earth did you know he was here?'

'No, I am not Mrs Carberry.' Mrs Shepherd stepped back a pace to peer at the number on the door. 'This is 4a, Elsa Dolli's flat. Who are you?'

'Madame, I do not know who you are except that you are not Mrs Carberry and apparently he is not the son for whom you are looking. Could you be more explicit? We are busy.' Henrietta waved a hand at the two people standing in front of the table. 'Squadron Commander Carberry, you don't know. Mrs Cordle, presumably you do … '

'That slut was never married to Jack Cordle. Or to anyone else with a decent name,' Mrs Shepherd said staring at Elsa. 'I hope the lie sticks in your throat and chokes you.' She turned to Henrietta, looked her fiercely up and down and said. 'I believe there are a lot of women like you in London. G'day.'

As they reassembled round the table, Shepherd ambled out of the kitchen holding a cup of coffee and a slice of toast and marmalade.

Henrietta glared at him, one foot beating an ominous tattoo. Shepherd raised his cup like a schoolboy offering teacher an apple to avert the impending storm.

'Richard. I have seen you at work. I share the view of the Department that you have a first-class brain, but you are striking proof that the intelligentsia do not have enough common sense to come in out of the rain.'

'What have I done wrong? I made some coffee while you and my mother had a slanging match … '

'You called this meeting in York. We would have been far safer meeting in Berlin. Idiot! You could have ruined all of us. As it is you have compromised Elsa in a most unfortunate way. I fancy your mother is a woman who could excuse almost anything except being made to look a fool.'

147

Carberry's laughter brought the meeting to order. He had just finished Henrietta's summary on Schiller and Beibedecke. Most of the information had come via Beibedecke's girlfriend.

'We don't need a council of war. The answer is here, in this folder. All we want is a ticket to Zeebrugge – we'd have to go via Amsterdam – and a catapult.'

He reopened the file. 'After his drinking bouts in the officers' club Schiller always walks back along the top of the sea wall, stopping halfway to urinate into the sea ... There you are. Half a dozen ball-bearings and a stout catapult and your man is in the drink. Pick the right time of the tide and he will never get out. Not with a bellyful of schnapps inside him ... '

'Your idea is not original, Mr Carberry,' Henrietta said coldly. 'It was first tried some weeks ago. It failed because of our side, not because of the Germans.'

'I'm sorry,' Carberry closed the file with a slap. 'You know I've never seen anything like this about Jerry. I almost like Otto Schiller. I can see him enjoying himself on one of our guest nights. Not von Beibedecke. I know one or two like him on our side. Mostly captains, RN, or more senior by now.'

'I remind you of two things, Mr Carberry. This is not a jolly romp in the wardroom,' Henrietta said. 'On your word of honour you have not read those papers and you know nothing about Schiller or Beibedecke other than what you have read about their murderous exploits in the newspapers. The smallest comment by you could jeopardize the life of the, er, the person who got that information. If this is the effect such information has on you I can understand better why it is buried in the archives.'

'It makes you wonder whether old Bart would have got away with it,' Shepherd said.

'Richard, hold your tongue,' Henrietta snapped. 'You have done enough damage already. Before you do any more, explain our plan for dealing with Schiller.'

'You have read the paper Henrietta and I prepared showing that this new "secret delay action mine" is actually an ordinary mine used by a cunning U-boat skipper. Schiller looked at the way the minesweepers work and he is now laying his mines between the sweepers and the ships following them.'

Shepherd swept his hand over the chart of the North Sea. 'Two out of three of Schiller's patrols start at the Humber. He seems to know his way through our minefield. But it does not matter. He uses the wireless so frequently that we can plot his course and forecast where he will make his first attack.'

'That makes it easy,' Carberry said. 'Take any patch of fifty square miles of open sea – north, south or east of the Humber – and drop a bomb on something ten fathoms underwater and you have got him.'

'It is easier than that. We are going to let him blow himself up. And that is where you, Elsa, through your father, come into the act. We want to arrange a surprise sweep, a back-up of dummy minesweepers to pretend to sweep up Schiller's mines as soon as he has laid them. We will spot the mines from the air. For every mine there would have to be an explosion. A small depth-charge or a grenade would do. When the dummy sweepers have done their work Schiller will try to relay his mines ... in his own minefield. Boom!'

Carberry whistled and rattled a pencil against his teeth. 'I like it, I like everything about it except the job of selling it to the Navy. They do not have all this background stuff. We have to start from cold and you are asking a lot. You are asking them to believe that they have brought a lot of experts in for nothing. That they have been diddled. You are asking them to hold back a convoy for at least half a day. They'd lose a tide. Twenty-four hours' delay. An extra pair of sweepers, they are worth their weight in gold. Believe me, you are asking a lot. All apparently based on a hunch by a RNAS wireless operator who had only been in the Service three weeks ... '

'That was unfair,' Henrietta said.

Carberry shrugged his shoulders. 'And now you are being silly. When I put this scheme, that is the question I will be asked. Who thought of it and where is the evidence. We might get away with it. There is a grisly sense of poetic justice about it that would appeal to the anti-U-boat people. The

149

little ship people. But nobody above the rank of lieutenant-commander would listen to you.'

Henrietta glared at him but he went on. 'I'll give it a try. Can I borrow that chart?'

'Yes, but keep it in a safe place and do not tell anyone where you got it. There is one thing in our favour. Alec Jervis is in overall command of the minesweepers at Whitby.'

'And four of my father's skippers are in command there,' Elsa said. 'I think he will listen to you.'

CHAPTER EIGHT

It was after midnight when they got back to Cleveland Hall. Carberry had been preoccupied as the train crawled through the sleeping countryside. By default he had joined the quest for Schiller. Firstly by taking no action against Shepherd and now by agreeing to put the case to Jervis. His own fault. It was he who had pointed out that neither Henrietta nor Shepherd could put forward the plan and that Jervis would not dream of listening to a civilian, let alone a woman like Elsa. So he had got the job although he warned them he had little hope of success. Shepherd slept, awakening only at each stop when the motion of the train jolted him off the seat.

Reluctant to face Miller's suspicious stare Shepherd accompanied Carberry to the Flight Office. He was feeling increasingly guilty about Miller's plans to desert and the possibility that some blame might be attached to Carberry. He was still dithering about Miller when he rang Tregarron to find out what was happening. There were two U-boats off the Yorkshire coast outward bound, and another north of the Tyne returning home with empty tubes. An old coastal minelayer, UB16, had cleared the Mole outward bound from Zeebrugge. Two Zeppelins had been plotted on a reconnaissance about the Dogger. A quiet night. He had seen the up-to-date figures of sinkings. They were terrible. March was going to be by far the worst month of the war. Tregarron sounded old and tired. He brightened up when he asked to be remembered to Elsa. He recalled her personal triumph in some sordid revue in '15. Then the Zeppelin scare had closed the theatre and she had simply dropped out of sight. Tregarron could understand how a gel newly widowed might not want to continue playing in shows like that.

Shepherd nodded. He had his own ideas about what had happened in '15. Jack Cordle was dead and then Elsa found

151

she was pregnant. West End success or not she would never have had any money put by. He was sure she had gone away to have the baby. He was equally sure that she and Jack had not married. With no heir to the name the Cordle family would have pounced on a legitimate son no matter who their late son might have married. Poor old Elsa, she had been literally left holding the baby. Not that it made any difference to his feelings. She ought to realize that and be open about it.

Carberry joined him at the window. The rain had stopped after sunset as the wind swung round to the east. The cloud was breaking, showing patches of starlight, and a three-quarter moon went on and off like a lighthouse. He had never known the weather to play such a part in his life.

'Convoys are not a cure-all,' Carberry said. 'Two U-boats had a go at one of the Scandinavian convoys a couple of hours ago. Brave lads, there was a strong escort. A destroyer rammed one but they got two ships. And there is a flying boat down somewhere between here and the Texels. Poor sods, it'll be a cold night for them.'

Shepherd nodded, his mind on the U-boat that had got away. He would be singing his story to his HQ as soon as the escorts and the convoy were out of the way.

'Can you fly a blimp at night?' he asked. 'If we were there we could look for survivors and maybe run down a bearing on that second U-boat.'

'They are easier to fly at night than in the daylight. There's no sun to expand the gas, no expansion for cloud to cool and contract. That makes it easier to hold a steady altitude without fiddling with the gas-valves and ballast. But that's not much use if you cannot see anything.'

At that moment the moon found a gap in the cloud and flooded the parked airships with light.

It was 2.30 before a bleary-eyed, cursing handling party dragged SS 19 through the trees on to the moonlit aerodrome. The cloud had blown away. They were heavy on take-off with two depth-charges and extra petrol. There was nothing cloud-like about SS 19 as they ran the full length of the field, the wheels bucking and juddering over the rough grass until

152

Carberry wound on the elevator, the nose went up and the blimp sailed over the trees and out across the bay.

There were no survivors in the water nor any bodies when they reached the reported position of the attack. Someone had picked them up. It must take a peculiar cold-blooded courage, Shepherd thought, to stop your ship to pick up survivors knowing that there were U-boats about. There had been plenty of examples of the cost in the past three years since the poorly armoured cruisers of the 'Cold meat squadron,' the *Aboukir,* the *Hogue* and the *Cressy,* had gone down within little more than sixty minutes of each other.

Soon after, Shepherd picked up a U-boat transmitting. He looped the aerial again, but although they flew down the bearing until the message stopped they saw nothing. Only a cold sea with the wave-crests glittering under a waning moon.

Shepherd made a routine position report to Howden. There was a message for them. An exhausted pigeon had been found carrying a message from the flying boat. Carberry turned east as he plotted the position on the chart and tried to estimate how far the boat would have drifted since the men aboard released the pigeon.

It was just before dawn and they were well to the east when they found the wreckage. A broken wing, one wing-tip float and a petrol tank washed over by the waves. Nothing else. The sun appeared over the horizon as they circled. Carberry dipped the nose in salute and turned west for home.

A flash of light on the horizon caught Shepherd's eye. He focused the binoculars but it was on the limit of his vision. A flicker of white or of light, he could not be sure. But there was something there. Carberry pointed a pencil to a spot on the chart. Their position. The enemy coastline was just over the hill. And they were getting low on petrol.

'We have an east wind,' Shepherd said stubbornly. 'It will blow us home.'

Carberry shrugged and turned towards the flashes. 'Keep your fingers crossed and your eyes open. And offer a little prayer that the Jerry seaplane pilots are having a long lie-in.'

They flew on for another ten minutes before Shepherd realized he was watching a flock of seagulls, dozens of them.

They settled on something too low in the water for him to make out and then, as though alarmed, whirled upwards in an explosion of white.

'They are only birds,' Carberry shouted.

'Another ten minutes will not hurt us. I can't understand why they don't settle.'

Carberry stared at him. He had been flying over the North Sea for three years. Three years that had taught him what it was that brought a cloud of seagulls together. Food. It would not do Mr Shepherd any harm, he decided, to let him see what happened when men slaughtered men at sea. He might realize that his quest to kill Otto Schiller involved the man's crew dying with him. He lifted the binoculars to his eyes again. Put them down to remove a glove and rub his eyes. Lifted them again. The seagulls leapt into focus as his fingers stroked the adjustment, a cloud of snowflakes touched with gold. He felt his stomach heave and a cold sweat bead his forehead. You never get used to it, he thought. There would certainly be a lot of extremely fat seagulls in the North Sea before this war was over.

SS 19 was climbing again. The blimp was very light now after burning so much petrol. And the sun was at work heating and expanding the hydrogen. The stability of the night flight was over. Once again he would have to juggle with gas-pressures and gas-valves, ballonnet pressures and crabpot valves, to try to maintain a constant altitude. It was hardly worth going on just to make a raw recruit sick. Not with so little petrol left. If the wind dropped they would finish this trip as a free balloon again.

The object beneath the seagulls suddenly came in sight, a waterlogged ship's lifeboat lifting soggily on the crest of a wave. As it rolled, seawater poured in through the shattered port gunwale. Three bodies sprawled half-submerged in the bows. One man was folded over the tiller. They were too late, Shepherd thought, as Carberry valved gas to approach at fifty feet with the engine throttled back.

The gulls, unaware of their silent approach, whirled round again preparing to settle. One, bolder than the rest, dropped on to the Samson post in the bow. A cruel yellow beak slashed at the body lolling against the rail. A dozen followed, stabbing down again and again. The rest followed until the bows were covered with jerking white birds.

The man in the stern sat up as one pecked at his outstretched arm. He brandished the tiller at them, his lips parted in a soundless scream. The birds stirred, took alarm and exploded upwards and outwards.

Shepherd threw himself half out of the cockpit, bent double as his stomach reacted violently to the scene in the lifeboat. The heads and shoulders of the bodies in the bow were shapeless lumps of raw meat. Something indescribable floated head-down in the bloody water between the bows and the centre thwart. In the stern the survivor, a crimson slash down one cheek, waved the tiller again before fitting it back on the rudder post. He used a baler to scoop out a couple of pints of water before crumpling sideways.

Shepherd turned, wiping the vomit from his face. 'How do we pick him up?' he shouted.

As Carberry eased back the throttle to hold the blimp in line with the stern, Shepherd clipped the Lewis gun on to its spigot and sprayed an angry, ineffectual burst at the gulls. Stationary, nose into wind, the blimp was light again. It rose slowly up like a soap-bubble into the wheeling, screaming flock of birds. Shepherd turned angrily. The colour was coming back into his face. It was the shock of seeing war as it was and not as it was pictured in the newspapers, Carberry thought. The physical effects wore off quickly but the scar in his mind would remain. It would break open every time they flew in the coming weeks. And sometime in the months ahead he would wake up in the night screaming with anger ... and fear.

Carberry put his operator's rage out of his mind as he concentrated on his own problem. The man in the boat would weigh twelve stone or more, say 170lb. He had to take that weight aboard without dragging the nacelle into the water. If their propeller touched either the boat or the waves it would break. And then there would be two more carcasses for the ever-hungry gulls.

The blimp was light. But he had to approach slowly, which

155

would rob them of the dynamic load that balanced their lightness. Too fast and Shepherd would be dragged over-board. Without his weight SS 19 would climb away quickly. He would never get back. And there was no friendly boat within a hundred miles.

Shepherd climbed out of his cockpit on to the skid. Hand over hand. One hand for himself, one hand for the ship. Carberry raised his thumb. But for this operation he did not want a gentleman ranker, a frightened young man with an imagination being brave. He wanted a horny-handed sea-man, bred in sail and used to running up the braces to free the halliards, and who could do handstands on the yards. Someone who could hang on the axle by his ankles and pluck that chap out of the lifeboat. A daring young man on the aerial trapeze. But he would have to make do with what he had got. He closed the throttle. The blimp drifted slowly backwards, rising. His hand reached for the gas-valve but he took it away. They were going to need all the lift possible.

'Shepherd, get behind the wheels with the grapnel. About twenty feet of cable. Take a turn round the axle. As I fly over the boat, hook the grapnel under one of the thwarts. Got that?'

Shepherd nodded. Carberry checked the two depth-charges to make sure the safety-pins were in the fuses. As Shepherd took the man's weight he would drop the bombs.

He was too slow the first time and never got within twenty feet of the boat. Too fast the second time. The grapnel bounced off the gunwale, hooked into a peajacket and ripped off a bloody sleeve as they raced by. Shepherd slipped as he retched again and almost fell.

A gust of wind plucked them off course on the third run, the grapnel bouncing along the side of the boat. Then Shepherd was too slow as another gust spun them out of reach. Carberry stood on the rudder bar and blasted them round with the throttle wide open. SS 19 spun on its axis, moving slowly across the boat but beginning to accelerate with the engine at full power. Shepherd hooked the grapnel under the centre thwart.

The shock as they hooked on slammed Carberry's head

against the leather padding round his cockpit. He saw Shepherd jammed into the vee of the undercarriage as he groped for the throttle and the propeller flicked round lazily as he closed it. He could hear the clatter of the valve gear and Shepherd trying to be sick again as he hauled the blimp down to sea-level hand over hand on the grapnel rope.

Boat and airship rose together on the crest of a wave and then fell back into the trough with an enormous splash. Shepherd slipped again. The blimp lifted as the rope slid through his hands. He hauled them down again and snubbed the rope round the axle.

Carberry took up the lost motion in the bomb-release toggles as he leaned out to watch Shepherd. The man in the boat seemed to be unable to help himself. Shepherd's first attempt to lift him failed. Now he had the trail rope, a three-inch grass line. He knotted a loop in the end and the seaman hooked his arms through it. Shepherd took the strain by pulling the line over the skid. He waited until they were rising on a wave, and raised his thumb to Carberry.

The blimp sank down towards the boat. Carberry winced as the propeller tips cut through the crest of a wave. He pulled the bomb release. SS 19 sank as the weight of the man came on the rope, but it recovered as the bombs fell away. Shepherd got his arm under the man and hauled him over the axle.

Carberry dropped some precious ballast and cracked open the throttle. The two bombs had crashed through the bottom of the boat, breaking it in two. The blimp lurched upwards a few feet but the stem of the boat still hung from the grapnel. It spun slowly as the blimp began to sink.

'Cut that grapnel free!' Carberry shouted.

Shepherd was too exhausted to do anything but hang on. The seaman recovered first, plucking a sheath knife from his belt to cut the rope. SS 19 slowly floated upwards. An arm came out of the sea as one of the bodies, rolled over by a wave, gave them a parting salute.

They turned west. Helped by Carberry, Shepherd pulled and shoved the seaman into his cockpit. It was going to be a long, cold, cramped ride home.

They were all lucky. Halfway home a destroyer took the seaman aboard and found a dry uniform for Shepherd. He was only aboard ten minutes, much to the relief of Carberry, because the captain of the destroyer was demonstrating the capabilities of his ship by towing the blimp at thirty knots.

'I talked to that seaman,' Shepherd said after they had landed. 'It was Schiller who sank his ship. The man is like a mad dog ... '

'You have Schiller on the brain, he's not the only U-boat commander in the North Sea,' Carberry said. 'It could have been any one of a hundred men.'

'No. That man was the first mate on a little Dutch cargo boat. He was on the bridge. The second shell blew him into the water. The time and place tie up with that last message from UC62. And the method. No warning and a continuous barrage until the ship blew up. It was Schiller.'

'Was it Schiller, or the war? What would you have done if you had been skipper of a British submarine limping home damaged in the Baltic and that ship had been German. Eh? You'd have expected a DSO.'

Cleveland Hall was like an empty shell with the two Zeros out on patrol. Shepherd could not sleep. Every time he dozed off he dreamed that a seagull was stabbing him with that vicious yellow beak. Then he would lie in his bunk listening to the scrabbling noises of the gulls walking about the corrugated-iron roof. He got permission to leave the camp to walk down to Cleveland Bay in the hope that Elsa would be there. But she was still working her final month with the Ambulance Corps. Her little boy was asleep, and the woman looking after him made an oyster sound like a village blabbermouth. Just as he had decided that the woman's vocabulary only included two words, yes and no, a mechanic arrived on a motor cycle to take him back to the aerodrome. Flight Sub-Lieutenant Dutton was in trouble with his Zero and Carberry was taking SS 19 to look for him.

He nearly missed the flight. The mechanic believed that intensive reading about the TT was an adequate substitute for experience. Nobody had ever said to him before, 'Fetch

Shepherd and don't hang about. Every minute is vital.'
Going round the final hairpin bend on the road up the hill,
the back wheel of the Douglass slid outwards on the
windborne sand that drifted on the road. Shepherd picked
himself out of a gorse bush, asked the mechanic for an
invitation to his parents' wedding and ran up the hill. He was
still picking spines out of the protruding parts of his anatomy
when he staggered up to SS 19.

An impatient Carberry had the engine running. Shepherd
had to struggle into his flying gear as the blimp was walked
out on to the aerodrome. The men on the nacelle were grinning
as they saw Carberry swearing, although the words were
inaudible over the noise of the engine. Shepherd went on
methodically tucking in the ends of his scarf, pulling up the
fur-lined collar of his long leather coat and then retrieving the
skirt from where it had caught on the outside of the cockpit. He
shuffled his feet into the big sheepskin thigh-boots, fastened his
lap strap after a final wriggle, and raised his thumb.

'Hands off,' Carberry shouted. He had ballasted up as soon
as Shepherd got aboard. They were light. As the nacelle men
let go the blimp bounded a few inches into the air. Carberry
opened the throttle. The wheels kissed the ground ten yards
on, hopped another thirty yards and then they were going up
like a silver bubble, momentarily lit by a ray of sunshine
cutting through the layers of stratus.

The nose moved off course, as a gust deflected off the
cliff-face hit them. Carberry trod on opposite rudder to drag
the nose back on course. He eased the throttle back at 300 feet
and played with the crabpot valves, trimming the blimp to
fly level by the amount of air let into the fore and aft
ballonnets. It was a busy time for the pilot – setting course,
trimming, notes in the engine log, times in the navigation log.
He was glad to be busy. The euphoria of the past few days
since he had found out what Shepherd was up to had finally
blown away.

It had been amusing to watch two amateurs, civilians,
twisting the Admiralty machine to suit their own ends.
Watching Shepherd, the epitome of the plodding Establishment man, come to life as he expounded the summary of

intelligence on Schiller, and describe how the man's own creation could be used to engender his destruction. And that incredible schoolmistress, coolly ransacking the most secret files in the country to feed her weapon. Shepherd might not realize it but that was how she saw him. They made a dangerous pair. Carberry had enjoyed imagining the look on the face of Captain Botham had that martinet found out what was going on in his command.

The Establishment would win, it always did in the long run. Any one of a hundred little things could bring the project down around their necks. Like that telephone message this morning. Then the Establishment would have its revenge; it always did on those that flouted it.

He eased the throttle back and tapped Shepherd on the shoulder. 'You owe Mr Dutton a drink. His engine problems saved your bloody silly quest from sudden death this morning. You are a hero. Officially. That seaman we picked up told his tale well. Just what their Lordships needed to stimulate recruiting. There was a photographer and a newspaper reporter on the way. Until I stopped them … '

Carberry snorted with disgust as Shepherd shook his head and went on wiping a speck of oil off his goggles. The damn fool is so cocksure that he has never considered the consequences of failure. To himself and those who had helped.

'That's torn it. Can we land somewhere else? They'll be waiting for us when we get back.'

Carberry shook his head impatiently. 'Don't be an ass. To be a hero in wartime you need Admiralty authority and you need to be where the newspapers can get at you easily. They'll be back in a month or so … if someone jogs their memory. Heroes are two a penny in wartime. It is time you packed it in. This nonsense. Too risky a game to play just to feed your ego. Go back to your job.'

Shepherd's lips tightened and his jaw jutted out stubbornly. 'Now, when we are so close … '

'That is the time to go, when you have done what had to be done. You have made the trap and baited it. It has to be dropped where Schiller can spring it. I can place it, you can't.'

Shepherd shook his head but the morse in his earphones stopped the argument. 'It's Dutton. The engine has finally packed up. It boiled dry and seized. He's sending a position report.'

He kept an old chart in the cockpit to plot U-boats. He put a cross on it and pushed it back to Carberry. The wind was from the south-west. There was nothing between them and Sweden but a lot of sea. As Carberry swung on to a course to intercept the crippled Zero, Shepherd fashioned his aerial into a loop. It might help and he saw no point in continuing their earlier discussion.

Carberry swung SS 19 through a ninety-degree turn to the right, butting through a thin curtain of rain while Shepherd listened to the morse dying in his earphones. Mark the bearing. Carberry swung back the other way. Mark the bearing. Now do it again. The change in volume was not as clear-cut as he would like. Shepherd raised his thumb.

Carefully Carberry plotted the bearing. Either it or Dutton's reported position was wrong. Dutton's position would have been calculated using a forecast wind invented by some weatherman last night. The bearing was the better bet. How much would Dutton drift with the wind before they reached him? Now he had a track to which he could apply the forecast wind to give him a course to steer to find the Zero. There was an awful lot of estimation, he thought, to carry the lives of three men.

Shepherd had released the aerial and he was bent over the key again. He raised his thumb in triumph before passing a message to Carberry. 'I got on to T4, the triangulation station. They have plotted his position. 54°15′N by 02°20′E. And there is a U-boat twenty miles NE on the surface transmitting. T4 plot its course as being straight for Dutton.'

Shepherd marked the positions on his chart and guessed how long it would take them to reach the crippled Zero. In about an hour, give or take five minutes, all of them would be together.

It would be a relief, Shepherd thought, if Miller was taken prisoner. He would not have to tell Carberry about Miller's intention to desert. Or why Miller had joined. That might be the last straw, turning Carberry against helping in the future. He might feel compelled to protect his own hide by giving the game away. And letting Schiller off the hook.

The binoculars quivered in his hand, blurring the seascape below as a blind rage flared up at the Carberrys of this world. The men doing their duty, a job of work, keeping the war going by their observance of the minutiae of war, the administrative inertia that kept the fighting forces, once started, grinding away until one of the opposing sides disintegrated. They swear at Brass Hats but they create them. Somebody has to organize the parade, bring all hands to attention, the Fleet cannot leave harbour without being properly dressed. They made war civilized, tidied it up to hide its basic objective. To kill more of the men on the other side than they can kill on yours. Simple arithmetic.

He, Shepherd, had been one of the civilized killers, keeping office hours, playing literary games that killed men he never saw in ways of which he had never dreamt. Now he was a real killer, a primeval man with a club in his hand intent on bashing the brains out of some hideous night prowler after his woman. No, killing Schiller was too important and personal to leave to men to whom war, The War, was just a dirty daily business.

Carberry shook him back to cold reality. Over to port, shipping it green over the bows, a trawler butted through a veil of rain.

'Can you raise him on the lamp? Doubt whether he will have wireless. Get him to turn back for Dutton. They are about ten miles nor'east.'

While Shepherd got the lamp ready SS 19 dived for the trawler. They had been fishing. This was one the Navy had not commandeered. He could see the men gutting and filleting fish. A man in oilskins came out of the wheelhouse to wave as they swept alongside. Shepherd had no need to use the lamp. Carberry took the blimp in a wide sweep through the stinking smoke trailing from the funnel to position SS 19 by the wheelhouse on the windward side.

'Fling them the trail rope,' he shouted. As Shepherd unhooked the coil of rope and threw it on to the deck of the trawler he heard the engine telegraph ringing, 'Stop engines.'

The big man by the wheelhouse waved his sou'wester, freeing a mane of red hair to the wind. He had not shaved for four days but Shepherd recognized him immediately. They had never met. But he had lived for six months in a flat dominated by photographs of the man. Portrait studies, a wedding group, launching a trawler, standing in the wheelhouse with his red-haired daughter at the wheel. Elsa Dolli and her father had been very close. Shepherd knew that he had to get aboard that trawler somehow.

'Skipper, there is a blimp down in the sea or maybe drifting in the wind about ten miles nor'east of you. Can you give them a tow? Steer zero-five-eight. Follow us.'

'Tell him about the U-boat,' Shepherd hissed.

'Keep your eyes skinned for a U-boat. The wireless people reported one about an hour ago.'

Will Dolli cupped his hands to shout back with ease, 'Right. We steer zero-five-eight. Ten miles. We look for the airship. You look after the U-boat.'

The screws were already turning. As the trail rope was flung clear a froth of white water boiled under the stern as the *Elsa Gabrielle* – it was named after Elsa's mother – spun on her heel to head back into the rainstorm.

The rain was in thin curtains half a mile thick and two or three miles apart. A cell, Shepherd thought. First the wall, water drumming on the envelope weighing them down, flung back by the propeller to bite at the exposed skin underneath the goggles, running off in sheets to splash over the wireless set and drip through his wickerwork chair. Then empty sea, grey, featureless, a froth of foam at the base of the receding rainstorm, another under the one approaching. No sign of the Zero.

It had to be in the sea now. Miller's last message had stopped suddenly, as though the aerial had been torn away. Or they had met the U-boat.

They saw the U-boat first. Not the boat, the white bow wave and the wash as they poked through one of the rain curtains. A mile ahead of the U-boat the missing Zero, SSZ 86, was still airborne, the boat-shaped nacelle riding just above the wave-crests to a couple of sea anchors and the trail

163

rope. It was not going to last long. The movement due to the sea would have the gas-valves chattering. The gas-pressure was low, the envelope crinkling and bowed, about to buckle in the middle.

The slow bark of a heavy machine-gun stopped Shepherd's speculations. A Maxim had been rigged on the conning tower. It would not matter about the chattering gas-valves now. The envelope of the Zero was a target the gunner could not miss even at 2,000 yards. The bullets would not set it on fire unless he had special ammunition, but each hole made it more certain that she would never fly again.

Shepherd clipped the Lewis gun on its spigot and reached for a drum of ammunition. The range was too great for him to do any harm but it would attract the U-boat's attention, force it to dive.

Carberry's hand clamped on his arm as he dropped the drum in place and took aim. 'Belay that popgun,' he shouted. 'We have not been seen. I am going to sink them.'

'While Miller and Dutton get perforated by that Maxim ... '

'You are the one who is always going on about the horrors of war. Unship that gun immediately. Dutton and Miller will have to take their chance ... like that U-boat crew.'

He took SS 19 round in a sweeping curve to bring the blimp in over the stern of the U-boat. A no-deflection shot that could not miss.

It seemed incredible to Shepherd that no one took any notice of them as they overhauled the U-boat. The engine was howling at full power, pushing SS 19 along at 45 mph. Every cable screamed at its particular frequency. A jazz band in full flight, with the twin exhaust pipes rattling in their brackets for the timpani.

It must have been the closed-room effect that hypnotized the U-boat crew. With their view limited by the rain they had seen nothing but the crippled Zero, therefore there was nothing else but the target. Shepherd craned his head out into the slipstream with the binoculars glued to the submarine as they overhauled it from astern. He suddenly realized that the noise of her diesel engines would drown the puny rattle of the 90-hp OX 5.

164

The captain, naval cap rakishly tilted, a white scarf round his neck, pointed at the Zero. The Maxim gunner bashed the cocking handle with a copper mallet. A jam. He cleared it. The gun fired, the gunner swinging the barrel, pounding a short burst into the envelope. The two look-outs had their glasses trained on the Zero. It looked to be in a bad way. The envelope was beginning to buckle. That would spill the occupants of the nacelle into the sea.

Carberry took the safety-pins out of the bombs. SS 19 was overhauling the U-boat at 30 mph. There was no bomb-sight but it looked as though they would be able to drop them down the conning-tower hatch.

Then the OX 5 blew two exhaust valves. Instead of the petrol-air mixture burning as the designer intended it in a robust cylinder, the rising pistons pushed the explosive mixture past the hole in the valve into the red-hot exhaust manifold. The manifold opened like a peeled banana. Three feet of yellow flame flashed back into Shepherd's face. The binoculars saved his eyes. He saw the horror written on the faces of the men on the conning tower as the noise whirled them round to see their destroyer poised over their stern.

But they were quick. Once the shock of seeing the blimp hanging there evaporated, their training took over. One look-out leapt down the hatch followed by the second. The captain waited. The Maxim loader tripped over the ammunition can, trapping the gunner. The captain waited no longer. He jumped through the hatchway. The cover slammed shut. Shepherd thought he heard the klaxon blaring as the vents sprayed water vapour and the hull slid under water, leaving the two machine-gunners.

Carberry kicked the blimp straight and pulled the bomb-release toggles. He was a fraction short. The first one hit near the stern as it was submerging. It bounced ten feet into the air, breaking into a dozen pieces. A dud. The second fell to one side, exploding underwater. The sea boiled as a geyser of white water climbed fifty feet in the air.

'Get on to the wireless, Shepherd. Raise some help. We've got the bugger.'

The nacelle was vibrating like a tuning fork again from the

misfiring engine, but Carberry kept the blimp circling over a widening patch of oil. The bodies of the machine-gun crew rolled over as the oil slick damped down the waves. Carberry had seen too many men killed by underwater explosions to look at them. The oil slick grew but it did not move. U202 was either crippled or dead. Finally he cut across the centre of the oil to drop a smoke-float and a buoy before setting course for the crippled Zero. Away to the west the *Elsa Gabrielle* butted through the rain into the arena.

The nacelle of the Zero class of blimp was shaped and built like a boat. On SSZ 86 it was behaving like one. One with a variable weight. Each time the nacelle lifted on a wave the partially inflated envelope held it until the wave had gone. Then it dropped sickeningly into the trough. Miller was in the front cockpit, immobilized by sea-sickness. The mechanic was dead, killed by a stray Maxim bullet. Dutton, in between bouts of vomiting, was trying to cut away the engine bearers with a hacksaw.

By the time the sea boat from the *Elsa Gabrielle* had reached the Zero the rise and fall of the nacelle had hopelessly entangled the cables. A bad bounce and a gust of wind twisting the envelope jerked the ripping panel-control cable. Immediately a 14-foot-long panel in the top of the envelope opened, releasing the hydrogen. Almost empty of gas the envelope draped itself over the nacelle like a winding sheet. A body popped out of the water on the edge of the fabric. One of the trawlermen jumped into the sea to pull another man to safety as the heavy engine dragged the waterlogged nacelle down.

Shepherd was leaning over the side watching the rescue. Suddenly he was deluged with hot water as the vibration of the damaged engine split a cooling water hose. They had a few seconds of life left before they emulated the Zero. Carberry opened the throttle and headed the blimp for the stern of the *Elsa Gabrielle*.

'Grab the trail rope,' he shouted. 'Get it aboard that trawler. It has got to be made fast before the engine seizes.'

But there was no one watching the blimp. Everybody was concentrating on the men in the lifeboat hauling the survivors of the Zero on board. The trail rope dangled on the deck of the trawler while Carberry held them at mast height with the last seconds of the engine's life. Shepherd scrambled down on to the skids.

'I'll jump.'

'No. You will kill us both. She'll float off once your weight comes off. Slide down the rope. Shout for help.'

The rope slithered across the deck. Shepherd looked down on the sea behind the trawler's stern as he started to go down, hand over hand. Will Dolli had seen them. He jumped down on to the deck, running clumsily in his sea-boots. Carberry turned the blimp sharply, flinging the rope over the handrail round the stern. Ignoring the pain as the rope burned his hands Shepherd slid the rest of the way. He had taken a couple of turns round the handrail when the OX 5 seized solid.

'I know you, by God I ought to,' Will Dolli said after he had made a more professional job of lashing the trail rope and the grapnel. 'My Elsa has been telling me about you. And some damn fool idea for getting a U-boat to blow itself up with its own mines. I like ideas like that.'

The boat returned with Dutton and Miller. They were stripped, rubbed dry and, well fortified with rum, put to sleep in Dolli's cabin. Shepherd sipped treacly rum from a glass that seemed to refill itself and waited to get Will Dolli alone. Carberry stayed in the nacelle of SS 19 as they wallowed westwards at five knots with the blimp bobbing astern.

It was warm in the wheelhouse once you got out of the draughts. Shepherd coughed and prayed that his stomach would hold out against the rum, Dolli's pipe and the corkscrew motion of the *Elsa Gabrielle*. He told Will how they planned to make Schiller kill himself.

'You can see mines from your airship? Moored mines under the water?' Dolli asked.

Shepherd nodded. 'It's not too difficult, especially if you know where to look. There will be one or two lines of them. It will be easy.'

Dolli chewed his pipe-stem, growling at the back of his throat as he bit through the mouthpiece. 'I was mined once,' he said, packing tobacco into another pipe. 'Two year ago come August. The Navy took all my boats but two. They took my ships but they would not take me. So I skippered the *Miss Elsa*, my lucky ship. The fishing was good, we got catches we had never dreamed about. Then one morning just after daybreak, the abbey on the horizon, I hand over to old George Tebbutt, the mate. Damn it, he was nearly as old as my father would have been if he had lived, God rest him. I step out of the wheelhouse to yell to Bert Potter to fetch me a cup of tea. Next thing I know I'm in the sea with my thigh-boots taking me down for the third time. No ship, no crew, just me in a puddle of dead fish.'

He patted Shepherd gently on the shoulder, almost breaking his collarbone, and grinned at the stricken look on his face. 'Outside for you, behind the funnel to lee'ard. Shut your eyes and sleep. Come to see me when you are ready to put this Schiller to sleep.' He chuckled and dug an iron finger into Shepherd's aching ribs. 'Don't worry about the Navy. If they won't do it your way, we'll do it our way … '

They did not go into Whitby with the trawler. Carberry had them taken off the beach in Cleveland Bay and a handling party walked them up the hill to the aerodrome.

Carberry beckoned Shepherd into his office. 'I did not say you could sit down,' he barked. Shepherd stood to attention. He did not know how long his legs would hold him upright. 'It will take all day to fit a new engine, so we will not be flying tomorrow. You will oblige me by spending at least one day without doing anything to draw attention to yourself. Just for twenty-four hours. I will see this SNO, the chap in command of the minesweepers.'

'Alec Jervis.'

'Lieutenant-Commander Jervis. I've heard of him. Ex-submariner. I thought they had given him a desk somewhere … Give me a letter written so that he will think you are at your normal job, that will convince him to help with this hare-brained idea. Right. When I get back I expect to see you packed and ready to travel. Back to your office. Then I will find some way, God only knows how, of getting you off the books.'

'I am not going. Not until the job is done.'

'Don't argue with me, Air Mechanic Shepherd. If I lift that telephone you will be under arrest for, I don't know, desertion in the face of the enemy for starters.'

'Then I'll state the defence right here. Deserting towards the enemy? Running away towards the shooting war? What sort of a case is that?'

Carberry showed a row of teeth like that of a shark. 'You still talk like a civilian. If your case did come into a court, that defence would get you shot out of hand. Just imagine all the worthy gentlemen shining their arses behind official desks, lamenting that their importance to the war effort makes it impossible to join the dear boys in the thick of the fighting. They would have to put you in the deepest dungeon and throw away the key.'

Shepherd hunched his shoulders and stubbornly held his ground. According to his rough calculations Schiller should be back on patrol within two days. Two bloody days. Carberry had to be bluffing.

'Why are you still here? Before you write that letter, check when your German friend will be coming out. Then you can start packing.'

Shepherd raised his hands. The rope-burned palms were shrouded in yellow-stained bandages. 'And how do I explain these? To say nothing about the state of my face and my strapped-up ribs. Damn it, for your sake you have to keep me here until I look half-presentable. I reckon another week should do it. But I will write that letter. Right away. Permission to leave, sir.'

He stamped his tired legs to attention and waved a hand in a salute that was a cross between a boy scout and a hall porter waving down a taxi.

CHAPTER NINE

The U-boat section of OB14 tended to sleep from lunchtime onwards, as there was seldom anything left to decipher or to check or to refer back by the end of the morning. Tregarron felt a stir of unease as he saw Henrietta Talbot bearing down on him just before midday. He bitterly regretted having got involved with her and that idiot boy, Richard Shepherd. He missed the acrid comfort of life with Molly and this nonsense of Shepherd's would not bring back the wit that punctured his pomposity or the warmth of her body that repaired all wounds. Vengeance is mine, said the Lord. God, that was true. He was too old for this caper. While Talbot was in York he had lived and slept in the office dreading that someone would discover that files were missing. And he could not look Villers in the eye. No wonder the Secretary was still suspicious of him.

'Don't go to lunch too early. We are to have a visitation from the Lord High Admiral's bum-boy, Mr Villers himself. He wants a few words with the section. In half an hour.'

'Your language, Miss Talbot, is deplorable.' Tregarran wriggled uneasily. 'What is it about?'

Henrietta laughed at him. 'Stop worrying, Bart, it's not about you-know-what. I think it's about that telegram from Zimmermann. There have been a lot of big-wigs coming and going between here and the FO. All of them with that stiff-upper-lip, M'God-it's-too-good-to-be-true look about their faces.'

'The Zimmermann telegram had nothing to do with us.'

'No, but if it brings the Americans into the war there will be enough kudos about for some to splash over peasants like us.'

Tregarron waved a summary of merchant ship sinkings at her. 'Don't count your chickens. I think that Jerry has decided that he does not have to worry about the Yanks joining in. There are 3,000 miles of water between them and us. If the sinkings go on at this rate the Americans will have to row over.'

Miss Talbot was right, Tregarron thought, as he watched Villers. The Secretary did look more than usual like a complacent seal with a barely suppressed air of triumph about him. But Villers always went about looking as though it was only by superhuman effort that he managed to contain the secrets struggling to escape from his bosom.

They were, Villers reminded them, the first line of defence against the U-boat and the Zeppelin. From the triangulation stations and the intercepted messages their Lordships depended on them for knowledge about where the enemy was lying and what he was going to do.

The man was pouring pap over them. It was nauseating.

But they were, Villers burbled on, part of a larger sphere. Here his audience pricked up its ears. They must be aware that through the efforts of the Department a vital telegram from the German Government had been deciphered. The contents of that message had been passed to the Americans in a manner that did not concern them, except that the security of OB14 and its work was unbroken.

True, the Americans had not yet declared war but he was authorized to say that President Wilson had recalled Congress to hear a message of importance on 2 April. The next few days were the most crucial of the war. If the Americans learned of the existence of OB14 they would suspect the telegram of being a British plant; if the Germans knew they would replace their code-books. Therefore the message from the Admiral was this: Well done, but take even greater care, no matter what the cost, to maintain the secrecy of what went on in OB14.

'The man is an idiot, that speech was an insult to every man who works in the Department,' Tregarron said.

'And to the women,' Henrietta said. 'Look out, we are going to get a special pat. He is coming over.'

Villers waved to them. 'I would like a word with you two. About this young man, Richard Shepherd. When are we supposed to see him again?'

'You have the doctor's certificate,' Henrietta said. 'There was a date on that.'

Villers rubbed his face in the palms of his hands. 'Yes, that doctor's certificate. Very adamant about his condition. Very odd. You see, I've had a letter … ' He looked sharply at Henrietta. 'You saw him in York. How did he look to you?'

'Terrible,' Henrietta said truthfully. 'Far worse than when he left us. I am not surprised that the doctor insisted on him having a long rest.'

'Oh.' Villers rubbed his face again. 'Did you by any chance see his parents?'

'Yes, I saw his mother. She was very distressed; in fact she was angry. And rather rude to me.'

'Who else was there?'

'A number of people. A friend of Richard's, a pilot in the Naval Air Service. And a lady friend of his … '

'A lady friend. My God, I thought he had had a breakdown because he blamed himself for the death of his fiancée. Off with the old, on with the new … '

'Mr Villers, I did not enquire about the relationship between the two but I gathered that the young woman was an acquaintance of long standing of both Richard and his late fiancée.'

Villers produced a letter. He gave it to Tregarron. 'Read it. I find these things sick-making. From a sick mind. Some crank with his knife out for Shepherd. One of the disadvantages of our job.'

'Of course,' Henrietta said. 'We all have that cross to bear.' She leaned over Tregarron's shoulder.

The letter was addressed to 'Admiralty Intelligence, Whitehall'. It started with the letters crooked, almost childish, but as the message went on the anger of the writer overcame the clumsy attempt at a pretended uneducated hand. By the end of the message the words were written in an excellent copperplate hand.

Sir, I want to tell you about the goings on of one of your clerks, a fellow called Richard Shepherd. It is disgraceful what he gets up to while his betters gets killed out in france. How is it a fit young man like him can idle away his time at home in York. He is the talk of the town. It is a disgrace. Now he has taken up with the whooer he used to live with although his intended, a charming gel, was murdered by a Boche U-boat only a month ago. He was strutting round the town with his whooer Elsa Dolli, the actress as was, although she is besmirching a good name calling herself Mrs Cordle these days. That is a lie. Jack Cordle would never marry the likes of her not after her being Shepherds kept whooer. He has taken her on again. They was walking through the town as bold as brass, arm in arm, kissing in the railway station in full view of everyone. And why is he allowed to pretend to be an airman? How is it that a clerk in Whitehall is allowed to wear the uniform of the boys fighting to preserve our homes and liberties? With the girl he was to wed not cold in her grave.

In the name of justice and common humanity you should stop this man spitting on his fiancée's grave.

Pro Patria

Henrietta shuddered. 'Ugh, it's dirty. It's like looking into a cesspit.'

'For a schoolmistress you have a surprisingly wide field of expression, Miss Talbot,' Tregarron said. 'All anonymous letters are the same, the product of a sick mind.'

'Well, that's as maybe,' Villers said retrieving the letter. 'I'm not responsible for the feller's mind or Shepherd's morals. Somebody's got it in for him. But what is this nonsense about him wearing an airman's uniform.'

Tregarron said quickly, 'He was probably wearing his uniform. He is a lieutenant. You know how obtuse civilians can be about uniforms.'

Villers pursed his lips, glancing sharply at Tregarron as he got up to go. 'It's a damn funny business, Tregarron, damn funny. We'll sit on this. But you tell Master Shepherd that if he is not back here at work in the next seven days I want him here for a medical board.'

'That's it then, the game's up,' Tregarron said to Henrietta, trying to keep the relief out of his voice. 'There will be the devil to pay when they see him. How do you get two black eyes recovering from nervous exhaustion.'

'We are not done yet. Schiller should be on patrol within a couple of days. I'll check the I. file. That damned girl should have written again by now.'

'If your Intelligence section lived up to their name they would have had something to say to you by now about the way you go rooting about in their files.'

'I'm only the lidy wot tidies up the piper,' Henrietta snapped bitterly in a mock cockney accent. 'Jolly good show and all that. Carry on, Talbot. If I am to be a filing clerk, then I will be a conscientious one. Coming to lunch?'

'You saved my neck, mate, an' nobody ever said Shag Miller welshed on a debt,' Miller said, pumping rum fumes over Shepherd. He looked better than he was, Shepherd thought. There was only a piece of plaster over his broken nose but he would get a shock when he tried to bend over.

'Look in my paybook, mate,' Miller gasped, reeling against his locker. 'Told you this job was bloody dangerous, didn' I?' Carefully he lowered himself on to his bunk. 'Look in the paybook. Should be an address. Got it? Nah then, I 'ad a hundred quid off you. Thought I'd pinched it, did'nya? Not true, mate. It was an investment. For us to buy our way outa this mob. Ship to Aussie. Listen. In case summat happens to me. Two days' time after nine o'clock at night you go to the Keelie's Rest. Near the fish quay, anybody'll tell you where it is. Ask for Jake Padham. Tell him who sent you. There'll be two sets of papers, identity cards, discharge books, the lot. Yours is in the name o' Shelton, Paul Shelton. Twenty-five quid in the hand it'll cost. Your ship should be leaving within two days. Any longer than that, tell him nothing doing.'

He fell back exhausted and was asleep and snoring before Shepherd had left for Carberry's office. He had been told he could use it to call Henrietta while Carberry was visiting Alec Jervis.

He was unable to get in touch with Henrietta or Tregarron, and he guessed that they were lunching together. To kill time he wandered out on to the flying field. A big Coastal-class blimp, C75, had dropped in to repair water leaks in both Sunbeam engines. He felt frustrated, angry at the way things had suddenly started closing in on him. Carberry wanting him to go, Miller's talk about deserting, and why had Henrietta failed to confirm when Schiller was due out? It had to be soon.

Petty Officer Riggs called to him. 'Where the hell is the Old Man? We have trouble on the way. I've just had a tip that there are two coppers at Howden asking for your mate Miller. They are on the way here.'

Shepherd swore under his breath. Miller would never believe that he had not told the police. Especially after this morning. 'Carberry has gone to see the minesweepers. Something new he wants to try on the next patrol. He won't be back until late … '

Riggs gave him a funny look. 'That man is going to kill himself. Why can't he let the young 'uns have a go. And you aren't much help. He's been a damned sight worse since you came.'

Shepherd stared at the big nacelle of the Coastal. Plenty of room there. 'It's hard luck on Miller, getting picked up. Mr Dutton is going to be mad at losing a wireless operator.' The pilot of the Coastal was walking towards them. Shepherd said, 'Could you persuade him to take Miller along? For experience. Carberry might be able to sort something out if Miller was still free. He could get a sudden posting … '

Riggs grinned. 'Leave it to me. You get Miller here inside ten minutes. They are doing a long recce with a couple of light cruisers. As far as the Texels, so they'll be glad of a relief dogsbody. And the pilot was talking about going in to East Fortune on the way back. Convenient place for Miller to start his leave. Get him.'

Miller took a lot of persuading. He wanted to start running. And be picked up within two hours, Shepherd said. If he went in the Coastal they would simply say he was flying. The police would wait at Cleveland Hall. No one knew that the pilot was intending to see a friend at East Fortune on the way back. Miller would be in Scotland before the police knew he was missing. He went.

The policeman was in plain clothes, an elderly detective sergeant, accompanied by a local uniformed sergeant. Air Mechanic Miller was flying. The CO was away. The Deputy CO was flying. He showed Riggs a photograph. That was Miller. He was satisfied. He could wait. That was one of the things you learned in police work. Waiting.

He left the following day when there was no point in waiting. Carberry had returned the previous night in a foul temper. Nobody told him about Miller and the police until Riggs mentioned it just before the morning parade. He rang Howden for the Coastal's ETA. Howden wanted to know what it had to do with him. The Coastal had been scouting ahead of the cruisers when three seaplanes attacked. They had set 170,000 cubic feet of hydrogen alight. There were no survivors. Howden had not realized that Carberry was involved. No one had told them Miller was aboard.

'You can forget your stunt,' Carberry said when Shepherd joined him after the parade. They had to test-fly the new engine before going on patrol at midday. 'The Navy does not want to know about crafty U-boat captains. No one is going to admit that a German naval officer could outsmart British naval officers. They are going to do it their way. And if they did not tell me to mind my own business it was because I did not get a chance to state my interest.'

'Let me go to see Alec. He will listen to me.'

'Get your ouija board out. He's dead. Blown overboard by a mine. It's an occupational hazard of minesweeping. They got him out of the hoggin alive but the exposure was too much for him. He was not a fit man. It's like a bloody pantomine now. There's a snotty young lieutenant acting in command with a dozen hard-nosed trawler skippers under him. He doesn't know his arse from his elbow and he could not care less for your ideas about mines. He has an expert. The solution of the new fully-patented Delay Action Mine Sinker is in the hands of the mine experts from Mount Vernon. They have sent up a twenty year old to get one of the mines and take it apart. He's wetting his nappies waiting.'

'But they are no different from any other mine. It is the way they are dropped.'

'Save your breath. Our expert knows that after the next attack he will be either a hero or a greasy scum floating on the surface. He has screwed his nerve up to accept this and he does not want to hear anything that might deflect him. He is beyond hope.'

'They always take an NCO with them. Can't we get at his man? They usually have their feet on the — '

'You are a civilian, Shepherd, a stupid, logical, bloody civilian. Yes, he has a CPO with him. Twenty years on mines, man and boy. And where the orficer goes, he goes. And if the orficer says, "Lasso that mine," he lassoes the mine. It's the Navy way, you bloody civilian. And don't knock it or I'll kick your bloody arse from here to Whitehall.'

'So, it looks as though I had better stay. At least long enough to see Will Dolli. With your permission, sir.'

Carberry scowled at him. 'I do not see anything humorous about two gallant if misguided men killing themselves and putting an entire crew at risk. But I didn't have the benefit of your broad education. What the hell can Will Dolli do?'

'Those minesweepers were his trawlers. He had them built. And their captains were his skippers. The Navy has them for the duration. They have commandeered their brains and their seamanship but their souls were not on offer. If there is a clash between the Navy way and Dolli's way they will do what Will Dolli tells them to do.'

Carberry shook his head, staring open-mouthed at Shepherd. 'God almighty, you are a menace. Damn it, man, you'd subvert the entire Service to suit your own ends. I suppose you are on our side.' He laughed bitterly. 'I wonder. Our side, your side versus Schiller, is losing hands down. You set a trap for the man. We lost three ships, several hundred men and women and a few children. And your fiancée. So you decide to run the action yourself. We lost an airship, that Zero. We lost Mr Dutton's Zero and his mechanic. The aerodrome has been shelled. Your pal Miller goes missing with four experienced airshipmen and one Coastal-class blimp. You are a one-man disaster area, Shepherd.'

'I still think our only hope is Will Dolli.'

'All right. After the patrol. You can have thirty-six hours. Not a minute longer, is that clear ... ? Well, what are you waiting for, a medal?'

A gust of rain lashed against the shuttered windows. Beibedecke stirred in his sleep and rolled on to his back. The clock in his brain told him it was time to go. The girl beside him wriggled closer, but when he made no move she went back to sleep. The rain pattered on the roof, trickled along gutters and spouted out of leaking drainpipes.

It was music, Beibedecke thought, better than Beethoven. There was no chance of Tommi's night bombers disturbing them tonight. He would have to find a room like this in Kiel. Or Heligoland. Drowsily his eyes took in the blackened beams high in the ceiling with rosettes carved in the joints; the heavy curtains; the big English armchair by the stove; the glint of firelight on polished wood and silver; the luxury of space and silence.

You had to live in a U-boat to appreciate this. The days in a cramped iron box; the everlasting drip-drip of condensation and flaking cork chippings; the stench of thirty men on restricted water breathing the same air for ten hours or more; cold iron; and the glare of bare electric light-bulbs night and day on standard shipyard paint. And Schiller.

The smell of real coffee mingled with the girl's perfume as he breathed in the spaciousness of the room. Space, room to move, to think, be alone with your thoughts. In UC62 even Schiller did not have that. That coffee ... His dry mouth salivated. He had looted it from an American ship. The one with the newspaper headline that set Schiller off with his treacherous talk about losing the war. With all his experience the man did not realize that in the close community of a U-boat the captain was the essence of the crew's spirit. Perhaps he did and did not care. The man had lost his nerve.

Very few Americans would reach Europe ... alive. And he, Hugo von Beibedecke, would be out there sinking them. Coffee. There would be all the coffee he could drink. His hand stroked the girl's rounded belly. She reacted immediately but he pushed her away. 'More coffee. I may as well get my share of it before you squander it on the rest of the flotilla.'

That was unfair. She knew better than that. She crawled over him, letting her nipples tease the hair on his chest, a provocative twitch of her crotch over his flaccid genitals. She stayed there as his penis began to harden. He pinched her bottom.

'He'll keep, now you have woken him up. First the coffee.'

Her rounded buttocks swayed in the glow from the stove as she minced her way into the kitchen. It was a pity he could not move her to Kiel. But there would be problems with Security even though she was half-German. And it was too near home to risk making a fuss. There was always another room, another girl. Maybe it was as well he was moving. After the horrors of his second trip he had been moved to mention marriage while he was drunk. She had never referred to it but you could not be too careful.

He wondered if Schiller knew. It would be better if he was not told until after this last patrol. If it had not been for sickness and a couple of accidents Schiller would have done his last patrol. The fool, it would never occur to him that his First Officer was reporting on him. The man was a menace. His nerves were in shreds. He ought to be grateful. Plenty of captains would jump at the chance of a summer in the Baltic as instructing officer. One more patrol.

It was amusing the way the girl had got the wrong end of the stick. She must be fond of him. She really thought that Schiller was kicking him out. Instead he was getting the Atlantic boat. Schiller? If he did not take the instructor's job he could stay on minelayers until his nerves led him into making one mistake too many. But it would not do any harm to let the girl go on thinking that. She would see that Schiller's stab in the back became local gossip. And those in the know would look at what happened to Schiller and think twice about crossing Hugo von Beibedecke.

What was the lout doing now? Copulating with one of the whores in the Officers' House? Drunk for a certainty. Standing on the sea wall pissing over the boats moored below? One of these days he would fall in.

'Are you in trouble? Or is the ceiling more attractive than me?' She was kneeling by the bed holding a cup and the coffee pot. The loosely-belted silk wrap had slid off her shoulders, exposing most of one breast. The fabric seemed to be suspended on the other nipple. She really was a delightful thing. It was a pity he had to go in an hour ... or two.

'I was thinking about Schiller, drunk as usual, boring the pants off everyone in the officers' club. He has a new scheme to break Tommi's convoys. Admiral sur Zee Schiller.'

The coffee was hot, sweet and strong. No need to hold it with one hand and brace yourself with the other. It burned his lips.

'*Ach!* Too hot. We shall have to find something to do while it cools. Something to warm ... '

Her hands reached out to stroke him. She giggled as the robe slipped over the restraining nipple.

When he had gone she sat for a while thinking about him and Schiller. He was not a bad sort. Dull. But he had made things easier for her. Damn that bastard Schiller for spoiling things. The drunken sot ought to fall down and break an arm. They would never get a replacement at four hours' notice. Then Beibedecke could take command. Then he might stay. Picking up a new man was always difficult. She did not want the police sniffing round. He had to be a U-boat officer. They were not all gentlemen like Beibedecke.

She took a picture postcard, ran a fingernail into a prepared slit and opened it like a lettercard. Carefully in minute letters she wrote out the scheme Schiller was proposing. She added sailing dates, numbers of U-boats thought to be missing, flotilla gossip. Who was being promoted, who was getting a command or a transfer. She did not know what use the British made of such trivia but it paid well. After resealing the two halves together she wrote a short note to her aunt in Amsterdam on the back assuring her that she was well, looking forward to the summer and seeing her again. For the first time in four months she did not mention Beibedecke or UC62.

The rain had stopped when she went out to post the card and the sky was clearing, but it was cold and wet. There were few people about. No moon, but that would not stop the night bombers from looking for U-boats and the canal.

She moved slowly through the darkened town after she had posted the card. There was plenty of time. She knew the sailing time of UC62 and she knew Schiller's habits better than the man himself. He would be drawn to the waterfront like iron filings to a magnet. He would mount the parapet to piss into the sea. She had watched him often enough. Perhaps tonight there would be no one about.

'T4 here, give me the Duty Officer, Room 156, OB14.'

'Duty Officer.' Shepherd raised his thumb to Carberry. Suddenly he could feel the anxiety and frustration falling away. He knew that everything was coming right. 'Henry, I got your telegram. What is the panic? Has Schiller sailed?'

'Villers is on the warpath. Somehow he got to hear about that wireless man getting killed. Miller. He went through your records. You did not tell us you had been a signals lieutenant in the Territorial Army, but I suppose it was just as well. We were not acting when he threw it at us. Poor old Bart is practically under open arrest … '

'What about Schiller?'

'UC62 cleared the coast an hour ago. Two of them. U75 is with her. It may be a coincidence but we do not think so … And don't change the subject. What are we going to do about Villers?'

On the rare occasions when he was asked what his job was, Frederick Jamieson Villers would make a deprecatory cough that he was only 'the Old Man's secretary, a bit of a plumber, oiling the cog wheels, y'know'. Confusing the questioner, hiding behind a camouflage of mock self-denigration, ignoring his self-appointed role of administrator to OB14. He thought Admiral Hall the most brilliant man alive and that it was his privilege to see that the machine the Admiral had created worked smoothly. He did it well.

He looked like a seal, rounded rather than fat, sleek in the formal dark suitings he always wore in town. His complexion was more sallow than golden. He wore a spiky moustache and

181

his thin blond hair was brushed close to his pink scalp on either side of the central parting. Like a seal he looked harmless. Only those who came or appeared to come between him and the Director of Naval Intelligence knew the viciousness of his bite.

And today he was in a mood to bite. The unease he had felt about young Shepherd's disappearance was crystallizing into an unpleasant certainty. At any minute the young fool would be uncovered doing something stupid. Something that would expose OB14, something that would make Frederick Villers look a fool. The thought made him dab his forehead with a silk handkerchief. He knew only one sure remedy. Find the bastard and shut him up. Any convenient way.

He opened the file again. What could he be up to? A pre-war commission in the Territorial Army did not mean much. A few evenings in a drill hall and two summer camps. No wonder he wanted to get out of the Department. Most of his companions at those camps had given their lives. He picked up the anonymous letter. Hate. The letter reeked of it. And something else. The Dolli woman, whatever she called herself, was involved. Wherever she was, Shepherd would not be far away. Well, he had a machine that could find out and settle once and for all whether she was married and to whom. He passed the order to his secretary. He wanted results today. And as an afterthought he told her to get him Mrs Cordle, the Cordles of York, on the telephone.

There was usually some truth in anonymous letters. He would work on the assumption that the writer was telling what he, or she, thought was the truth. Shepherd would not be the first young man to throw his hat at the wrong sort of woman. Or to be relieved at release from a marriage contract. It fitted. A few weeks' drink and debauchery would explain the strong language that doctor had used.

But Miss Talbot had been with him for a day. A schoolmistress with her background, would she be capable of judging the relationship between a man and his doxy?

The telephone rang. Lady Cordle was on the line.

'Whitehall? What is it, have you got some news about my son?'

'I am sorry to have raised your hopes, Lady Cordle. I'm afraid that we have no new information. I am endeavouring to trace the whereabouts of your son's widow.'

'I do not know who you are, sir, but I will not have this impertinence. My son was not married and therefore even if he was dead he could not have a widow. Good day.'

Desperately Villers racked his brain for some excuse to keep the conversation going. 'It is most important, Lady Cordle, for us to find this young woman. Where an officer has been killed we have a responsibility to the children.'

'My son was not married.' The call ended with a decisive click that made Villers glad he had not given his name. But unless he was mistaken there had been a tiny pause before the line went dead. A child. Suppose the Cordles had been left without an heir? Now he remembered that this Elsa Dolli had a son. Someone had sniggered over it. Suppose her story was true. In wartime young men did strange things.

Villers rubbed his face in his hands. He could feel a weapon being forged, and it was time to crack the whip over those people seeking the material needed to complete it.

CHAPTER TEN

It was difficult to tell where Will Dolli's house began. The entrance on the fish quay led off the cobblestones into a high-roofed shed draped with nets and cordage and smelling strongly of tar. Otter boards, fish boxes, dan buoys, spars, a spare winch drum and an assortment of navigation lamps merged into the gloom beyond the curtain of nets. A wide stairway of varnished yellow pine, black with age, led up to a gallery surrounding three sides of the shed. On the gallery were a couple of offices, empty apart from a couple of elderly women and a man in a dark blue reefer-jacket with the right sleeve pinned to his chest.

More stairs, steeper now, twisting upwards as the house climbed up the hill behind the quay. Stair carpet clipped in place by triangular section slats of pine in brass clips. Pictures on the wall. Ships. Sepia-tinted photographs of trawlers, drifters, a two-masted sailing ship, waves breaking over a hulk on the wrong side of the North Tyne pier.

The stairway came out into a long living-room, bow-framed windows overlooking the river, pitch-pine varnished walls studded with more photographs of ships, an oil painting of a tea clipper running for the Horn with everything stowed apart from a couple of storm jibs and a mizzen. Over the mantelpiece in the place of honour was a painting of Will Dolli's wife. A semi-circle of armchairs ringed the big coal fire.

Although it was only mid morning two paraffin laamps hanging from the ceiling beams brought a sparkle from the polished wood, the crosed narwhal tusks on the wall and the knick-knacks strewn over every flat surface. Will Dolli and the two skippers with him, burly thick-set men in blue reefer-jackets and roll-neck navy-blue jerseys, were smoking pipes and drinking rum. He filled glasses for Carberry and Shepherd as he introduced his men.

The rum was like treacle. That, the heat from the fire and

the pipe-smoke made Shepherd's eyes water. Carberry refilled his pipe as Dolli topped up their glasses.

Dolli lifted his own glass in salute and said. 'Let's have it. What do you want us to do and when?'

Carberry started to speak but the trawler owner cut him short. 'Not you, Admiral. We've had a bellyful of the Navy. The *Three Brothers* went down last night trying to tow one of those mines above the low-water mark. Blew the stern off. Your lieutenant and his mine experts went down with her. And Bertie Simpson, smartest lad we ever had. Let the young fella tell us what he wants.'

Shepherd sipped his rum, trying to collect his thoughts. It had been a long day already. Tregarron had roused him before midnight. UC62 was sailing west in company with U75 and there was an indication that the two were going to work together. There were enough intercepts to plot her course accurately and there was a long message to be deciphered. He had copies of them at his feet. Tregarron, angry at the way Villers was regarding him as the villain of the piece, decided that he would rather be hung for a sheep. He had boarded a northbound express at King's Cross. Two hours later he had stepped from the northbound at Doncaster and crossed the footbridge to return on the waiting south-bound express. Shepherd had been on the footbridge to take the night's intercepts. Characteristically Tregarron had reminded Shepherd that up to now there had been no hard evidence of any illegality. But if they were caught with the transcripts they could be shot.

He looked at the waiting fishermen, realizing how many of his 'facts' were hunches surmised from inadequate data, theories derived from reading between the lines and the pricking of his thumbs. All they really knew was that two minelaying U-boats were on their way to the east coast. And now he was going to ask these men to risk their lives, and their reputations, on his inspired guesses.

'There is no new secret mine,' he said. 'Only a U-boat captain using his eyes and common sense and prepared to take a chance. He moves into position in the War Channel and waits for the sweepers to come out. Once they have passed him he goes across the Channel and back laying a double row of mines between the sweepers and the convoy. Those UC-class boats can carry thirty-eight mines, they have two 500-cm torpedo tubes and an 85-mm deck gun ... '

'Aye, that's as maybe but what do you want us to do?' Dolli repeated.

'I want to convince the U-boat captain that his mines have been swept, so that he will try to lay more and while doing that he will hit one of his own. Mines have no respect for battle flags. To do this I want you to steam along the line of mines pretending to sweep and destroy them. Chuck hand-grenades overboard, one for each mine. Then turn and carry on as though you were doing a sweep.'

'Twice through a bloody minefield,' Dolli said.

Shepherd nodded. 'We'll spot the mines from the air for you. We'll put a flare over each one.'

Carberry butted in to say, 'There will be three of us, two spotting mines while the other looks for the U-boats. We don't know how the two U-boats will operate, if indeed they are going to work together.'

They ignored him. The Geordie skipper said, 'What d'ye want tae play wi' grenades for? Nasty bloody things.'

'They'll be listening to you on their underwater listening gear, their hydrophones. We'll blow a real mine first to deafen the operator. They'll take the thump of a grenade for the real thing.'

'How do you know he'll be there to lay fresh mines?' Dolli asked.

'At four knots' underwater speed he can't go very far even if he wanted to. Charging across the Channel at full power will have exhausted his batteries. But he wants to be there. This chap has bigger ideas than just mining a couple of ships. He expects the convoy to break up and scatter. Then he can use his torpedoes and, with luck, surface to shoot his deck gun.'

Suddenly Dolli began to laugh, rocking backwards and forwards, slapping his huge hands on his knees. 'By damn, boy, we'll do it. Without the bloody Navy. We'll do it. Three drifters ... '

'They've no sweeping gear,' one of the skippers said.

186

'They don't need it,' Shepherd said. 'That is the idea. Not to sweep up the mines. You ought to stream something in case they get a good look at you although we hope the third airship will keep them on the bottom.'

'It makes sense to me, lad,' Dolli said. 'It sounds as though you have thought it out. When and where?'

Shepherd shuffled his papers. His heart seemed to be thumping indecently loudly in the quiet room. This was the crunch. If he was wrong they could be playing charades outside one harbour while the U-boats were organizing their ambush somewhere else. He could feel their eyes on him.

They knew what it was like. Dolli had been mined and the other two had been torpedoed. Each of them had waited through long hours to be rescued, had seen their companions die. They knew the North Sea at its most cruel. Would they ever forgive him if while they waited elsewhere their friends were killed somewhere else? Because of his mistake.

If he gave way to his imagination they would sit here for a week. Facts. They had good intercepts. The tracks were converging on one place. He pointed to the chart in front of him. 'Here,' he said. 'This is the most probable place. High water is at 06.15. Jerry will expect to see the sweepers going off at first light. We have to start looking as soon as the minesweepers have passed. If they come back you'd better think of a good excuse.'

Dolli stretched and walked to the window overlooking the harbour. He opened a window. The wind came in like a knife.

'Glass is going down,' he rumbled. 'Dirty night tonight. There'll be a nasty sea running.'

'Squalls. Snow showers according to the met. forecast,' Carberry said. 'Blowing half a gale by tomorrow evening.'

'Hey up,' the skipper with the Geordie accent said. 'You'll not be there, then. Your gasbags are damn all good in a bit o' wind.'

'There is no point in us turning up if we cannot hold our postion,' Carberry said. 'We can't help you if we are blown halfway to Germany every time we zigzag. Apart from that there is nothing to beat a blimp for escort duty. We have never lost a single ship.'

The trawlerman sucked in a lungful of smoke and spat accurately into the fire. 'Mebbe. Ah've hord yor lads taakin' aboot this afore now, hinny. Ye niver lost a ship when you were there but how many went down when you should hev bin there and worn't?'

'We'll let you know in plenty of time,' Carberry said doggedly. 'I will telephone the SNO before you cast off.'

'An' who'll tell the U-boats?' Dolli said. 'We'll need to be there between five an' six. If you can't get there we'll have to take a chance ... '

Shepherd let out a startled squeak of protest but Dolli waved it down. 'Shut up, boy. How do you think mines get swept. We'll be using drifters. No draft, we sail over them.'

Shepherd stared at him, realizing that he had started something he could not stop. He imagined the drifters sailing down the lines of anchored mines, pitching up and down in the short rough seas off the estuary. He shuddered.

'What about the convoy, the escort? Can you get them to hold off long enough ... ?'

The skippers laughed. Dolli's eyes were twinkling. 'Don't worry your head about them. They'll have terrible trouble getting them ships closed up. I wouldn't put it past one of them auld relics to break down in the main channel.'

He refilled their glasses. The three of them stood up in front of the fire. For a moment Shepherd thought he was going to propose some stirring Scandiwegian toast, but he only tilted his glass briefly in their direction.

'We've all a lot to do. 'Til tomorrow.'

As they went down the twisting staircase Dolli held Shepherd back.

'What's up betwixt you an' that lass o'mine? She were here yesterday wi' the bairn crying her eyes out. Y'know I don't remember her ever crying afore.'

Shepherd shook his head. 'She seems to have disappeared. I enquired at the hospital and at Cleveland Bay. I was hoping to find her here. We are going to be married,' he announced.

Dolli shook his head gloomily. 'What about the bairn? She's not married, you know, for all there's times she takes it

188

into her head to wear a wedding ring. Yon fella Cordle wasn't the marrying kind. Not for the likes of Elsa.'

'I guessed that but it makes no difference to me. We should have married before the war.'

Dolli chuckled. 'And have her give up the stage an' settle for warming your slippers by the fire? She might find the prospect more pleasing now. Ach, she's too damn stubborn for her own good. She wouldn't wed you then an' mark my words she'll not marry you now. There's too much of her father in her.' He poked Shepherd with a finger like a baulk of timber. 'Like me, no damn good. You know what I was doing when her mother died? God curse the day. I was climbing up a trollop i' Bergen like a salmon leaping in the spring. By God I have a feeling in my bones. Whatever that gel is up to will do no good to either you or me.'

Carberry was waiting for him by the Crossley. Shepherd started it on the crank. As he got in Carberry said, 'You have natural ability, Shepherd. Stay in the Navy and become an admiral. People will kill themselves for you. If I had asked those men to sail through a minefield twice in a half a gale they'd have thrown me in the harbour. As I deserved. It takes a bastard like you to get away with it.'

Shepherd thought he was having a nightmare. He had barely closed his eyes when the door was whipped open. Somebody was shouting, 'All hands, rise and shine. Jump to it. All hands to the picket ropes on the double.'

The hut was shaking, windows rattling, sand and pebbles peppered the roof. The noise of the wind was an inhuman scream that curdled the blood. The weather forecasters had been wrong. The gale promised for the following afternoon had arrived.

As Shepherd forced his way out of the door into the wind he gasped for breath, lost his balance and was blown down against the brick supports. The wind racing in from the northeast was a live monster tugging and buffeting everything in its path. Ice particles stung like needles and it was hard to breathe. A two-gallon petrol can hurtled by his head as Shepherd pulled himself up and a man cried out behind him. A flying branch raked his face as he struggled to join the stream of torches and hurricane lamps heading for the airships.

The wind was screaming across the tree-tops, pouring over them like a waterfall. The envelope of SS 19 jerked and twisted as it struggled to escape from the extra cable tying it down. A white blur of a face looked up from the two men hauling at a cable.

'Shepherd. Grab that Scrulex anchor. Just behind you. Screw it in as far as it will go.' It was Carberry and Riggs wrestling with an extra cable snaking up into the darkness over the envelope.

Flashing his torch around, Shepherd looked for something like an anchor. There was a thing like a three-foot-long corkscrew. He picked it up.

'Don't stand there looking at the bloody thing. Screw it into the ground. Not there, a yard or more this way ... '

As he screwed in the anchor the two men slowly backed towards him. When he had everything but the eye screwed into the ground they slipped the cable through the eye and lashed it. SS 19 was now enmeshed in a cat's-cradle of cables that hauled the envelope down on top of the nacelle.

Carberry plucked at one of the ropes. He pointed over Shepherd's shoulder, shouting above the noise of the wind, 'Far end. The Zero is getting away. Z42.'

The trees made an effective shelter for SS 19 and Dutton's Zero, but as the wind veered the tail of Z42 had been exposed to the gale roaring through a thin part of the wood. Now the envelope was bouncing like an enormous rubber elephant. The wind pouring over the tree-tops slammed it down on to the nacelle. It bounded up, twisting as the gale caught the tail and pulled it further out of the shelter of the trees. The nacelle lifted. Then the envelope bounced down again, slamming the nacelle over on to its side, straining the guys. Before it could bound up again a cable snaked over the tailplane while half a dozen men took the end of the rope round a tree. The tail shook like a rat in a terrier's mouth. The tree with the cable round it suddenly bowed and ripped out of the sodden ground, flailing through the surrounding men.

190

The Zero swung through ninety degrees into wind. The tail rose. Cables snapped as it reared up vertically, tearing away the aft car suspension. A fistful of wind slammed it back on to the ground. The bottom fin and rudder, a crumpled mess of broken timber and torn fabric the size of a barn door, broke away. A broken control cable coiled round a man and dragged him across the clearing. Two men ran to his aid but the wreckage sailed on to slam them against a hut wall. The handling party ran back as the envelope bounded up and down, each twist flinging cables outwards like scythes.

Carberry thumped Shepherd on the shoulder. 'We'll have to rip it before we lose it altogether. Come on.'

The envelope bounced up, dragging the nacelle further from the trees. A rope parted and whipped Shepherd's legs from under him. As he struggled to his feet he saw Carberry running ahead of him, and he started to chase after him. The nacelle was still held by the forward suspension cables but the mooring ropes had nearly gone. If they were in the nacelle when the last rope went, the battering as the car was dragged across the clearing and into the trees would put them in hospital for the rest of the war.

The envelope was coming down again. Carberry had his hand on the nacelle. This time the bounding envelope was sure to snap the last mooring rope. The nacelle slammed back, jolting Carberry off the footrail. It leapt sideways. He rolled away from the keel just before it smashed into the ground.

The gasbag dropped on Shepherd, flattening him on the ground. The noise of the wind went, replaced by the noise of the envelope. It was like something alive, creaking, groaning, rustling as it squashed the breath out of him. His torch was still on, a sliver of silver in the blackness two feet ahead of him.

The weight came off his chest, and the beam shot out to illuminate the nacelle as the gasbag bounded up again. This would be their last chance. He pulled himself up, sucking air into his tortured lungs. Ten steps, that was all. Carberry was down by the rail, hopelessly tangled in broken cables. The nacelle quivered as the tangled ropes lifted. Shepherd jumped for the pilot's cockpit. As he tumbled over the side he felt the nacelle snatched upwards. It checked, jumped up a foot as the cable slipped. He groped for the rip-cord among the tangle of cables. It was special, coiled with red twine, distinguishable by sight or touch. Pulling it ripped a panel in the top of the gasbag fourteen feet long. Useful now or after a bad landing but not a repeatable mistake at 1,000 feet.

Another snatch at the mooring cable slapped him down into the bottom of the cockpit, still holding the bundle of ropes. A double jerk. Nothing. They were starting to move across the clearing at the speed of the wind. The nacelle dangled vertical, held only by the front cables. His questing fingers found the rip-cord. He yanked it hard.

The nacelle fell ten feet with a crash that slammed him back into the bottom again. Now the deflated envelope was a sail dragging the car across the clearing at 30mph. Until it hit the first hut. The impact shot Shepherd the length of the nacelle through bracing wires and struts until his head lost the argument with the engine bearers. He was knocked out.

He woke up in the sick-bay. Hoskins, the sick-bay orderly, had thrown a bucket of ice-cold water over him. Petty Officer Riggs leant over him. 'You all right, old son? That was a hell of a crack you got.'

He struggled to sit up. A fist the size of a small ham pushed him back none to gently. 'But that is nothing to what you are going to get if you have got the Old Man into trouble. Who the bloody hell are you and what are you doing down here?'

The fist slapped him back on to the stretcher as he tried to sit up stuttering his rank and number.

'Balls, pull the other one, mate. You 'aven't been in the Andrew long enough to find your way to the heads. Bloody hell, you salute like you touches your hat ... when it comes to mind. Now you've got the Old Man in trouble with Whitehall ... '

Pushing the fist aside Shepherd rolled on to his feet. His legs almost gave way under him, and the pain of dozens of cuts as the dried blood cracked made him realize that his slacks and tunic had been cut to ribbons.

'What the hell do you mean, trouble with Whitehall?'

'The Old Man got a gale warning early on. Orders to get everything back to Howden. For shelter. When the Court of Enquiry sits they'll have that order in front of them. The

192

salt-water bastard at Howden will see to that. He hates the Old Man's guts ... '

'What Court of Enquiry? I don't know what the hell you are talking about.'

'Jesus wept! Get him out of my sight, Hoskins. You stupid civilian, you. When one of His Majesty's officers loses one of His Majesty's ships, be it sea or air, their Lordships instigates a Court of Enquiry to see why the poor sod did it. An' gawd knows why but we think it was on account of you. An' if we loses the Old Man on your account it 'ud be best for you to get orf the camp afore we catches you ... '

Shepherd grinned and flexed his sore muscles. 'Forget it, Mr Riggs. By tomorrow afternoon Mr Carberry and this station will be on top of the world. Oh my God, if the gale dies away. If we can fly at daybreak.'

Riggs' face was as black as thunder. 'We'll see about that when the time comes.' His voice rose to a bellow. 'Meanwhile, your Highness, get out of those damned rags, put on your number ones and report to Mr Carberry's office at the double. Come on, move yourself.'

The wind was dying away as he hurried round to Carberry's office. Starlight shone through a rent in the racing clouds and a faint radiance from the moon showed how thin they were. But there was rain in the wind and more to come once the gale had blown itself out. He wondered why Carberry wanted to see him so urgently. He needed sleep and they were due to take off in three hours. This was one stunt where they had to be in position before first light. And they would be one blimp short before they started. Even the weather was on Schiller's side.

There was a Rolls-Royce outside the door to the Flight Office. A long low tourer with the hood and side-screens up, the silver paint glinting dully in the starlight. And an armed sentry at the door. The rifle and fixed bayonet dropped to the parry.

'Shepherd?' It was Harris, a mechanic on the wrecked Zero.

'No, it's Kaiser Bill. Who the hell else would it be at this hour of the morning?'

'It's your fault, mate. They're all in there waiting for you.'

'Who?'

'The Old Man and some civvy … '

He did not have to go on. Shepherd knew only one civilian who would want to see him here at this hour. In a Rolls-Royce. Villers. He had been rumbled. Forewarned he marched up to Carberry's desk, ignoring the little man in the chair on his left, and saluted like a sergeant-major. Like the sergeant-majors he had seen in the theatre.

'There is no need for the music hall act, Shepherd, the game is up. Squadron Commander, put this man under close arrest immediately.'

Carberry stared at Shepherd. He nodded towards Villers. 'Do you know this man?'

'Nay, never set eyes on 'im,' Shepherd replied in a broad Yorkshire accent. 'What's 'e say ah've dun?'

'He claims that you are Lieutenant Richard Peter Shepherd, an interpreter lieutenant in the RNVR, a deserter from his post in Whitehall.'

'Bloody 'ell, beg pardon, sir. But who'd want to desert from a cushy job in Whitehall towards the enemy?'

'This is ridiculous, I demand that you arrest that man.'

Carberry ignored him. 'A deserter, Shepherd, is a man who leaves his post, wherever it may be, without orders and with no intention of returning to that post. If he intends to return he is entitled to plead that he was only absent without leave. Desertion in war is a very serious offence. Men have been shot for it. You can prove who you are?'

'Nay, not at two in t'morning, I can't. But it's up to 'im to prove I'm who 'e says I am. It's like I told you when I fust come here an' you said as you knew me. It's me cousin, well, second cousin, this gent is on about. There's money on 'is side o' the family. Not by rights, it isn't. Posh school, cushy job in Whitehall. There's no call fer him to desert to be a wireless operator. There's no bloody sense in't … '

Carberry brushed aside Villers' objection. 'It's a reasonable point, Mr Villers. What dreadful crime makes a man desert a pleasant office for an open cockpit above the North Sea? We are not pampered, Mr Villers. It is damned important work but there is nothing glamorous or exciting about six hours in the cold looking at the sea.'

Villers glared at him. 'This man is a member of a most secret department, the existence of which is unknown to the Germans. It has a very significant effect on the conduct of the war. This man has made numerous requests for a transfer to a fighting post, all of which have been turned down because of the risk of him being captured. A clever interrogator, a chance remark, might reveal our secret. I do not exaggerate when I say that such an event could cost us 10,000 casualties. You must place him under arrest.'

'We call them deaths, but then we know them.' Carberry drummed his fingers on his desk. 'And your part in this?'

Villers slid his card across the desk. 'As private secretary to Admiral Hall, Director of Intelligence, I am, *de facto*, the senior administrator.'

'A civilian.' Carberry sniffed, turning the card over and over between his fingers before turning to Shepherd. 'You will wait outside with the sentry, Shepherd. He has been given his orders. You will at all times remain within sight of the man until you are told to return.

'Now, Mr Villers, what the devil am I to do with you? You arrive here with no warrant, no authority and make allegations against one of my men. You are a civilian with no authority to order me to arrest one of my men. So far as I am concerned the man is a competent wireless operator and I do not have spare men available. We too play our part in this war. We know something about preventing casualties. No ship escorted by a blimp has ever been sunk by a torpedo. And I have a convoy awaiting me soon after dawn. You have five hours to produce something more substantial than you have produced so far. Otherwise Shepherd will be in his usual position in my airship. He happens to be my wireless operator. But ... '

He pulled open a drawer to take out a Webley .38 revolver. He broke the cylinder to load five cartridges. He closed it with a flourish and put the loaded gun on the desk in front of him.

'I understand your predicament. You have my word of honour that should we fall into German hands I will shoot him. Right. Now, if you don't mind you can send him back in to me as you go out. Good-night, sir.'

The sentry leaned his rifle against the wall, slapped his

arms around his shoulders and then tried to rub some life into his hands.

'Bloody cruel it is out here, mate. An' all on account o'you. Got a fag, mate.'

Lighting the cigarette cupped in his hands he nudged Shepherd in the ribs with a spare elbow.

'The toff is her father, the geezer in with old Carbers? You shoulda joined the real Andrew, mate. They keep 'em outside the dockyard gates. Now they've found you you might as well say "Hello" to the gel. She's in the back of the motor car with the kid. You might do worse … '

She was lighting a cigarette as he opened the door, the flame of her Tommy lighter illuminating the oval of her face. It was kind to her, hiding the lines, the shadowed eyes, the fingers stained brown, and firing the colour of her hair, curling from under the close-fitting cloche hat. Her earrings glittered in the shadows of the high-collared fur coat pulled up behind her head. One arm pillowed a small boy fast asleep.

'You look as though you are going to a first night,' he said breathlessly. 'Or an audition for the Lady of Shalott.'

She moved over, taking the child with her. He rested between them. Suddenly he knew how Villers had traced him. She drew heavily on the cigarette, and exhaled twin plumes of smoke through her nostrils before stubbing it out.

'I shall have to give up smoking. The family do not approve of such coarse habits. In public … '

'I've never objected to you smoking.'

'Richard, you never had the right to object to me doing anything … '

She smiled at him, and all the old fascination turned his guts to water. She had sold him to Villers for her equivalent of thirty pieces of silver, but she had only to snap her fingers and he would start running to her. However, he knew she was not going to snap her fingers.

'Don't be such a damned fool, Richard, we have no future together. There's twelve years between us and two different ways of living. As you observed I'm dressed for a first night. My last role in what I hope will be a record-breaking run. Jack and I take up residence with the Cordles in the morning.

196

I shall have the Dower House and he will be brought up as all the Cordles before him were. It's his birthright.'

'You'll go stark raving mad locked up with the hunting, shooting, fishing set.'

'Don't be melodramatic, Richard. We had our fun in a garret. It would not have lasted a second winter. You have a future, what about me? How would you choose, given the choice between living with the Cordles or going back to twice-nightly Rep? And let's face it, darling, I'm not a second Sarah Bernhardt ... '

'Is that why you told him?'

She blushed. One hand moved over to rest on his. 'I'm sorry, Richard. Your Mr Villers is not a nice man. He found out that Jack and I were married. Jack had flown over from France when he heard about the baby. We got a special licence and had one night together. He knew he was going to be killed sooner or later, and before he could tell his people he was dead. I kept quiet because I thought they would take the baby away from me. Your Mr Villers told them. A legitimate heir changes a lot when the family is as old as the Cordles. Then he told me what he could tell the Cordles about "our affaire". The cottage down in the bay. You lured from your key job just to be with me. It made a good story. Because of it the Cordles could have taken young Jack away from me. That was a risk I could not take. I'm sorry ... '

The door swung open. Villers said, 'Your commanding officer wants you back in the office. You fool, I think you will find that your juvenile antics are over. I cannot see Squadron Commander Carberry risking his career on your behalf.'

Shepherd did not hear everything. The soft unctuous voice told him he was a failure, he had made a fool of himself, he had lost Elsa and failed Henrietta and Tregarron. He threw himself out of the seat slamming Villers in front of him up against the hut. But the soft flabbiness of the man beneath his fists sickened him. It did not need the sentry's bayonet to make him let the man go. He put his head in the car again, touched his fingers to his lips and held them out to her.

'Goodbye, Elsa. I hope it works out for you and the boy. You will always find me ready if you need me.'

Carberry kept him standing in front of his desk while he cleared some of the pile of paper that had accumulated. Requisitions, leave-passes, promotions, fines, record sheets, a few splattered with red ink for drunkenness. An Operations Order – the only form Shepherd could recognize. Two blimps. Five names. Convoy patrol, Spurn to Flamborough.

Carberry looked up. 'Apparently you are as important as you always said you were. I did not believe you.' He looked at his watch. 'Better get your gear. I would like to be away within forty minutes. Mr Dutton can follow.'

Shepherd sighed with relief. 'Thank you, sir. I appreciate what you are doing. You'll not regret it. For a moment I thought you were sending me back to the office.'

'Shut up, Shepherd. You are everything that man said you were. A stupid, irresponsible idiot. You don't think he is taking you back to the office, do you? Pick up your work, be a good boy and don't rock the boat again … Oh God, you do. Now I know why this impossible stunt worked. You are so stupid you don't know what you have done … and what others have risked on your behalf. Your Mr Villers is going to put you in jail, Shepherd. You are an officer in the Royal Navy, you hold the King's Commission. You deserted your post, broke the Official Secrets Act and suborned officers, men and material essential to the conduct of the war for your own ends. Damn it, Shepherd, they'll lock the door and throw away the key. With me and your friends in cells on either side of you. So we are not doing it for you, Mr Shepherd, we are doing it for three little ships sailing twice through a minefield because you told the skippers it was important … '

As he spoke he strode round the room collecting things: a plotting board with a chart pinned to it, recognition signals for the day, helmet, goggles, three pencils, and a loaded revolver.

'And the other reason is a selfish one, to get me and your friends off the hook. You can rot in jail as far as I am concerned. It will teach you that a war that drowns 3,000 sailors a month has no place for your schoolboy vendetta. But a victory, a sunk U-boat, is something tangible. One planned successful sinking, two would be better, might be sufficient to keep our lords and masters away from our throats … and yours.'

198

CHAPTER ELEVEN

It was three in the morning before they got away. The moon had gone but there was some starlight shining through rifts in the cloud. The wind had backed round to the west, bringing with it the smell of rain. They walked SS 19 along the drive and stopped in the shelter of the trees to ballast up.

'Take off a bag, Riggs,' Carberry said. His hands went up. 'Hands off.' SS 19 remained solidly on the ground. The men on the nacelle stepped forward to hold it as another seven-pound sack of sand was dropped.

This time, as Carberry's hands went up in the air and the nacelle was released, the wheels lifted and settled rustling in the grass.

'Take her out, Mr Riggs. Down to the bottom hedge. She'll need a good run.'

The coxswain picked up his megaphone. 'Guy ropes, stand by. Bowmen, stern, take up the slack … '

Slowly the men pulled SS 19 out from the shelter of the trees and turned the bows towards the blackness that hid the seaward face of the Cleveland Hills.

Cloud Nineteen was still heavier than air, and the wheels rumbled through the rough grass, shock cord squealing as they hit ruts that the bulk of the envelope could not soften. Carberry would not sacrifice any more precious ballast. They were loaded to maximum weight. Two bombs, the rifle, Lewis gun and spare ammunition, a full load of petrol. He would fly it off like an aeroplane and keep it low as they flew through the hours of darkness to meet the drifters.

Carberry waited. The men hung on to the nacelle, heels digging into the turf as he ran the engine up to full power to burn oil off the plugs. A spark glittered at the far end of the field where a mechanic swung a hurricane lamp at the foot of a tree.

The handling party stepped back. Bow and stern lines free,

nacelle men clear, the engine speeded up to full power. SS 19 trundled off. Faster. The wheels smashed back after bouncing off a rut. Again, but softer as the envelope took the load. Carberry wound the elevator wheel back. The night was so dark and the swaying gasbag so large that the 100-hp engine sounded no louder than a farm tractor as the airship lifted, a silver bubble with a sting.

As the blimp turned gently to the south-east Shepherd morsed a routine airborne report to Howden hoping that no one was going to get the Captain up at this hour to report that the nutters from Cleveland Hall were doing convoy patrols in the dark.

Hastily he tuned in to the U-boat band. Someone was transmitting. The harsh note going on and on filled him with despair. Clever Dick Shepherd had made a balls of it. If he had been in the office that message would have been deciphered in minutes. Now it was just a stream of unintelligible rubbish. Because of him their grand scheme was going to be an almighty flop because they did not know where the U-boats were. Tyne, Tees, Wear or Humber?

If only Villers had not turned up they might have got something from Henrietta or Tregarron. Surely Schiller would need to talk to his number two boat?

The message stopped. A different fist chattered a short reply. An acknowledgement? Order to number two?

A spot of rain hit him on the cheekbone. The blow seemed to pierce the thick grease caked over the exposed flesh. The wind blowing from the Wolds thumped them up and down, twitching the nacelle from side to side.

Another message. Automatically he translated the stream of morse into letters and wrote them down. He had written the first sentence before he realized that the message was in clear and beamed at himself. Tregarron, it had to be Tregarron, must have gone mad. He of all people knew the importance of not compromising OB14 and equally he knew that there was no code that could not be broken given a long enough message and time.

T4TOC LOUDN INETE ENXXX. COMEI NCLOU DNINE TEENX OOO

Hastily he sent the acknowledgement. Then the message came in, a little slower as though the operator was trying to make sure there were no mistakes. It was in the same five-letter groups.

TREGN CLOUD NINET EENXX OOO USEYO URSEL FVULG ARCHE
ROOTS MOKER COUSI NJACK ANDAD JECTI VALSE CRETA
RYXQE DXXXX OOO MESSA GEBEG INSIN 5MINS OOO

What the hell did that mean? T4 must have picked up and translated Schiller's message to UC70. Tregarron must be out there. Before he could do anything the message started coming through.

MZCTK GZRBK LTKKT OBKEY YAQGO FKJBJ OOO KYDBD
YLIZO YGCOF ZKBRV GKAJB OGZFK FZDRC IRTGO BYQXX OOO
ZAGBO BGVOD OFZUZ OXXXX OOO QFKYG KGZBO FPEGR
GADTJ AZGBG VOKJB DOFZH ZOMRG LRXZR GAXXXOOO TDLTB
KKVMG ZMGRG LRXZR GARBH KMHKO OBKGK VZKRV RQXXX
OOO GOZMZ PBRGG CNTLL HRDGZ DZKGK EMLBH RYYDT
ZTBPD ZOLVP OTBPA OOO
ACKNOWLEDGE. IF IT TAKES YOU LONGER THAN TEN
MINUTES WE DO NOT WANT YOU BACK. TREGN.

The paper fluttered in his hands as the slipstream tugged at it, and despite the cold he began to sweat. The message must be from Bart and it had to be in an unbreakable code. One he had to solve in a few minutes.

A literary parlour game. Except the nacelle of SS 19 was no parlour but a flimsy structure of vibrating timber and fabric. The pencil he had laid down hopped and quivered over the little ledge he used to steady the message pads. A piece of string retained it. Alternately he was bathed in hot air laden with oil smuts from the engine and the bitter blast from the propeller. A raindrop exploded on the message pad.

Carberry pummelled his shoulder. 'What have you got? Do you know where the drop is going to be?'

He held up the message pad, shining his torch so that the pilot could see the gibberish. Carberry's face mirrored his disgust. Shepherd scowled back at him, suddenly angry. His friends were not fools and they must have confidence in his ability. Together they had tackled worse problems. Of course, the preamble to the message told him what to do. It was a simple substitution code. Safe enough used only once. A short message, probably full of simple slang and abbreviations, a minimum of Es and no repetitive 'the'.

USE YOURSELF. An instruction. He wrote down his name.
VULGAR CHEROOT SMOKER. Henrietta. No. Why vulgar, this was no slanging match? Henry.

COUSIN JACK, a Cornishman. Tregarron's christian names were fearsomely rural. If he could remember them.

ADJECTIVAL SECRETARY. Villers of course. x and QED would be in to round off the alphabet.

Carefully he wrote the names down, leaving an extra line between each one.

Richard Peter Shepherd
Henry Talbot
Bartholomew Ezekial Tregarron
Frederick Jamieson Villers
X
Quod Erat Demonstrandum

Starting at Richard he wrote down the alphabet above the letters, crossing out the duplicated ones. Then he tabulated the results. He had a coded alphabet. R in the message represented A, I stood for B, C for C, H for D and so on until Z stood for R.

He leaned back to ease his neck muscles. It was difficult to hold the torch in one hand, steady the message pad and write with the other. He pushed up his goggles to rub his eyes, but a flying blob of hot oil started them watering. It was time he decoded the message. Perhaps Carberry might have a bit more respect for him and his friends if the message contained what he was expecting.

PRCIS TRANS MISSI ONSHL LEYTO USVNV ... SLFNF LMBRO
LTCOU RSNAW
TSEVN OTRUS URFAC BAITO NLY--...RETNO NTWOF OURZR
O----...

   YUSLT STRNO UGHTA TEFIV ERTNT WOSVN FOURD ROPAT
MAXRA TE---...

IFMIN SSWPT RPTAT MAXRA TEAND SPDSO ONSTS WRSAW
AY---...

TORPR GNATT CKIMM DAFTR FRSTS HPMND ALLFI RINGF
ROMWG OINGE OOO

ESTNS ANDSN CNVOY PASSE FLMBR ONINE HUNDR EDAM-
...LKHEN

Automatically he glanced at his watch, wrote out his acknowledgement, transcribed it into the code and sent it to T4.

ODDKM ZBPIZ BTBJK GZQVT GEGVO LTBKG OKMRZ AGBNF
ZMKMEOOO

Hastily he transcribed his acknowledgement and passed it
with the expanded message back to Carberry. At that
moment he would not have changed places with any man in
the world.

Offspring brn in vstry with two mins to spare. Tnk WRP
5ph. Precis of transmission from Shelley (Schiller) to U75
(minelayer 38 mines). Self north (of) Flamborough Light
(will steer) course 070° true. Surface bait only. Return
(course) 240° true.

You (should be) south (of Flamborough) light steer 085°.
Return on 274°. Drop at maximum rate. If mines swept
repeat at max rate and speed as soon as the sweepers are
away. Torpedo or gun attack immediately after first ship
mined all firing from west going east. Estimate north-south
(convoy) and south-north convoy (will) pass east of Flamborough 09.00. Luck. Henry.

He was so pleased with himself that he had passed the
message to Carberry before realizing that he had made a
ghastly mistake. He had sent drifters everywhere except
where the ambush was laid. Off the Humber and Tyne the
crews of a dozen drifters would be bracing themselves against
the hazard of sailing through a minefield while the balloon
went up off Flamborough Head. The two blimps would be
able to save the convoy but their last chance of sinking
Schiller had gone. There were no drifters left at Whitby. The
message had come too late.

203

Carberry prodded his shoulder. 'See if you can raise Dutton. He should be airborne by now. Tell him to meet us off Whitby.'

Dead ahead of them a couple of searchlights swept the sky. A copse, black against a field of winter wheat, was suddenly lit by sheets of flame as an anti-aircraft battery opened fire. The battery rotated in the disorienting fashion of ground objects at night as the airship turned. Carberry was setting course for Whitby. The guns stopped firing and Shepherd realized that SS 19 at 500 feet had been mistaken for a Zeppelin at 15,000 feet.

Carberry brought the airship into the inner harbour at Whitby like a tired soap-bubble. He came in from the sea with the engine throttled right back until they were barely making headway against the wind coming out of the west. Fifty feet above the black water he stopped outside Will Dolli's house. SS 19 pitched and slewed in the turbulence above a forest of masts. Any one of them could wreck the airship by spiking the nacelle, hitting the propeller or spearing the envelope.

'Are you any good on a rope?' Carberry asked. Shepherd shook his head. The thought of sliding down the trail rope into the black water terrified him. Carberry said he would go but Shepherd knew that would be disastrous. Carberry had taught him to handle the airship after a fashion but holding their position with throttle and elevator needed the delicate touch of an expert.

'Lower me on the grapnel,' he said. 'Slowly. I should be all right standing on the flukes.'

The grapnel was dropped over the starboard side with Shepherd's feet on the eighteen-inch flukes. The coil of rope was on the port side but Carberry took it under his arms around his chest and over the right-hand skid.

'I say again. Do not let go until the rope is secured. You should be able to find a watchman,' Carberry said. 'If your weight comes off she'll be away and I will not get back without valving gas. Get a couple of chaps to haul her down.'

Harbour, river, houses and masts spun dizzily beneath him as Carberry let the rope slide over his shoulders. The turbulence made him swing like a pendulum. A deckhouse rushed towards him. Only his frantic shout and the wind pushing SS 19 back as Carberry slammed the throttle shut saved his legs.

But on the next swing he caught the standing rigging of a boat moored next to the quay. With the help of a couple of startled watchmen they hauled the blimp down. Carberry switched off the engine while Shepherd ran round lashing the fore and aft guys to convenient bollards.

There was no need to waken Dolli; the trawlerman was waiting for them, tousle-haired with a peajacket and a pair of serge trousers thrown over his nightshirt. Despite their pleading that there was no time the big fisherman insisted on them going into the house. A poker broke up the banked fire and set the flames flaring. The heat reminded Shepherd that even his bones seemed to be frozen. When he had poured them glasses of rum Dolli said, 'That should unfreeze you. No good ever came of a decision made by a block of ice. I suppose the rendezvous is changed ... '

Carberry thrust the message pad at him. 'For God's sake, Mr Dolli, there is no time for this. We have got to get three drifters down here before it is too late.' He drained his glass, coughing as the raw spirit caught his throat.

'Shut your gob, man,' Dolli said. 'The boats'll not have gone s'far as ye think. Yon gale last night saw to that.' He glared at them over the tiny steel-rimmed glasses perched on the end of his nose. 'I'm going wi' ye ... '

Carberry snapped back that it was impossible before accepting the inevitable. They would signal Dutton and have him switch his mechanic for Dolli from a boat in the outer harbour.

'Flamborough,' Dolli growled, reading the message again. They heard the rasp of his beard as he stroked his chin, then the chuckle rumbling in his guts exploded like the last trump.

'By damn, I could do wi' you fellas round every night. Two of the bastards. With news like this you will always be welcome in my house.'

The words brought Shepherd out of his rum and fire-warmed trance. He plucked the flimsy out of Dolli's hand

and threw it on the fire. 'You never saw that note. There was no message. Just two chaps in an airship who had spotted a couple of U-boats. So forget it. It's important, Mr Dolli. It could send me and Mr Carberry to jail and the good friends who got us the information.'

Dolli growled his assent but he went on, emphasizing each word with a poke in the chest from a finger like a gun barrel, 'Aye, hae'it ye're ain way, but you remind them fellas, whoever the buggers are, that they aren't figures on a chart getting drooned out there. They're men, husbands, sons and mates. Frien's o'mine. It's time you stopped it.'

It took them over an hour to find the drifters pitching and rolling, a plume of smoke streaming to port, red mizzens set away south of Flamborough Head. A pallid grey light was outlining the eastern horizon. Grey stratus bled rain as it scudded across at 1,000 feet, driven by a fresh breeze from the west. Despite the rain the previous night's gale had left an angry sea inshore. A drifter dipped her bows into a wave and disappeared as green water swept the decks clean. As the ship shook itself Shepherd plugged in the Aldis lamp and began flashing AAA at the bridge. A big man peered out of the wheelhouse, pushed his sou'wester up off his eyes and waved.

Dolli saved the day. Dutton took his Zero down to sea-level and slowly moved between two of the drifters. Dolli sat in the mechanic's cockpit behind the pilot. He took his helmet off, his red hair streaming in the wind like a Viking. He had a megaphone but his message could be heard without it.

One after another the ships turned, rolling on their beam ends, exposing scabrous red bottoms. As they settled on course to the north for Flamborough they streamed their otter boards. Sailing in a flat vee formation no U-boat could mistake them for anything other than the morning sweep ahead of a convoy.

Shepherd blew on his fingers, and clapped his hands together to get them warm enough to hold a pencil. He began to do some elementary arithmetic on the corner of his chart. In about forty-eight minutes U75 would see the drifters, and assuming they were the forerunners of a convoy she would set off across the Channel to lay her mines while Schiller laid a few mines near the surface to convince the sweepers that their morning had not been wasted.

There was no dawn. The darkness leaked away until they were flying through a cold grey sky with tendrils of dark stratus scudding across the featureless overcast at 500 feet. Occasional patches of rain whipped the heaving sea into a white frenzy.

As Shepherd strained to see the bulk of Flamborough Head thrusting out to sea SS 19 suddenly yawed violently to the left. Hastily he glanced back at Carberry. The pilot had pushed his goggles up to rub his bloodshot eyes and the slipstream had whipped them over the back of his helmet. The elastic strap broke and before Carberry could grab them the goggles bounced off the fuselage and spun down to the sea. Hastily Carberry pulled on a spare pair, shouting that he had used those since his first flight. The pilot, Shepherd realized, had had no sleep. Neither had he unless his spell after being knocked out was counted.

He saw a flicker of red out of the corner of his eye. A can buoy marking the inner edge of the War Channel. He rubbed his own eyes, unable to focus on the white letter as it bobbed through the waves. His eyelids were full of gritty marbles. He licked the corner of a grubby handkerchief to wipe his eyes and the lens of his binoculars.

'R'. Each can buoy from Spurn Head to Flamborough was marked with a successive letter. The Head was a mile further on. He turned to point it out to Carberry. The pilot nodded then, and as his eyes swept through his patch of sea he pointed ahead through the disc of the propeller at the feather in the sea below.

It was the arrow-like straightness, a geometrical anomaly amid the tumbling curves of the sea, that betrayed the path of the periscope. It slid back underwater. Behind it something heaved up to break the surface and fall back. The mining had started.

Below the surface the crew of U75 were muscling the weight of the mines and the anchor frame along a track, through a hatch into a chute. Mine and framework dropped together from an airlock in the belly of the U-boat. As the framework dropped towards the sea-bed the salt water attacked a soluble lock. The lock dissolved, allowing the mine to float up to the length of its anchor cable. Now it was armed. 500 kilogrammes of high explosive. And as the crew heaved the next one into the chute they kept their fingers crossed, hoping that the U-boat had moved far enough ahead before the mine floated upwards. The armed horns knew no nationality.

Not that they had any time for reflection. It was hot brutal work in the mine gallery, a contest between the cold inertia of the mines and the sweating viciousness of the Mine Petty Officer. Heave, hold. Hatch open, heave. Hatch locked. Haul the next one along. 750 kilos of metal had no mercy on the minor appendages that men use to control it. By the time the first pattern had been laid two men had lost fingers, another had a broken bone in his foot and there were three with torn muscles. The machinist's mate who doubled up in the sick-bay handled them with absent-minded competence, his eyes and ears on the Captain. This new game that would bring the Kapitänleutnant a medal and his picture in the paper was going wrong. Those damned airships again.

Shepherd logged the mines appearing underneath as Carberry conned SS 19 on to a course over the line of them to get a bearing. The tide was taking U75 north of her intended course. Two miles further north the Zero turned in lazy circles as the crew looked for the mines laid by Schiller. A squall of sleet swept between the two blimps. If the wind dropped the rain would turn to snow, and snow settling on the vast bulk of the envelope would bring them down. There was no future in looking for mines in a snowstorm.

The Zero appeared again, a pinpoint of light flickering from the nacelle. They had found the northern line of mines. A green flare arced away from the Zero to bring the drifters back for the charade.

There was something else on the horizon. Smoke. The convoy was early. Thirty ships wallowing north at eight knots towards the mines. He pointed them out to Carberry.

The pilot nodded. 'Send to Dutton. Imperative. If plan fails, explode mines before convoy approaches to within one mile. Repeat message to acknowledge.'

Blowing some warmth into his frozen hands Shepherd scowled at the haze on the horizon. His stomach was tying itself in knots and it took a conscious effort to hold the signal lamp steady, aiming the light at the distant Zero. Everything was going against them – the light, the snow squalls, Villers and time trickling away as they waited. They needed the patience of a hunter to ambush the ambusher, patience to wait until the U-boat had completed the reverse leg of his pattern. To wait until they were back in position with the convoy growing large on the eastern horizon.

Carberry was rubbing his eyes again. Without continual attention the blimp yawed to the left like a lame elephant. Then instead of the oily, smelly but warm slipstream blowing over the engine and through the radiator over him, Shepherd's left side was assailed by an icy gale laden with half-melted snow. He flinched as an accumulation of slush hit him in the face and a patch of cold damp began to penetrate down the back of his neck. Suddenly the sheer lunacy of what he had done and what they were trying to do made him giggle. Facetiousness was a sin much effort by his tutors had failed to suppress.

The two latest weapons of the twentieth century were in mortal combat, yet neither of them could see each other and neither of them had the means to harm the other. He had little faith that their bombs, even when aimed by two good eyes, could seriously damage a U-boat. Fortunately the U-boats were reluctant to put them to the test. Just as with the bow and arrow and with primeval man's club, victory would go to the one with the most cunning.

There was no doubt that the U-boats were winning their private war with the admirals. Already several well-founded careers had been blighted by the cold blast of the mounting shipping losses. And the scuttlebutt had it that even the C-in-C himself was in queer streets with his civilian masters. Lord Nelson had left no guidelines for dealing with U-boats. Only the convoy system. And adopting that was not possible, because for two years the professionals had been telling the civilian advocates of the system that it would not work.

Yet in the early days of convoying they had succeeded far better than all the panache of the destroyer flotillas or the cold bravery of the Q ships. It struck at the heart of naval principles to preserve merchantmen instead of seeking to destroy the enemy.

And while the professionals failed, the amateurs – a school-mistress, a couple of lawyers, a vain old man trying to hide his failing eyes and the men on three dirty old fishing boats – were going to make two of those triumphant U-boats destroy themselves. Their Lordships would not be amused.

Something moved in the tumult below, a mechanical purpose alien to the confusion of natural forces. A black sphere, copper horned, burst out of the wave-tops and sank back. Shepherd pointed. As they swung round to follow and plot the bearing another mine broke the surface ahead. U75 was on the return leg.

He heard the first explosion above the noise of the engine. A plume of white water spouted up behind the stern of the drifter as the first grenade went over the side. Dutton's Zero nosed through a thin squall, following the line of mines. He was dangerously low, Shepherd thought, looking at the Zero enviously. Carberry's decision to give Schiller to Dutton and have SS 19 deal with the bigger U75 still rankled. This stunt was his, his and his friends in OB14, and the stunt was to kill Schiller, to avenge their personal losses. U75 was for the Navy.

Now Dutton was barely ten feet above the sea, nosing ahead of the drifter like a dog putting up game. Puddles of dead fish surfaced belly-up where the grenades had gone down. Schiller would be furious ... No, this is how he had planned it. They were expecting these to be seen and dealt with. Schiller would be counting, unwilling to move until all his first drop had been accounted for.

Suddenly the Zero had gone. It happened so quickly that it was impossible to say how it happened. The Zero was low. Perhaps a grapnel or the trail rope uncoiled and fell. And hit a mine. The nacelle of the Zero disappeared in a column of white water, a hand reaching out of the water to pluck them down. The propeller broke, the blades scything into the envelope, while the column of water thrust the buoyant nacelle with its red-hot exhaust into the rent. Into the spilled hydrogen.

The column of water spouted flame. 70,000 cubic feet of hydrogen burning. Falling as the water fell back into the sea. Dropping like a deadly blanket over the bows of the drifter, the *Sarah Armitage*. The white-hot glare of the burning hydrogen was shot with the dull red flame of burning timber, oil and tar. And the crew. Something, the grenades or a fuel tank, exploded.

By the time SS 19 reached the scene the gutted carcass of the *Sarah Armitage* was slipping under the litter of charred planking. A couple of blackened bodies rolled in a hideous parody of living. There was no sign of the Zero, or Dutton, or his operator, or Cap'n Dolli, master mariner.

SS 19 flew along the reciprocal of Dutton's course, counting the number of mines by the puddles of dead fish. Carberry plotted them before turning south to where the remaining two drifters were getting ready to hoodwink U75.

Oh, we're bloody clever, Shepherd thought. Bloody marvellous clever Shepherd. If this was a boxing match Schiller would have taken every round. Every round a knock-out. He was killing every one on Shepherd's side. Except Shepherd.

With the throttle wide open SS 19 raced back to the two drifters as they started to run along the first line of mines. Carberry pulled the blimp round in a tight turn, juggling with throttle and rudder so that for a moment Cloud Nineteen hung motionless over the most easterly mine. Shepherd dropped a smoke-float within three feet of it and flashed a course to steer to the *Annie Shaw,* the nearest drifter.

They soon evolved a technique. Warned by the fate of the Zero, Carberry held the airship at about a hundred feet, crabbing along a track of 95° about a hundred yards ahead of a drifter. As Shepherd saw a mine he aimed a flare at it from the Very pistol. One of the drifters dropped a grenade over the stern as she steamed by. Shepherd put a tick on his chart. Jerry, he thought, would be doing the same thing because

211

they would not move until they were sure that each mine had been dealt with.

It took nearly an hour, fifty-eight nail-biting minutes to simulate clearing twenty-four mines. A double row of twelve. The trap would have broken up the convoy, especially with Schiller's mines two miles ahead. But now the haze on the horizon had resolved into hulls and masts and an armed trawler dashing ahead to find out what was happening. The *Annie Shaw* turned south to meet it while SS 19 and the *Maid of Shields* turned north to deal with the remaining mines laid by Schiller.

There was smoke on the northern horizon now as the southbound convoy, colliers with their decks awash, Scandiwegian timber boats like floating castles, butted and wallowed through the squalls hanging like curtains from the cloud base. Unless their plan worked this could be the biggest disaster in the North Sea since the loss of the 'Cold Meat Squadron'.

Shepherd swallowed hard and concentrated on finding the trail of mines beyond the charred planking that commemorated the crews of HM Airship SSZ 88 and the *Sarah Armitage*. He visualized an imaginary court with the judge leaning towards him saying, 'You actually had the knowledge, Mr Shepherd, to prevent the loss of these fine ships and gallant men but you suppressed it in order to use it for your own purposes ... '

He knew now why Carberry had carried on at him after the meeting with Villers. Folkestone and the loss of Jennifer seemed events that had happened in another lifetime. The copper-tipped horns of a mine rolled in the trough of a wave. He flashed the lamp at the *Maid of Shields* until he got an answering wave from the wheelhouse. Then he put a red flare exactly where he had intended it to go, three feet in front of the mine.

To the south, nothing was happening on an apparently empty sea. Perhaps U75 had gone home scenting a trap. Or maybe the captain was not as keen as Schiller. And the convoy was getting nearer.

They had dealt with Schiller's mines on the eastern leg and

they were halfway along the return leg when the trap was sprung. Shepherd heard the explosion and felt SS 19 shudder from the shockwave. Either U75 hit two mines or the second one was a sympathetic explosion. A huge pillar of water boiled up from the sea until it seemed that it must reach the cloud base. It hung in the air as the shockwave hit the airship.

Like a toy manipulated in slow motion by an invisible fist the black hull of a U-boat lurched above the surface, bows down, deck gun canted, U75 on the conning tower. It was turning like a Catherine wheel, the stern rising, propellers still spinning. It went over the vertical before it plunged back into the sea.

Carberry broke the terror of the moment by punching Shepherd on the shoulder. 'Leave that one alone, he's done for. Get on with catching the other bastard or you will go to jail for two lifetimes.'

They finished the last row of mines. Carberry nudged Cloud Nineteen into wind and slowly eased back the throttle until the airship was hovering above one of the can buoys marking the western edge of the Channel. They were midway between the two rows of mines. Somewhere beneath them Schiller must be getting ready for another dash laying mines to replace those he thought had been cleared. Shepherd wondered whether he was swearing at U75 for making the first score.

He trembled as though he had the ague. They were so near to the quest he had so lightly started so many lives ago. Because an old man hit him across the face with a riding crop? A quest that had killed everyone but the quarry. Miller, Dutton, Dolli, the fishermen, Alec Jervis ... The crew of the U75. The names tolled in his mind like a great bell. Down below, the quarry was still untouched. Shepherd rubbed his aching eyes and turned to scan the grey waste again, looking for the arrow-straight anomaly that would show that Schiller was there.

He could still get away. If he surfaced now he could bolt for home because there was nothing that could match his speed on the surface. Not the foul-bottomed armed trawlers doing escort duty. That left an old airship with an engine that would not run at maximum power for ten minutes without boiling. With a Lewis gun, two 100lb bombs and a half-blind pilot behind a useless sight. And in the past weeks Shepherd had learned what a vast lonely place the sea was.

A thin line of rain lashed the water below and a gust buffeted SS 19. The airship turned slowly like a balloon on a string, stirring fragments of stratus underneath the cloud base. At this speed Carberry could not hold them down. They had drifted up to the underside of the cloud.

Over to the left about 200 yards away the sea frothed and bubbled as a black hull came up out of the sea. The hatch in the conning tower opened. Kapitänleutnant Otto Schiller, Captain of the UC62, pushed his cap on to the back of his head as he lifted the binoculars to his eyes. A puff of black smoke from the stern. One of the diesels had started to charge the batteries. One of the look-outs bent down to take a Lewis gun from the hatch. As he dropped it on to a pipe-mounting at the rear of the conning tower he skipped sideways to dodge the spray from a breaking wave.

Shepherd held his breath. There was something obscene about watching the three men below carrying on their business. Schiller scratched the dirty bandage on his hand. One of the look-outs wiped his nose on his sleeve. The other bent down to take an ammunition drum from below. His teeth flashed as he looked up at his mate, laughing at some joke. The grin froze on his face as he saw the airship hanging above them half-hidden in the cloud base. He pointed, shouting an alarm.

Schiller turned to stare at them, his lips moving, mouthing unheard orders. One of the look-outs tumbled down the hatch. SS 19 stirred into life as Carberry slammed the throttle open. The engine spat black smoke, twisting on its bearers. A couple of plugs had oiled up. It spluttered, picked up speed as the petrol washed them clean.

Schiller knocked the gunner aside to grab the Lewis, cock it and swing it at the menace above him. Spray blew into the air as the valves opened along the length of the U-boat for a crash-dive. A short burst of tracer bullets arced up into the nacelle of the airship. A hand reached out of the hatch to tug at his leg. The gun jammed. He threw it down the hatch, jumping after it and slamming the hatch shut seconds before seawater swirled over it and UC62 slid under water with the electric motors at full speed.

SS 19 reeled into the clouds, like a boxer hit hard as he went in for a knock-out. The engine was roaring away at full throttle but the pilot hung unconscious over the cockpit coaming. Without Carberry to hold it down, and light now because of the petrol burned and the ammunition fired, the blimp drifted slowly up into the cloud.

Schiller changed course as soon as UC62 was underwater, turning back through 180° to edge closer to the western side of the War Channel. No bombs fell. He remembered the enormous bulk of the airship filling his gunsight, and came up to periscope depth. There was nothing in sight. Nothing but a smoke-haze on the northern and southern horizons that revealed the approaching convoys. His batteries were low after the minelaying run and his escapade with the airship, but there was still time to kill two birds with one stone. A quick dash across the Channel, hull down on the surface, would dispose of his remaining mines and charge the batteries for a torpedo attack and underwater withdrawal. And it would look good in his report now that U75 had scored first blood.

UC62 was halfway across the War Channel doing ten knots when she drove through the charred planking remains of the *Sarah Armitage.* From his position a few feet above water-level Schiller thought he had the German ocean to himself. He could not see the approaching minesweepers, and the armed trawler and the *Maid of Shields* were hidden behind a shower of rain. Even the elements, he thought, were combining to provide the conventional trappings of an ambush. Today would be the high point of the war against Tommi's shipping, the end of the convoy system before it had really started. UC62 did not give any sign of hitting the twenty-foot length of deck planking but a huge wave creamed over the bows and the submarine started to slow. Schiller stooped to the speaking tube, cutting their speed and ordering men on deck to clear the obstruction. He lifted his head in time to see *Sarah*

Armitage's planking hook the mooring wire of his own mine and slide along to the waiting horn.

In that split second he knew that he had been trapped. That U75 had been the first blood. Then the mine exploded. UC62 reeled from the sledgehammer blow, rolling on to her beam as the sea swelled up against the hull before toppling over to swamp the conning tower.

Four torpedomen died, swatted like flies as the spare torpedoes broke the lashings and rolled on to them. The duty cook in the galley broke his back when he was flung from one bulkhead to another. Two machinists writhed in agony, impaled on the hot diesel exhausts, and the duty electrician was crushed under the batteries.

The water drained quickly from the conning tower. It had been peeled open like a discarded tin-can. Schiller was still there, huddled in one corner with his arms locked round a stanchion. The two look-outs had gone and so had the jumping wire, the port forward hydroplane and the periscopes. With no power UC62 was a dead ship rolling sluggishly as she awaited the escorts drawing closer from north and south.

Schiller shook himself, stifling a scream as a broken rib knifed into his insides. He could not stand but he pulled himself upright. There was no pain, nothing from the chest downwards. But he was still alive. Automatically he scanned the horizon as he reached for the speaking tube, but saw only the smoke-haze forecasting the coming escorts. Under the circumstances they were unlikely to have time to think about taking prisoners. And if his guess was right his mines were still there.

He blew down the tube. 'Bridge here. Captain speaking. Damage report. Is there anyone there? Give me some power. Quickly ... '

'Henne, sir. It's like a butcher's shop down here. And leaking like a sieve. We're turning over a diesel. Give us five minutes ... '

'Five minutes be damned, Henne. Tommi is about to fall on our necks. If you don't want to swim home give me an engine now.'

As if in answer a diesel barked into life, blowing smoke from the exhaust like a coal-burning tramp with a soot-caked flue.

'Course to steer,' he croaked as the bows punched into the choppy sea. What course would keep them clear of their own mines? He could not think any more. East and to hell with the mines. 'Steer 090°. And I want more speed. And less smoke, a lot less smoke.'

'No compass. Most of it is mushed up with Mr Beibe-decke's head. I can't do anything about the smoke. We'll clear some bodies away and try to give you another engine.'

That was that, no need for an adverse report. Goodbye to a glorious career in Kiel. No battle of wits, his against Beibedecke and his friends in the Kriegsmarine.

'This is no time for giving me burial details. Not if you want to stay alive. Starboard helm 10°. Bring me a bearing compass. And an oilskin, a dry towel and a new cap.'

There was no sun visible under the lowering cloud but he could tell they were moving clear of the trap. However, that smoke would bring down on their heads every Tommi destroyer within miles. The second diesel started up. More smoke. And this one was vibrating itself to death. The first one stopped. Then the second. Before he could scream at Henne, first one and then the other diesel started up. They were not going to last. But they were alive, pulling clear of Tommi, heading for home at six knots. Tonight they would fix the wireless set and call for help. If they saw the night. Please God, let there be no destroyers with those escorts.

CHAPTER TWELVE

A spray of hot water woke Shepherd. He thought he was dying as he stared at the blood on his gloves and the mess on the front of his leather coat. He patted himself, looking for a wound, before he found that his helmet was stuck to his hair by congealing blood. A bullet had grazed his scalp and given him a centre parting for life. And a broken nose, more blood. And a scratch up his side from knee to shoulder that started to hurt like the devil as soon as he found it. His right hand had been hit by a ricochet that was still burnt into the leather of his gauntlet. He cut the glove away, watching the blackened hand swell as the leather peeled off. Flexing the swollen fingers was torture. Bruised but not broken, he thought.

They were in cloud, a grey shapeless passage that had him completely disoriented. As he squirmed away from the water spraying from the radiator vent he saw Carberry hanging out of his cockpit with blood dripping from his sleeve. He forgot his aches and pains.

Twisting round he reached into the pilot's cockpit to close the throttle. The OX5 always boiled at full throttle. And it was missing on two cylinders, which was not surprising as it had absorbed a drum of Lewis gun ammunition at 200 yards' range.

He climbed out on to the skid and shuffled along to look at Carberry. The pilot was still alive but he had been hit three times, twice in the fleshy part of the shoulder and in the chest. Holding on to a strut with his injured right hand Shepherd poked and prodded with his left until he had a couple of field dressings in place to halt the bleeding. Then he could lean his shaking knees against the fabric skin of the nacelle and consider what next to do.

There was no sense of movement. SS 19 and its crew were contained in a featureless mist. The engine ticked over, the propeller blades lazily clop-clopped round and the scale of the compass slowly rotated. They must be going round in a circle, drifting eastwards at the speed of the wind.

Sinking. Shepherd could hear the suspension ropes creaking, and the ballonets looked flabby as the air pressure dropped without the blast of slipstream. And there had to be holes in the envelope. Somehow he had to get into Carberry's seat to fly them home. Neither of them was fit for a long swim. The mist thinned beneath his feet, giving him a momentary glimpse of a cold grey sea. He grabbed the inert body of the pilot and tried to lift it. They had no time to waste.

There was no way by which the time it took him to move Carberry could be measured. He went on and on, slipping, kicking holes in the fabric sides, pushing and pulling with his left hand, bracing himself with the crook of his right elbow. He wrenched out part of the side when he found that he was unable to lift Carberry over the coaming. After his first slip he lashed the body with two pieces of rope, never leaving it untied. Using the ropes he inched the unconscious pilot from the rear cockpit to the front one. It was easier getting him into the front cockpit because he could bend his knees and get his shoulder underneath the body. Harder because his hands, and the front of him, were slippery with blood and sweat. Once he had the pilot in place he shuffled back to sit, shivering, in the wreckage of the pilot's cockpit and staring stupidly at the dials, pressure gauges, gas-valve controls and engine instruments.

The slowly rotating compass attracted his attention. Feet on the rudder bar. Press. The graduated disc slowed, stopped. He wiped the blood and sweat out of his eyes with his left hand and saw the sea, 500 feet below. The statoscope showed they were sinking. The compass was rotating in the opposite direction. Press with the other foot. A long way ahead he saw a smudge of smoke. A ship. Damn fool, a smoke-pot like that was an open invitation to a U-boat. Despite that it was something to steer for in this desolate waste.

He opened the throttle, wincing at the vibration, and trod on the rudder bar until SS 19 was heading east of north towards the smoke. Winding on elevator did not stop their sink so he sacrificed some ballast. With something to steer for

219

and roughly holding height he began to teach himself to fly. Cables, suspension cables, gas-valve controls, red and white to the top gas-valve, blue to the bottom, brown to the crabpots. Red, leave that alone: it goes up to the ripping panel. Use the controls, rudder, elevator wheel to go up or down.

He flew like a drunken traction-engine driver, over-controlling the elevator wheel backwards and forwards, setting the gas-valves rattling as the blimp shot up and down, losing irreplaceable gas. He tried trimming, pumping air through the crabpot valves into either the fore or aft ballonets. Sweat and blood ran together before he realized he was trying to do the impossible. Hold a sinking airship up without dropping ballast. But Carberry had always impressed on him that only novices threw away their ballast, that to an airship pilot ballast was as important as petrol for the engine. He was the novice of novices.

He began to throw things overboard. Four drums of ammunition followed by the Lewis gun. A spare can of oil. Wait, count up to ten. They were still sinking. Open the throttle. The vibration from the engine suddenly increased, the compass rose and disappeared in a blur, and the suspension cables swelled into strange patterns. Reluctantly he eased the throttle back until the vibrations were tolerable. The statoscope showed them sinking again. The bullets that had done for him and Carberry had gone on through the envelope. And he did not have the strength to climb up and apply the patches in the repair kit.

And that damned ship did not seem to get any nearer. There was nothing else on the empty sea but that smudge of black smoke. The skipper seemed to be working at it, sometimes it died away altogether. It was going to be a gamble whether they could reach it. But the cloud was breaking. A bit of sun to heat up and expand the gas would help them stay in the air.

To drift on into the North Sea? They were gaining on the ship now, where the hell was he going? But the wind was steadily pushing them eastwards. Towards Germany and the seaplanes from Heligoland.

He sacrificed one of the bombs, remembering at the last

minute to re-insert the safety-pin to make it safe. Not that there was anything below, but a few fish might be grateful. Then a small bag of ballast and his heavy thigh-boots to avoid jettisoning the last one.

Carberry recovered consciousness, staring at the strange cockpit before turning to look at Shepherd. The rough bandaging seemed to have stopped the bleeding. He peered over the side estimating their drift, then he groped under his coat for something and produced his revolver.

'Word of honour,' he croaked as he tried to pass it over. 'You have to shoot yourself before Jerry catches you.' The effort of holding the heavy gun was too much. His face twisted with agony, and as he fell back unconscious again the revolver dropped over the side. That must weigh five pounds, Shepherd thought, it'll save dropping that much ballast. He was beginning to get light-headed. What was that about shooting himself?

The ship had disappeared. Shepherd rubbed his eyes. No smoke. No ship. It had gone. There it was, the wind had drifted them off to starboard. Only a wisp of smoke. Her skipper had realized he was in dangerous waters. Black smoke, a huge puff. Bloody fools, or were they in trouble?

The binoculars were too heavy for him to hold, producing nothing but a blur when he rested them on the windscreen. Left rudder, push her upwind, brace your elbows on your knees. Now focus.

The image swam in and out of the grey fuzziness with a rapidity that made his senses reel. The long low line of the hull, the squat tower amidships, the deck gun, that was no ship. The exhaust smoke stopped, a miniature cloud of it drifting across the shattered conning tower. UC62. It was his U-boat. The diesel engine started again, blowing smoke from the exhausts. The bow wave curled away along the hull as the submarine started to move.

There were three men in the conning tower. One of them was Schiller. Half a dozen were on the foredeck working on repairs, and the flame of a welding torch sparkled between their stooped bodies.

Shepherd opened the throttle, ignoring the vibration, the

221

leaking gasbag and Carberry's need for attention. UC62 and
Schiller were just ahead and below him, crippled, concentrating on repair work. And he had one bomb left, one chance to
finish what he had started. He jettisoned his last bag of
ballast and leaned hard on the elevator wheel as he began
nursing SS 19 up towards the shelter of the cloud base. This
time he would stalk his prey like a hunter.

It took him twenty minutes of patient stalking before he
was in position upwind of the U-boat and skimming through
the lower tendrils of cloud. He was talking to himself, half
delirious, and he had had two attacks of double vision. The
engine was boiling, the hoses leaking, spraying hot water over
the pair of them, the vibration was breaking up the nacelle,
his seat bearers had collapsed and he was crouched at the
controls with his stockinged feet wedged on the longerons.
But UC62 was 300 yards ahead as he closed the throttle and let
the wind drift him up to the U-boat. He had five gallons of
water ballast left, fifty pounds, and he had to sacrifice some as
Cloud Nineteen sagged downwards when the power came off.

Schiller saw him the moment the diesel failed and he heard
the noise of the engine. White faces turned up at him in alarm.
Except for Schiller. He lifted the Lewis gun to his shoulder like
a rifle. It was jammed. Slowly the airship moved towards the
crippled U-boat. The hatch was open. Shepherd could see the
lights inside, a figure climbing the cat ladder. He needed no
bomb sight; from this height at this speed he could drop the
bomb down the hatch. The diesel engine restarted but there
was barely enough power to give them steerage way. Carefully
he pulled the safety-pin out of the nose-fuse on the 100lb bomb
and took up the pressure on the release toggle.

Propped against the buckled rail Schiller had been trying
to cure the jammed machine-gun. Now he grasped the
muzzle with both hands and threw it at the airship in one last
spasm of defiant anger.

It was a good throw but it was 300 feet short. Shepherd
laughed. But the laughter undid him. Schiller was lying in a
heap on the deck below. The hatch slid beneath him and he
could not press the bomb release, not while he was still
laughing at their antics. There had to be another way. He

cracked open the throttle and turned into wind, hanging there just foward of the U-boat's bow.

Once again he got out on to the skids to shuffle along to the front cockpit. Starboard side this time. Carberry was lolling over the other side and the wireless set was to starboard. The germ of a wild idea was growing inside his half-delirious mind, something that would give him an excuse for decamping from his job. He was chuckling to himself as he fumbled for the key. A screaming bolt of pain as he pulled the headphones over his head and ripped the dried blood over his scalp stopped the laughter. But not the burgeoning idea. He and Carberry, and Henrietta, and Tregarron and the operators at T4, had done something new. They had used their skills to trap and destroy two U-boats.

Someone was standing by the hatch in the conning tower of UC62 waving a white shirt. One down and one in the hand. Civilian skills. Not steaming out with flags flying and guns booming. Just three men and a woman sitting in a draughty hut on the edge of a desolate sandspit.

He almost fainted from the pain in his right hand as the key stuttered clumsily. He should be tuned in to T4.

'Cloud Nineteen to T4. Emergency. Do you read. Fix my position immediately.' Then he held the key down, counting aloud up to ten and then back to one.

Faintly the reply filtered into his earphones. He was barely able to decipher the message but they could hear him. He fingered the key again.

'Cloud Nineteen to T4. Priority immediate. Object of the exercise below me at this position. Surrendered. Crippled. Send in the Household Cavalry to collect. Cloud Nineteen damaged. Sinking. Hurry. Send AAA if message understood.'

He could see two of everything again. AAA. Di dah, di dah, di dah. Screw the key down. As long as he was in the air they would know where he was.

SS 19 was sinking again and she had drifted away from the U-boat. He released some water ballast and cracked on a bit more throttle to get back into position. Immediately the white flag in the conning tower was waved vigorously. And a variation of his new idea started him laughing.

You did not need T4 and its complicated listening gear. Or airships or bombers. All you needed was an aeroplane. The sight of one would keep any U-boat underwater or make it crash-dive if it was on the surface. No one was going to stop to find out whether the pilot was a good or bad bomb-aimer or whether he had a bomb.

Soon Shepherd was flying mechanically, keeping SS 19 off the bow of the U-boat, watching the statoscope, grudgingly dropping a little ballast and finding something loose to throw overboard. He could watch those two things and compose his brief at the same time. To hell with clerks like Villers. This report was for the Admiral. Aeroplanes and airships with bombs working to directions from the triangulation stations. Backed up by any old training aeroplanes flown by pilots getting experience before going to the Front. This would be his justification for quitting the office.

It was an excuse. In his more lucid moments he knew this, but he thought it was one that would cover a multitude of sins. As Carberry had said, they had two U-boats to show.

He had lost Jennifer, and Elsa had deserted him, but he had found himself. He could do the hard thing and go back to being a clerk again.

He was rambling in a delirium, loudly presenting his summing up for the prosecution to a judge looking remarkably like Admiral Hall with an obstreperous clerk looking like Villers, when a boat from HMS *Ashanti* looped a line over the skid of SS 19. She was twenty feet up, sinking slowly, and there was nothing left to throw overboard.

Wrapped in a blanket, clutching a mug of cocoa laced with rum, he refused to go to the sick-bay until he had been to the wireless room. He dictated the message, the operators took one look at his hand and refused to let him send it.

'Cloud Nineteen to T4, Henry and company. Quest completed. Reporting to the office Monday to start work on part two. End of message.'

Still holding the cocoa in his good hand he slid slowly down the wall, down, down into a black pool. He was asleep. Grinning.

DATE DUE